Lizz Murphy, an award-winning Irish poet herself, is in the process of uncovering the great delights of work by contemporary women writers with Irish backgrounds. During her research she is connecting with writers in Ireland and its diaspora, and discussing issues such as immigration, language, politics, the influence of Irish heritage, and other concerns, across the hemispheres and down the generations. In *Wee Girls*, she shares just a taste of her discoveries with readers.

Other Books

She's a Train and She's Dangerous: Women Alone in the 1990s (ed. 1994)

Do Fish get Seasick: A Collection of Damn Bus Poems (1994)

Two Lips Went Shopping (2000)

Wee Girls

WOMEN WRITING FROM AN IRISH PERSPECTIVE

edited by

Lizz Murphy

Spinifex Press Pty Ltd
504 Queensberry Street
North Melbourne, Vic. 3051
Australia
women@spinifexpress.com.au
http://www.spinifexpress.com.au

First published by Spinifex Press, 1996
reprinted 1997
reprinted 2000

Edited by Jo Turner
Typeset in Adobe Garamond by Claire Warren
Reprint adjustments by Palmer Higgs Pty Ltd
Cover design by Soosie Adshead, The Works
For reprint, cover redone by Deb Snibson
Made and printed in Australia by Australian Print Group

National Library of Australia
Cataloguing-in-Publication data:
Wee Girls

Includes Index
ISBN 1 875559 51 5.

1. English literature – Irish authors. 2. English literature –
Women authors. I. Murphy, Lizz

820.8089162

Acknowledgements

"The Making of a Writer" and "The Marvellous Boy" © 1996 of Linda Anderson. "Sheela^Na^Gigging Around" © 1994 of Nuala Archer, first published in *Poetry Ireland Review, 41* and in *From a Mobile Home*, Salmon Press 1995. Design of Sheela-Na-Gigs based on an illustration from the Millenium poster titled "The Spirit of Women", designed by Cathleen O'Neill with illustrations by Marina Forrestal, reprinted by permission of Attic Press. Millenium poster dedicated to "An Caillach". Extract from *Echoes* © 1985 of Maeve Binchy, first published by Century Publishing, 1985. "Anna Liffey" © 1994 of Eavan Boland, reprinted from *In A Time of Violence*, by permission of W W Norton & Company, Inc., "Making the Difference" © of Eavan Boland reprinted from *Collected Poems* published by Carcanet Press Ltd, "The Emigrant Irish" © 1987 of Eavan Boland from *An Origin Like Water: Collected Poems 1967–87* reprinted by permission of W W Norton & Company, Inc. "Once Upon a Time", "Skeletons", "Coming Back Down to Earth", "Priorities", © 1996 of Bub Bridger, "A Wedding" © 1989 of Bub Bridger, first published in *Goodbye to Romance: Stories by Australian and New Zealand Women 1930–1980*, Allen & Unwin 1989, also published in *Short Stories from New Zealand*, Highgate-Price Milburn, 1988. "Seeing Stars", "Falling Asleep with Strangers" © 1996 of Joan Bridget. "To Whom it May Concern" © 1977 of Colleen Burke, originally published in *Hags, Rags and Scripture*, Cochon International, 1977. Extracts from *Outercourse: The Be-Dazzling Voyage* ©

"Millies", "Tatts", "Speaking of Eve", "Good Woman", "Dying" and "Wee Girls" © 1996 of Lizz Murphy. "Belief" © 1995 of Sue Reidy, originally published *Sunday Star Times*, NZ, 1995. "Loop the Loop" © 1996 of Francesca Rendle-Short. "Lamb-Marking" © 1993 of Bronwyn Rodden, originally published in *Scarp*, 1993. "Searching", "The Beginning", "Changing", "The Final Season" © 1990 of Robyn Rowland, selection of poems from *Perverse Serenity* published by Spinifex Press, 1990. Ailbhe Smyth, "Girl Beaming in a White Dress" © 1996 of Ailbhe Smyth. "Maybe it was 1970" © 1992 of Cherry Smyth, previously published in *Virago New Poets*, Virago, 1993 and *The Popular Front of Contemporary Poetry*, Apples and Snakes, 1992, "The Roadside" and "Summer Breeze" © 1996 of Cherry Smyth.

Jill Jones thanks Eavan Boland for permission to quote from the poem "The Oral Tradition" in "How I Might Write Irish" by Jill Jones. Thanks to President of Ireland, Mary Robinson for permission to quote from her speech. "Heritage" © Mary Gilmore reproduced by permission, from *Selected Poems*, published by ETT Imprint, Sydney 1996.

Thanks to the *Irish Echo* for permission to quote Minister Avril Doyle TD.

*For my grandmother Marya Jamison
in fond remembrance — may I be half as wise.*

*To my grand-daughter Michaela Murphy,
a delightful wee girl indeed.*

In some far, dim, ancestral hour
There is our root of power.

The strength we give is the strength we make;
And the strength we have is the strength we take,
Given us down from the long-gone years,
Cleansed in the salt of others' tears.

— from *Heritage* by Mary Gilmore
from *Selected Poems.*

Contents

Introduction   *xv*

Robyn Rowland   Searching   2
                         The Beginning   4
                         Changing   7
                         The Final Season   9

Mary Dorcey   My Grandmother's Voice   12
                         The Breath of History   15
                         The Gaelic Poets Warned Me   18
                         The Whiteness of Snow   19
                         Learning to Live With it   20
                         I Cannot Love You as
                             You Want to be Loved   22
                         I Saw a Fish this Morning   25

Helena Mulkerns   Famine Fever   27
                         The Whole Nine Yards   36

Colleen Burke   A Shadow on the Heart   51
                         To Whom it May Concern   53
                         A Joyous Day   57

Linda Anderson   The Making of a Writer   68
                         The Marvellous Boy   70

Nuala Archer   Sheela^Na^Gigging Around   91

Siobhán McHugh   Power Cuts   101

Maeve Binchy   extract from *Echoes*   122

Mary Daly   extract from *Outercourse*   134

Sue Reidy   Being Irish   150
                         Belief   157

Jill Jones	How I Might Write Irish	170
	Broken Language	173
	Lunch Music Café	177
	Among Trees	178
	Invisible Ink	179
	Ideas of Sirens	181
	Antipodean Geography	182
	The Pure in Heart	183
Medbh McGuckian	Drawing Ballerinas: How Being Irish has Influenced me as a Writer	185
	The Mast Year	204
	Road 32, Roof 13-23, Grass 23	205
	The Dead are More Alive	207
	Rathlin Road	210
Cherry Smyth	The Roadside	212
	Maybe it was 1970	214
	Summer Breeze	217
Joan Bridget	Seeing Stars	232
	Falling Asleep with Strangers	234
Ailbhe Smyth	Girl Beaming in a White Dress	239
Lizz Murphy	Growing a Language	250
	Paper Petals	253
	White Petals	255
	Good Fairy Bad Fairy	257
	My Irishness	258
	Wee Girls	260
	Sentiments, Millies, Tatts, Bobbing for Apples, Speaking of Eve, Sabbath, Good Women, Dying	262

	Deadmen's Eyes	266
	Time Out	267
	The Planet Next Door	269
Bub Bridger	Once Upon a Time	272
	A Wedding	275
	Skeletons	286
	Coming Back Down to Earth	289
	Priorities	291
Francesca Rendle-Short	Loop the Loop	293
Pam Lewis	Potatofah-Minirish	318
	Lifo	321
Bronwyn Rodden	On being an Irish Woman Writer	335
	Tomato Time	337
	Long Drive to Work Snowy via Canberra	343
	Lamb-marking	344
	Rites	345
	Bee Yellow Native	347
	Circling Dublin	348
Rita Ann Higgins	The Flogger	351
	Prism	354
	The Taxi Man Knows	355
	Mothercare	356
	Higher Purchase	358
	The Flute Girl's Dialogue	359
Eavan Boland	Anna Liffey	362
	Making the Difference	370
	The Emigrant Irish	373

Introduction

Well I have had the best time! I've been reading every little snatch of writing by Irish women today, that I can get my hands on. Everything from anthologies recently available in Australia, such as *Ireland's Women: Past and Present* and Dermot Bolger's *Picador Book of Contemporary Irish Fiction*, to Attic Press titles ordered in from Dublin, including, *Unveiling Treasures: The Attic Guide to the Published Works of Irish Women Literary Writers* and *Wildish Things*. Also special issues of journals like the *Feminist Review*'s, *The Irish Issue: The British Question* and a few novels and collections of short stories and poetry.

I'd already read a fair bit of James Joyce, a good deal of what Edna O'Brien has published, a few volumes of Seamus Heaney and of course some of the ever popular Maeve Binchy — including her amusing *Irish Times* column courtesy of Australia's *Irish Echo*. But having come to my own writing career belatedly, it's only a few years ago that I became really curious about contemporary Irish writing, particularly, but not only, women's writing and particularly, but not only, poetry.

Initially I didn't set out on a heavy-duty research path, just kept my eyes open during my favourite pastime, browsing in bookshops whether I can afford to buy books or not. It wasn't long before I realised that while there was plenty of Maeve, Seamus and Edna as you'd expect, that was about it. As much as these three very different writers can provide quite a smorgasbord between them, it did leave me wondering. I did find, *The Faber Book of Irish Poetry*, in Readings, Melbourne, which offered a selection of significant poetry beginning with Patrick Kavanagh (born 1904) and ending with Medbh McGuckian (born 1950). Of the ten poets represented, Medbh McGuckian was the only woman. This left me wondering even more.

Now I'd already made the delicious discovery of Medbh's work through a display of Irish books at a Bloom's Day celebration, in the Henry Gratton Inn in Canberra. That was the day everyone was reading everything except Molly Bloom's soliloquy. At that stage I hadn't got around to reading *Ulysses* and I was so looking forward to Molly, having heard the rave reviews. Okay, I said. Someone's got to do it, and before I knew it I was behind the microphone reading Molly "blind" so to speak. I remembered the good advice of English teachers when I was a wee girl and even if I was pointing to the words with my finger, I kept reading well ahead in my mind so I could present a smooth performance, anticipating all the places deserving of one emphasis or another. (If anyone there that day is reading this, you will now understand why my chuckles and raised eyebrows were all a few words ahead of your own!)

I had a great time reading Molly. The only difficulty was holding my breath long enough — the edition I'd pinched on the spur of the moment was unedited (as is our copy at home). I had hoped other women would come up and rescue me, take over at different points from one another like a relay. When this didn't happen I kept going as long as I could and finally, turning blue, I realised I just had to leave it. I fronted the bar for a well earned drink and a fella perched on a bar stool, head languishing over an open copy of *Ulysses*, turned his face slightly towards me and said simply, with the right eye still on the page, "You got about half way". I think his expression though, was one of approval or maybe even admiration, after all not many people outside an Olympic synchronised swimming team can hold their breath that long.

I thought it was very interesting that he had brought his own copy even though he wasn't going to be performing and had actually followed the text word for word as I read. Gosh. As I wended my way back to my table I realised for the first time that *everyone* else had brought their own copy of *Ulysses*. There were more open copies of *Ulysses* lying spine down in this pub, than all the Holy Bibles I'd seen open in my whole Sunday School and church-going childhood. It was my first Bloom's Day event. I've since been to others and they're all as bad.

The most intellectual was the one I read at in the State Library of New South Wales Mitchell Galleries. Great venue. Great event. A few intellectuals said to me soberly, "I do think there is great humour in *Ulysses*." I didn't think it proper to mention that I had laughed my way all around Canberra as I read *Ulysses* for the first time, on public transport. Or that I had written some quite irreverent poems in response. (No, they're not included in this anthology so stay where you are.)

Anyway, I bought Medbh's collection, *On Ballycastle Beach*, fell in love with her writing and decided it was some sort of omen since Medbh also, was born in Belfast in 1950. Another coincidence involving Medbh was the time I went along to the University of Canberra's Arts Lunch with visiting Spinifex Press author, Gillian Hanscombe. Afterwards a young woman came up to me and said how wonderful it was to hear a Northern Irish accent — I had asked a question brave soul that I am — in her own wonderful Northern Irish accent, which I couldn't quite pick. "Where are you from?" I asked. Or rather: "Where are *yoo* from?" having immediately dropped into Belfast Brogue. "Ballycastle." Well how could I resist — it's the only time I've been able to think quickly enough to make a literary quip — "On Ballycastle Beach?" But she topped me with: "That's my mother's cousin!" So Medbh did I ever tell you I met your cousin's daughter in Australia and she was doing just grand? (And yes, I'm delighted to say, you *will* find Medbh McGuckian in this anthology.)

I had the idea for this collection back in 1991, but I was up to my eyes in another project and thought I'd better leave it for a while. That was quite handy as it turned out, as since then people have gone to great pains to focus on the Irish, by organising Great Famine commemoratives, an Ireland and Its Diaspora Festival and the like, all just in time to promote *Wee Girls*. Anyway, I thought that if I was having trouble accessing Irish women writers, maybe other Australian readers were as well. Or maybe they were not even looking — maybe they didn't know what they were missing! And how much did they know about Australia and our writing, in Ireland? Was there as much growth and activity in the area of women's writing in Ireland as there has been in Australia over the last ten to fifteen years? (Yes it seems, there has.)

So that's where it started, but like most anthologies there was a process of evolution. *Wee Girls* began as a link between

Ireland and Australia with the thought of maybe going further afield. Susan Hawthorne of Spinifex Press, encouraged me to go into as many countries as possible and as a result, England, Canada, America and New Zealand are also represented.

The collection became not just a small taste of contemporary Irish women's writing, but an attempt to define just what "Irishness" is; what it means to *be* Irish. In particular it also looks at the influence that Irish heritage has had on writers — their work and their lives. There are stories and threads of heritage all through *Wee Girls*. It is addressed from many perspectives and in tangent with a range of other pertinent issues including the Famine, the Troubles, love and sex, family, education, immigration and what it feels like to be a part of the large Irish diaspora. (I hope all seventy million of you buy this book.) In this small but diverse collection, these writers contribute to the preservation of Irish heritage and invite other generations of women/writers to revel in this rich legacy.

Minister Avril Doyle TD who is responsible for Great Famine commemoration, told the *Irish Echo* during a visit to Australia this year, "it was not a simple task to recover in any meaningful way, the buried experience of the Famine or re-capture the culture of the time."

You will gain some insight though, through Helena Mulkern's graphic but sensitive treatment of this part of our history in her story "Famine Fever", while Colleen Burke shows how the Famine reaches down the generations through ordinary everyday rituals in her poem, *A Shadow on the Heart*. In "A Joyous Day" Colleen also paints a vivid picture of life in Sydney with a warren of Irish relatives, a shilling each way at the Chinese bookmaker's and St Patrick's Day — her mother's special day.

Pam Lewis' father often said to her, "'You're potato-famine Irish'. He always said this in a nostalgic, rather fond way, and the words ran together as one loving and exotic expression whose meaning was never explained. Like all words that are spoken together quickly, they blended into something else. I thought he was saying, 'Potatofah-Minirish'. It made me special in some mysterious way that would be revealed to me later. Then I saw a drawing of bodies lying at the side of the road during the potato famine. I still have a very clear memory of that picture because of the shock." Pam says that somewhere along the line, they were full Irish. "We'd apparently been Catholic too at one time, until the priest made a pass at one of my great aunts, and the whole family left the church at once."

In *The Emigrant Irish*, celebrated poet Eavan Boland, at once applauds from home shores the strengths of Ireland's expatriates and admonishes those who have stayed behind. "They would have thrived on our necessities." Others search out a place for themselves as members of the Irish diaspora, tenuous threads and memories linking them to their native land. Joan Bridget's story "Falling Asleep with Strangers", is a nostalgic walk in the twilight of Ireland, that will especially tug at the heart strings of twilightless Irish-Australian readers.

In *My Grandmother's Voice*, Mary Dorcey tunes in to the voices of all the mothers before her, and the histories they carry with them. She also shares with us in *The Gaelic Poets Warned Me*, the pitfalls of history and the dangers of love:

> *Snared by atavistic beauty,*
> *I fell into history.*
> *All the poems in the English language*
> *will not save me.*

Language is an issue for Jill Jones. This third generation Irish-Australian poet tries to analyse the Irishness in her own writing: "There is a sense that things must be said, spoken as well as read. A story that must be told: anecdote, history, voices. There are dreams — and the weirdness — even in ordinary things. As if access is given through language to the irrational. And then I write as someone living on an island (a very big one, no doubt) close to the sea using a language that came from some other place, that is my own surely but at times not quite."

Rita Ann Higgins, celebrates subjects around her, frequently employing a biting irony. *Higher Purchase* is the title poem of a recent collection:

> *We saw them take*
> *her furniture out,*
> *. . . When it was going in*
> *we watched with envy*
> *she told her kids out loud*
> *'You're as good as anyone else*
> *on this street.'*
> *When it was coming out*
> *no one said anything,*
> *only one young skut*
> *who knew no better, shouted,*
> *'Where will ye put the phone now,*
> *when it comes.'*

What people say to each other is a concern for Linda Anderson, born in Belfast but now living in England. She feels that her perspective is always influenced by her Irish background. The recurring obsession in her work is "the link between public and private kinds of violence. The way public violence seeps and deforms and creates what a man and woman say to each other in their own kitchen, for example . . . The way all our 'privacies' create the mutilating world." However, acclaimed poet Medbh McGuckian, who still lives in Belfast, feels that, "There's a determined search for the right language in which to say what we really mean, to each other and about each other, no longer behind each other's backs in each other's houses."

The violence experienced by the people of the north has certainly had its impact on writers. It features in Linda Anderson's short story, Medbh McGuckian's essay on her life and writing processes, and the contributions from Cherry Smyth. Events in the seventies are especially recurrent and Cherry's pieces show, not surprisingly, how the Troubles have filtered into the everyday lives and language of younger generations. The poem, *Maybe it was 1970*, begins,

> *Kids my age play real soldiers,*
> *dashing milk bottle bombs against tanks,*
> *binlids for shields.*

Still others are on searches of another kind. Journeys to seek out heritage, family roots, faces familiar. It didn't occur to Bronwyn Rodden that she was Irish "until I went to Ireland for a holiday in 1990 and found myself surrounded by people who looked just like my parents and brothers and sisters. I realised I belonged to a race of people after all."

In *Searching*, Robyn Rowland, succinctly expresses just why so many go to such lengths, go on such travels:

> *Dislocated to find location I come in search of family,*
> *traces followed with perverse avidity by those whose*
> *stories in their stolen land take short breath; counting*
> *stars for all the Irish exiled by famine, pain, or*
> *that great roving spark burning in their bloodline still.*

This legacy takes many shapes. "I'll take you to Dublin one day, Gabrielle says, we'll visit the gaol I was born in", writes Francesca Rendle-Short in "Loop-the-Loop". "And she tells you the story of her mother hiding three salt-boats, their delicate silver filigree, brilliant ultramarine glass."

"Do be a good girl" is part of the legacy handed down to Ailbhe Smyth, who finds herself "thinking about growing up in Ireland in the 1950s and 1960s, a good and proper middle-class girl." In her narrative poem, *Girl Beaming in a White Dress*, she discusses the restrictions and limitations of Irish girlhood, religion, education and home life.

For feminist philosopher, Mary Daly, it is Irish Luck. "From both parents I heard the rhetorical question, 'Aren't we Lucky to be Irish?' When I had to fill out forms inquiring about my 'nationality', I always wrote 'Irish'. It did not occur to me that I should write 'American'. Moreover, since I knew it was Lucky to be Irish I thought I must personally be Lucky. No matter how overwhelming the forces were that tried to disabuse me of this impression, it did, in fact, persist. Moreover, I believe that it worked as a self-fulfilling prophecy." All this and Mary's a third generation Irish-American. Where does this leave Sue Reidy? Still arguing her case?

"'Rubbish,' pronounced my partner crisply. 'You're no more Irish than I am English.' . . . *'Outrage!'* . . . 'Feeling Irish isn't enough,' he added. 'The whole notion is sentimental and misguided. You're not Irish. What you are is a fourth generation Pakeha New Zealander of Irish extraction.' I continued to feel Irish and indeed to staunchly defend my right to do so. I was surprised by the intensity of my response. Why did I feel so passionate about claiming the Irish identity as my own? Did it make more sense to focus on my New Zealand identity rather than hankering after a fragile thread of connection with Europe?"

These are the very questions that plague us all whether first, second, third, fourth generation Irish or more. Whatever the answers, one thing is for sure. Whether writing fiction, poetry, non-fiction or autobiography; young writers relatively new to the scene, award winning or best selling writers, they all tell a good story. Contributors were given a fairly open invitation. They could use their complete space allocation for current work or some of it to write about their lives and writing processes, the influence that being Irish has on them as women and writers, or any other related topic. The result is a rich selection of writing which takes us on an often moving sometimes humorous journey through many of the issues pertinent to the 1990s.

I look forward to the day when a wide, wide range of Irish women's writing is easily accessed from every corner. In the meantime, for drawing my attention to, or/and putting me in touch with various writers, I'd particularly like to thank: Jeremy Addis, Publisher of *Books Ireland*; Jessie

Lendennie, Managing Director at Salmon Press; Tom Kennedy, European Editor of *Cimarron Review*; Jenny Nagle of Addenda Publishing Sales and Marketing Services; Ailbhe Smyth, editor of *Wildish Things* and Director of WERRC, UCD.

I also must thank Susan Hawthorne and Renate Klein, Co-Directors of Spinifex Press, for their love and support, for broadening my horizons in more ways than one and for being mad enough to accept the *Wee Girls* proposal, on nothing but a title and one and a half pages of blarney. Thanks to all Spinifex staff especially editor, Jo Turner, for her expertise and friendship; Sue Hardisty, Export Manager, for her cheery support and for making me internationally famous (I fantasise); and Libby Fullard, Office Manager and Alison Bicknell, Finance, (may the mail bags be bulging with *Wee Girls* orders). Thanks to Spinifex friends Claire Warren, typesetter and her wee girl Gypsy, and designer Soosie Adshead for the classy good looks; and Samantha Isma and Marisa Stastny for enthusiastically promoting the book in many ways.

Thank you to Wendy King for yet again helping with the dreaded typing and for a gorgeous grand-daughter. Thanks indeed to Joseph Duffy, up and coming Irish-Australian muso, for assistance with music-oriented research. Special thanks to Helena Mulkerns for so generously translating my poem, *My Irishness*, into Irish and also to Barra O'Donneabháin for his assistance with this. And as they say, last but not least, thank you to my family — Bill, Aroona and Brendan Murphy — for their love and ongoing assistance and support, and to good friends who have also lasted the distance.

Mary Robinson said in her first address as President of Ireland: "symbols are what unite and divide people. Symbols give us our identity, our self-image, our way of explaining ourselves to ourselves and to others. Symbols in turn determine the kinds of stories we tell; and the stories we tell determine the kind of history we make and remake." I would like to think that *Wee Girls* will be included in some small way among these symbols.

I especially thank all the contributors who have been so welcoming of this project and whose voices — their poetry, their stories, their histories — bear witness to much of what is important to us, moves us and cheers us. And to women writing around the world, remember the words of Eavan Boland:

> *In the end*
> *everything that burdened and distinguished me*
> *will be lost in this:*
> *I was a voice.*
>
> — from *Anna Liffey*

— ★ —

Lizz Murphy
September, 1996

Robyn Rowland

Born in Sydney in 1952, Robyn Rowland grew up in the New South Wales seaside town of Shellharbour and has visited Ireland regularly since 1983. The inaugural Director of the Australian Women's Research Centre at Deakin University, Geelong, Australia, Robyn has taught Women's Studies for twenty years and written on women's human rights, women's identity, sexuality and feminist ethics. For fifteen years she has been a leading radical feminist voice against reproductive technology. Her books include, *Filigree in Blood* (Longman Cheshire) and *Perverse Serenity* (Spinifex Press); *Woman Herself* (1989), *Living Laboratories: Women and Reproductive Technology* (1992).

Searching

Dislocated to find location I come in search of family,
traces followed with perverse avidity by those whose
stories in their stolen land take short breath; counting
stars for all the Irish exiled by famine, pain, or
that great roving spark burning in their bloodline still.
Cappamore's Virgin centring the town would be enough.
Gazed upon mercilessly by her unflickering mother's scorn,
harassed by the toll of the priest's word and chafed by
the bleats of neighbours sure in numbers, prods in alien
pews remained only on sufferance. I see their exit written
like a psalm, accompanied by the weeping organ,
         full of the
ragged beauty of poems. And they grieved for the place,
pagan as it is; hills stabbed by crosses, crevices breeding
groves to the virgin. I place my hand on the grey rock of
an old barn, older than I have understanding for,
watching the turf cut. Long before, long after my shadow
has tossed itself in and out of life, the chunks will be
stacked and dried waiting for its slow burn of winter.
Nearby, Kathleen O'Neill spends each evening in this front
room, dark wood carved into the bar, roof thatched
against night, flags softened by old squares of carpet,
their pile trod soft. Two hundred and fifty years old
this room; older than my white country.
Clocks tick loud without hurry in rhythm with the
talk; up and down between laughter and the
worn worries of country life. The old black cat sleeps on

assured of its place. Evenings here bring parts
of a jigsaw to a whole, a place, a good fit, and the
musty smell of peat brings comfort on cooler nights, and
I take my pint of Guinness before bed.

    Rural Ireland rubs a
grain of memory. Green beyond belief, marked by age and
suffering, I feel it part of some old stirring: the place, the
voices so familiar. Reverent and irreverent alike

    know it when
the strings are played and the note is true.

    Fuschia, tree-tall,
drops its crimson purple flowers in tears onto the road.

The Beginning

1

There I entered Ireland —
down the long drive, circuitous
curled snug under colossus rhododendrons;
through that track by the farm
stinging nettles poised on each side;
past the lonely bull
torn from his heifers
shouldering each other
twitchy in the glens.

There were you by the hives —
that bee-loud stillness —
where all the sweetness of Glenstal is found.
You had tossed aside your Tunisian keeper's hat
reaching for the queen quite unafraid —
your fear waits in another glade.
And there was peace
beside the lake
green corners of it tranquil
green enough to subdue
even your bidden restlessness.

2

But up here
away from Limerick's lights
that stud the valley deepening below,

turf on Moher Bog is
softly jagged in twilight;
bog cotton whimpers white
brushing the dark peat;
that one star is planted into pale evening
calling in blackness
the taunting glow of night-sky
to shadow us.
Disquiet trembles in the coiling breeze:
"why are you here?"

Our talk twists and turns
like paths round the Abbey
always leading to the same beginning:
how the heart can quickly love,
how thought can spring so deftly to accord,
and hurt drive piston fast
to strengthening doubt.
Your agitation frets, disturbs.
Uncertain for the first time
I stir silently, begin to query all,
even that intimacy I breathe by:
to shine in the corners of the other's mind
to keep close in the twining tendrils of daily love
its wash and drain
in which the pace of my life
is measured, safe.

Must those threads flex and sometimes break
or like elastic bands entwining a wrist,

embed, curb circulation,
Both bound with raffia thread
into our divergent lives,
we only connect
knock each other in passing
accidental, surprised

and drifting
solid but unreachable
the misted possible
as Innisfree in hazy morning shimmers.

Changing

I stood uncertain among threads twisted at my feet
dropped haphazardly by the tangle of comfortable years.
Now I have plaited them fine and rough into this rope,
peacock blues and greens in Thai-silk flash, at its finest,
broken-brown of waves at the Heads when the river floods,
      at its roughest.
But this knurled cable is so heavy to lift.
Many times I could willingly have dropped it,
so much easier had it been a pebble in the sling of the mind
to whizz fast and light leaving me still with breath.
But now with one driving lunge and
muscle pain beyond snapping strength
I cast my line headlong from these cliffs,
watch it snake and spiral mid-air
splaying wild like a fall of coloured arrows
a tug tight, tense,
in some unseen landing place.

This edge of land where I balance
falls sheer to vanish in a raven-black pitch of sea
rocked, spiked with waves, hungry for seabirds that
shriek in skids down its face
only to rise screaming into the gulf of air.
Precipitous and thrilling,
Cliffs of Moher in the inner selfscape.

But there is no feathered safety for me to cross this breach
only these two hands, scarred

rope-burned, fretting at the task
gripping, ungripping, clutching
one grasp at a time.

How it would help at least to *see* the other side
its features, cliff and crevice, even if shrouded in haze,
to know this hemped advance is worth risking
that its knotted hook has firmly latched
round rock solid as Uluru, wide and earth-caught
      as Ben Bulben
and not some sycamore half-rotted in its core
that taking my weight on crossing will loosen
shake its soil to moaning winds, wrenching, uprooting
plummet me mute
leaden and wingless
to the pit.

The Final Season

You always thought
action is in the speaking of it
But speech is not the act.

The grey-white of snow skies,
the light-bloom of cold
into which these bare trees spread
free of leaf and
summer's torn glaze,
are those where my heron
had sought its peace.

I always thought summer the loving season,
but was wrong.
Look how naked winter makes us.

Now we join in releasing barbs
worn one-by-one through strength.
Slim steel dissolves, compulsion's scars heal.
But parting we draw close
as cold hands about a guttering flame.
Then touch
fires ebbing passion.

Rose-coloured loving —
curtain, sheet, lamplight,
the inner fragile flush of shells.

Blue eyes desire, confused.
Lines of your aging mirror mine.

I memorise
your feathery brow beneath my thumb,
each changing moment of this long last breath,
withholding endearment
the time long past.

Your breath will linger in my hair;
silk of me beneath you will wake you nights
hands searching the sheets, somnambulist in loving.

Bonds of ambivalence, the knowledge of ending.
Almost too late in this season between rain and sleet,
night has given us yesterday's promise.
We move toward something
we can neither touch nor keep.
And now, at last, I know that all my passion
cannot make sure your green will live.

I let go the last hook,
knowing you will remember flesh in flesh,
ache, now and then, for summers and springs;

for nights that were star-swollen over black turf,
bog cotton whimpering under whispering trees;
for those mountain climbs that fed
the flare of pain and struggle we burned
to feel we were alive:
for all we relished in the joy
and anguished raging of our hearts.

Mary Dorcey

Mary Dorcey was born and brought up in County Dublin, Ireland. She has lived in England, France, the USA and Japan. Her first collection of poetry, *Kindling*, was published in 1987 by Onlywomen (UK). Her work has been widely anthologised and translated. Her short story collection, *A Noise from the Woodshed*, (Onlywomen, UK), won the Rooney Prize for Irish Literature in 1989. An active feminist, Mary Dorcey was a founding member of Women for Radical Change, Irish Women United, and the Irish Gay Rights movement. Her latest collection of poetry, *The River that Carries Me*, was published by Salmon Press in 1995 and she is currently finishing her first novel.

My Grandmother's Voice

Sometimes
when my mother speaks to me
I hear her mother's voice:
my grandmother
with her Belfast accent
which carried with it
something from every town
the Normans passed through.
My grandmother,
mother of seven,
who will not be quiet yet
twenty years after her death.

Sometimes when I look at my mother
it is her mother I see
the far sighted gaze,
the way of sitting
bolt upright in a chair —
holding forth, the quick wit,
the fold her hands take in her lap.
The sweep of her hair.

And listening closely
or caught unaware,
I hear my great-grandmother
echo between them:
A glance — a tone.
My grandmother's

mother
who died giving birth
to her only child.
Whose words and stories
pent up in her daughter
flowed on
into the talk of my mother.
I catch them now in my own.
My head sings with their conversation

And hearing them —
this fertile
and ghostly orchestration
I am sorry to have brought them
to the end of their line.
Stopped them in their track
across millennia.
From what primeval starting point
to here?
A relay race
through centuries
from mother to daughter
an expression passed on
a gesture,
a profile.

Their voices reverberate in my head.
They will die with me.
I have put an end to inheritance
drawn a stroke across the page.

Their grace,
their humour,
their way of walking in a room.
The stoicism
that carried them all this way
has stopped with me,
the first of their kind
who will not bear their gift
and burden.

I lift my pen
quickly wanting
to set down all the stories
spoken by these busy, garrulous,
long lived women
who never had a moment
to sit down
or lift a pen.

I begin.
A young woman, a Protestant
from Belfast
married a sea captain,
a Catholic
who drowned at sea . . .

The Breath of History

I am not an ordinary woman.
I wake in the morning,
I have food to eat.
No one has come in the night
to steal my child, my lover.
I am not an ordinary woman.

A plum tree
blossoms outside my window,
the roses are heavy with dew.
A blackbird sits on a branch
and sings out her heart.
I am not an ordinary woman.

I live where I want
I sleep when I'm tired.
I write the words I think.
I can watch the sky
and hear the sea.
I am not an ordinary woman.
No one has offered me life
in exchange for another's.

No one has beaten me until I fall down.
No one has burnt my skin
nor poisoned my lungs.
I am not an ordinary woman.
I know where my friends live.
I have books to read.

I was taught to read.
I have clean water to drink.
I know here my lover sleeps:
she lies beside me,
I hear her breathing.
My life is not commonplace.

At night the air
is as sweet as honey-suckle
that grows along the river bank.
The curlew cries
from the marshes
far out,
high and plaintive.
I am no ordinary woman.
Everything I touch and see
is astonishing and rare —
privileged.
Come celebrate each
privileged, exceptional thing:
water, food, sleep —
the absence of pain —
a night without fear
a morning without
the return of the torturer.

A child safe,
a mother,
a lover, a sister.
Chosen work.
Our lives are not commonplace —
any of us who read this.

But who knows
tomorrow or the day after . . .
I feel all about me
the breath of history —
pitiless
and ordinary.

The Gaelic Poets Warned Me

The gaelic poets warned me.
They knew you of old —
your eyes like green stones
on a river bed,
the milk white skin,
the hair raven black
and its sheen.
For centuries they sang
your praise,

but I paid no attention
or had forgotten.
Until I saw you walking naked.
By then it was too late —
my past had caught up with me.
Snared by atavistic beauty,
I fell into history.
All the poems in the English language
will not save me.

The Whiteness of Snow

The whiteness
of snow
on a branch of pine
is the whiteness
of her skin
from shoulder
to thigh.
And the sway of the branch
under its
flesh of snow,
is the song of her hips
in the weight of my hands.

Learning to Live With it

They took my pulse
and my temperature
They told me to lie down
and be sensible.

They said all things
bad and good come to an end.
Half a lifetime of love —
let it be enough for you.

They said I must study the alphabet
and learn to read the writing on the wall
They said I must come to face facts —
they handed me the blindfold.

They said I must stop listening
for the last cry from the wilderness.
They said I must stop asking —
they showed me how to cut out my tongue.

And you? Well you, they said,
always made too much of things.
They saw the blood slipping from your eyes —
they offered you their handkerchiefs.

When the flesh withered on your frame
and your cheek grew haggard
They said: See — how shapely she is —
what fine bones!

They told me to lie down and be sensible.
They said all things come to an end.
I must stop listening they said,
for the last cry from the wilderness.

I must stop searching through grains of sand
for one grain of sand.
I must stop holding out bare arms
to stem the tide.

And when you cried out in your sleep —
Love me still love my only love
They said: See —
She's learning to live with it.

I Cannot Love You as You Want to be Loved

I cannot love you
as you want to be loved —
without wanting.
I cannot love you
without loving your black startled eyes —
without wanting them to look at me.
Without wanting to see them
catch fire
as they look at me.

I cannot love you
without loving your thighs —
the long lovely line of your thighs.
Without wanting to run my hand along
        the length of them.
I cannot love you
without loving your hands —
so strong, so talkative.
Without wanting them to touch me,
to touch my hand,
my thigh.
I cannot love you as you want to be loved —
without wanting.

You are a blade
I have lifted from my own hand
to put a stop to wounding.
Who made you so sharp?
so dangerous?

I miss your laughter
and your flights of fancy.
Your foolishness,
your wild untamable ways.
I miss your passion for things
your refusal to take life quietly.

You are a blade
I have lifted from my own hand
to put a stop to wounding.
Who made you so sharp?
so dangerous?
You whose love words
were like a bounty
a burst of grace,
oiled and perfumed
each one a healing,
a benediction.
You whose eyes were pools
the stars could bathe in.

You are a knife
I have lifted from my own hand
to put a stop to wounding.
You should be the earth I lie down upon,
the river that carries me,
the bright sky that covers me,
the wind that sings through the lilac.
Who made you a blade
I cannot dare to handle?

I Saw a Fish this Morning

I saw a fish
this morning
and it looked
like you.

Leaping
clear into air:
back arched
for joy.

And I wanted to be
lake water,
cool blue, slipping from its sides.
Green reeds washing clear

around its thighs.
I wanted to be yellow river bed
sand,
hollowed for its belly.

I wanted to be white, pure air,
waiting,
sucked by its breath.
I wanted to be

high
as spring summer sky —
sun gleaming
in its eye.

Helena Mulkerns

Helena Mulkerns was born and raised in Dublin. She studied at University College Dublin, the Sorbonne University and New York University. She moved to the United States and became Arts contributor with the *Irish Voice*. She has published in various publications including, *Rolling Stone*, *Music Express*, *Downtown Magazine*, *The Music Paper*, *Irish Edition*, *New York Perspectives*, *Entertainment Weekly*, *The Irish Echo and* corresponds from New York for *The Irish Times* and *Hot Press Magazine*.

Helena's first fiction was published in the *Sunday Tribune* and nominated for the *Sunday Tribune*/Hennessy Literary Awards in 1991. She is included in the anthology *Ireland in Exile*, and was featured in *Here's Me Bus!* She is presently completing a collection of short stories. Helena currently lives in Manhattan, escaping from the city on summer weekends on her motorcycle.

Famine Fever

He pulls me out of the cabin near the beach, and tells me the tide is alive. He says that out in the blue night a million tiny vessels are flowing along the current off to somewhere else, and he wants us to go with them. I say no. I am too scared. The hut near the beach is all we have, where we can rest in relative safety, considering the times.

His eyes are shining, like I haven't seen them in a long while now. And there is more to him that has changed. He seems whole again, not weighed down with the horror, the filth, and the fear of this plague. He is like he was before, when there was never fear on him. *Nuair nach raibh eagla ríamh air.* He fought hard through the hunger, but for all his handsome strength, he faded to a shadow like the rest of us in the end.

Yet tonight, here he is now, like a child with his talk of boats — and the sky coming down on us black as a grave, and something in the back of my mind shrieking loud and long like a storm. He is telling me that the moon will soon be out and I will see the boats. It is true — he has me laughing — I see no boats yet, but I do see the moon, scattering milky and gentle down the beach like a dancer. I begin to walk with him into its wake, except that I have a terrible pain at the same time, dragging me backwards into the hut, and I am tormented by this shaking in my bones and this fire over my skin, and I am looking at him, but remembering too deep for the sea to wash it from my head . . .

In Dublin and London, they said it was God's will for the

lazy, teeming Irish, stricken for our own good, and they couldn't interfere with God's will. Our own said it was a judgement on our sins, but I never could quite work out what they were, to deserve this. The first year, there was fierce talk of the blight, and it coming westwards. Then one morning, I woke up to the fearful screeching of them in Kelleher's, coming across the quiet fields, as they found the crop in the ground stinking black and mushy, like devils' spits, the flowers fouled. Since then it went from bad to worse.

I smell the salt, crisp in the air. It is strange, this sea — the soft sucking swirls of surf curling like cats around the rocks, and the biggest space in the world under the sky. Tonight, a silver mist seeps around him as we walk down the strand, and he says, "Listen: the bay is humming". It occurs to me that it is the fish, the ones out in the deep we could never reach, singing to us. Then I shiver. Maybe it's the dead-already, moaning from the night vapors. My mind keeps pulling back and forth between his light and my deepest horror, I am restless and dithering. But then I concentrate on my bare feet sliding gently into the sands, and it comforts me.

We weren't as bad off as some. We had sub-tenants, and a decent cottage and animals. But like the rest, we paid the landlord in grains and produce, and kept the potato for living. Oats, butter, barley, eggs, all went to him, even though we'd never seen him in all our days, an absentee. He only sent his bailiffs to do his dirty work. But still, the potatoes did us well enough, and the rents had to be paid.

I was married only a few months then, and Liam was

letting on of course, that it wasn't a serious thing at all. So just to be sure, we kept the seed potatoes and sowed even more for the next year, and less grains. We thought we might even make some money. We were wrong. But you see, nobody believed it would happen again, let alone a third time with the few seeders we had left for the '47 crop.

"So," he says to me, with that grin on him. "Are you coming?"

I peer out into the dark sea, pearl-speckled under the moon, and sure enough, he is right. You can just about distinguish an odd flurry of activity out beyond the shore's crashing wave line. I glimpse crafts tiny and majestic — some with lone mariners, some with groups, some with masts and riggings for to cross the ocean altogether, some just curraghs. They are heading in what seems like an out-to-sea and westwardly direction. The light is tricky, sometimes they seem not to be boats at all. But it is beautiful, and terrifying at the same time. "Why are there so many?" I ask. "And where are they going?"

I glance back towards the village, empty now. Where once was crowded and bustling, now is dead to the world, and for a moment, the huddle of bothies look like so many ancient burial mounds, from centuries gone. But his shining tempts me. Now he is unmooring a curragh from a stone on the beach with a ring in it, and he begins talking again, the voice low, smiling in that old way of his. I amn't hearing everything he is saying, and I think of just letting him go, and returning to my son, when it strikes me like a blow that of course, the child is gone. They took him away for fear of the fever, and because I had dried out like an old hag — without nourishment for myself, there was nothing to sustain my milk. I sink into a kind of paralysis, and he lifts me into the boat.

After the second year, we had nothing really. We survived awhile on savings and things put by. Then after the second crop failure we killed the sheep, then the smaller animals. Then we ate carcasses of cattle, rabbits, birds, even dogs for food. We made soup from dandelions, nettles, docks, charlock and when we could find them, we ate mushrooms. Through all that, we kept the holding, since to leave the land was death. You could see that in the eyes of the beggars that were coming to my door every day, bands of them. Those who'd been thrown off the land, those drifting souls whose families were dead, children orphaned and widows taken to the roads. The country was haunted by them, and if it wasn't the road fever with its relapsing fits that got them, it was the famine fever, that rotted and roasted a soul alive and emptied the body out like a putrid fruit, a human blight.

Then there were the dreaded corpse men coming round the houses to take away the bodies and throw them into the mass graves in the bogs away up from the roads. Worse: if a family couldn't afford that, or were too weak, they shoved the remains of children or parents into bog holes or ditches nearby, a shame never known before.

In the Spring of 1846, the fever hit the West, and I stopped giving to beggars, or even opening my door. The fear was terrible. The authorities had some schemes going, projects to employ people who could hardly stand, or soup kitchens where you had to give up your land for a bite. In the end, it sounds funny, but finally we ate the rent. That was the simple tragedy of it. I would not see us starve while the good grain was being shipped off to a landlord in England. The bailiff gave us an extra month, and then one day they just arrived with an eviction notice, and burned the house to the ground.

We came down from the mountains then, outcasts ourselves, thinking that maybe the seashore would provide us with some nourishment. You'd only want to have seen the sight of us, staggering along the boreens like bone-brittle ghosts, aching and red with scurvy. My sister's children had their bellies swollen out like pregnant dwarfs, and one was blinded with an eye-malady that seemed more to strike the small ones. We found this village deserted and wondered why, probably cleared by the landlord, we couldn't be sure. Then when the tide ran low, we discovered that the sea was no salvation.

The shore had been stripped bare from end to end, not a sliver of seaweed to put into a pot, not a shellfish or an old crab in a pool, nothing. And like the fishermen before us who had pawned their nets to eat after the first year, we had no fishing tools, nor craft to harvest the waters.

My brother-in-law wanted to continue along the coast to the workhouse, now only ten miles away. My parents said rather die out in the winds than lying screaming under two-day corpses, like the stories went. Nobody got out of there alive anyway. In the filth, the fever raged wild, and there was nothing to eat but the brimstone grain they tried to give us instead of potatoes, ground glass to the stomachs of the starving. We decided to rest a little, but then the fever took Liam, and the rest were afraid to stay in the village.

The water gleams silver and its coldness is a shock, I am shivering. On the buoyancy of the tide, once we get out beyond the rollers, the current is surprisingly strong. I have never left land before, and wonder at the waves, filled with enough life as if they were creatures themselves. I see faces under the surface, huddled close beneath the water, and am frightened. My shuddering increases, and I toss my head with pain. They are malevolent, and reaching for me. But then I look at Liam and feel renewed. He is facing me, pulling back rhythmically on the curragh's oars, and his silhouette is framed in deepest indigo speckled by a crowd of stars, and a growing glimmer from the West along the horizon. Which is strange, I think to myself, since dawn usually comes from the other way.

It was a desolate dusk, as I stood at the edge of the village, watching them walk away over the hill until they were gone. I gave my child to my sister, since she'd already lost two, and I stayed with Liam. What could I do. He suffered for days, the ghastly bloody flux, the fever, his voice gone and his face withered, until I felt he was almost beyond me. When my weeping wore out, and I so terribly alone, I screamed out loud at the Virgin, asking why I was left here with nothing to give him, only my own ragged arms and the sound of my voice, until I became so weak I lost that too. Only the shore-breaking of the waves answered me.

And now even the waves are far gone, and the humming sea soothes my terror. He is talking low again, that this will be a good journey. Maybe bring us somewhere the pest has not yet taken hold.

Alongside, towering over us or bobbing lowly, a huge fleet is moving now with some speed. It is magnificent, but quite sinister, because I cannot make out who exactly it is sailing with us, their faces are all indistinct and black, but it seems like we are all related, too. The faces on the boats, and the faces in the waves and even under the bogs.

Maybe it is America we were going to, there is always talk of that. On the estate down the road the landlord paid for all his tenants' passages to Boston, to get them off his hands, like. The land had emptied out entirely, and the cottages were razed, those too weak to travel shunted off to the workhouse. Liam said it was a lonely stretch after that.

I am leaning back in the curragh, with my shawl around my shoulders, although it is warm, warm, almost unbearably so. I am looking at all the boats, when suddenly an old woman leans out towards me from another craft, her face obscured by shadow, and inquires, "What are you doing here so soon, girl? Don't you know where we're all going?"

The dark stink of her comes wafting over to me, and the moment I realize what it is, I am pulled down into the floor of the boat, and I can't see Liam anymore, nor stars nor the milky glow across the heavens from the moon. I am tossed over, gnarled up into a knot of skirts, my shawl flung from me, my body burning again. I am on the floor of the hut, the cramps gnawing my guts, and a lashing pain all around my back and arms and legs, slicing through every bit of me like a fishmonger's knife. My skin is all aflame, but my clothes icy wet. The fire in the grate has almost gone out and as I get up on one elbow, the shaking takes me so badly I fall back again. *Dia eadrainn agus gach olc.* God between us and all evil.

Not long ago Liam was like this, the sweat on his head and body, the tossing and swelling rash. The stench fills me up, and with the new soreness in my fingers and toes, I know it is me. God Bless us, but I hadn't meant to fall asleep, only wanting to stay beside him.

I am crying for the sea — the blinding beauty of the open ocean, and all the tiny boats there, sailing steady, and Liam with his hands calmly on the oars. I'll not let that out of my head, I will fight the blackness with this beauty. The pain is battling to take over, it goes from the back of my neck through my eyes, engulfing me. I close them again, I swim back momentarily to the curragh, and he is as I've just seen him, blue-bathed, eyes out over the waters, alight with that old look of anticipation.

But this time, I am under the waves, within the pain-wracked hum of the under-creatures, and there is a terrible fear on me that he will be away off before I can ask him where it is they are all headed, because I know he knows. Pulled down yet again, I fall through black waters into a muddy bed, a muddy shack with a barren hearth, earth under me and an earthen roof to fall on me like a shroud.

I crawl, wretched as an animal, across the few feet of ground to where he lies, tangled in his own old coat, skeletal and still. Even through the wracking fever my heart breaks at the ashen, emaciated face of him, hollow as a holy statue. I start to ask him what place is it out there in the night that we are all off to, but he is already gone.

The Whole Nine Yards

The blue was a perfectly clear blue, no clouds, no haze. At least most of the time. It was outlined by an ancient frame, white chipped paint, rotten wood. There was an ornate grille that rose about a third of the way up the window, and being just under the roof of the building, if you lay on the bed you couldn't see anything else but the sky, which formed this azure rectangle. That way you could imagine you were just about anywhere, at any point in time. Almost pleasant was mid-afternoon, with the summer heat gently lulling her into a warm numbness. It dragged her into pasts real and dreamed, snippets of conversations far away long ago, or jagged bolts of surrealism, their strangeness prompting more flights into plains beyond comprehension, into morbid, shaky corners of mind.

Lately, lying on the bed looking at this shape had been her only real activity. The place was a total mess, clothes and scraps everywhere. Things just lay where they had fallen or been thrown the previous week, upon her arrival. Last week's newspaper lay under an unopened letter from three days back, a half carton of sour milk had become stinky, unbearable and then unnoticeable again. The garbage had overtipped and there were breadcrumbs and coffee stains in the sink. Empty wine and vodka bottles were in a heap under the window, a playground for an insect colony of indeterminate nature.

When she awoke each day, it was sometimes quite a while before she roused herself and went to wash over the tiny, ancient sink. It had a design like willow pattern plates, very old and pretty, but like everything around here it was slow, the hard scum-lathered water slugging torpidly down the pipe. She had run out of toothpaste now, and this was nasty. It was hard to steal, they usually kept toiletries near the checkout. Besides, she went out as little as possible, went hungry just lying there because she had no desire to move outside the door or down the interminable stairs to the street. She had little money in any case, and it was fast running out. The thought of this made the back of her neck ache and her stomach turn over, and a certain little list of items in her head came tumbling inevitably after: (a) no Ahmed (b) no money (c) no friends (d) no "plans". She called it the "angst list", and dealt with these eruptions by endeavouring to dismiss them as quickly as they came up. Easy. Sometimes. Or else she'd just have a few glasses of wine and sail off into the blue.

The first thing that came to her head every morning was the angst list. It took a lot to dismiss that, unless she was tired enough to go back to sleep. Then again, it would attack unexpectedly, at any time of the night or day, and was usually accompanied by jagged pangs of horror, which tended to rampage round her brain like a pack of rabid dogs. They wreaked varying degrees of damage, vanquished often by drugs or alcohol, or dreams. Then there was the nasty feeling that her brains had suddenly metamorphosed into gleaming white cotton wool, that rapidly changed colour as a liquid scarlet scream took over. The cotton wool, heavy then, throbbed under the scream: Tintinitus, maybe.

Something to do with the way the blood moves through the brain.

Sometimes, just lying there, everything else would disintegrate around the clear blue light, and it became the only thing in the world. There was so much light in the room, it was so hot, that the only sensible thing to do, she would advise herself, was to lie down naked on the narrow bed and remain quite still so there was not a creak. After all, they had told her in the hospital to sleep, so it was okay. Just to sleep. It was like an unexpected present, when the doctor said it. A gift that gave her the final order: "You don't have to do anything now for a little while." They didn't tell her how long for. They gave her sleeping tablets when she told them she couldn't sleep and Valium when she told them about the attacks. "Not to worry, fine in a few weeks, right as rain." They had found the scars on her arms and given her a letter of introduction to a psychiatrist in another hospital. Neat letterhead: illegible script.

But she did rest, sleeping solidly without movement for about four days, collapsing as soon as everything was dumped inside the confines of this bright cell. Lock on door, no phone. Waves of heat, waves of sleep: she got up now and then only in the good cause of going down to the store for the odd few bottles of wine, to tide her over. She bought some bread and pocketed some cheese and paté to go with it, which would do for a few days. She was glad the place had no phone and that it was so far from the city centre; there was nowhere to go here, no distractions. Nobody.

Her mind blazed into fantasy each afternoon, with the drink and the heat. Red wine and blue rectangle. Occasional muffled street sounds, intermittent dozes, intermittent headache. No Ahmed. No money. No friends. No plans. The cotton wool crammed her head, packed tight, tight into her skull — gnawed by the occasional rabid dog.

She had brought all her belongings here from Ahmed's house, not that there was much. But it seemed to take forever. And of course, it had to coincide with a heat wave. The trips bearing plastic bags and refilled-rucksack seemed interminable, and trying to get it all done in one day before he came back was a nightmare. Everything seemed so exhausting, Ahmed had really taken a lot out of her. She wasn't usually this out of whack.

The first time she saw Ahmed, he was very drunk. But what a laugh he was. A veritable bloody howl. Smart and smartass. Cute ass, Anthony Quinn voice, a taste for the scandalous and the chic. The life and soul of every party coming to you live in three languages. Dark curly locks and Italian boots, forget it. He took the "sudden onslaught" approach, arching her back down over her high chrome and leather barstool, a deep shameless kiss that ended even more shamelessly in a bathroom in some apartment near the Marais.

Pain in the ass, this memory thing. The cotton wool deal was unnerving enough, but the sudden explosions from these memory dogs would blast though every now and then: Ahmed falling over the Metro barrier with festoons of roses as she got off the train. Dragging her to the zoo to see a fucking Panda. Telling her exotic tales of Mohammed and Christ, of deserts and battles and slaughter, of love and Islamic art and learning and longed-for beaches where veiled mothers awaited their exiled sons. He was only abroad to study until he could go back to his father's house again, as soon as the government changed. Then he would bring her back, triumphant, into the bosom of his kindred, present her as a Queen in his regained homeland. The whole nine yards.

The last time she saw Ahmed he was also very drunk, surprise, surprise. Self-righteous, melodramatic and vicious. The worst of it was she was so out of it herself, she could hardly remember what the whole fight had really originated with, apart from the obvious. She gave as good as she got, of course, because by then she knew where to get him. She must have gone too far, though — she remembered catching the reflection of her own bleached, disembodied face in the bathroom mirror, just before he hurled the half-empty bottle of tequila right into it, missing her head by a calculated two inches. He yelled long and furious in Arabic, some words of which she recognized — woman, whore.

She carefully, systematically removed each bottle, container and jar from the cabinet, flinging each one at him as counter-ammo to the abuse, roaring away herself. A trip to see the parents my arse. Marriage arranged for years now. Second cousin the fuck. How could he deceive her? But how dare she question his action, he never promised her anything. She was deluded — a mere ignorant child — no idea of their way of life. "That's a home marriage — you are my modern girl!" Hello great white whore.

As he slammed the apartment door after him, she collapsed down in fury and frustration among the broken fragments scattered all around the grubby tiles. She remembered thinking how the bathroom was darker without the mirror, but the fluorescent light still shone — most spitefully — on the grey walls, and twinkled pathetically on the fragments. She wailed and cried for a while, she slashed furiously at her forearms with pieces of glass, feeling some kind of anguished release with the pain, but knowing she was too much of a coward to really cut herself.

Her hands, knees and calves were in ribbons when she woke up. Those she hid or excused easily enough, at work. But the long, fresh, thread like scabs on her forearms tended to protrude most dreadfully from beneath her cuffs every now and then. The other embarrassment in the light of day was her spectacularly bruised face which only Suzanne, the office lesbian, commented on. Suzanne invited her to lunch, which gave Paddy the perfect excuse to insist on paying for a bottle of wine she knew she would mostly end up drinking herself. She told Suzanne about Ahmed, and how she was better off without him now and everything would be fine. How Irish girls had this unfortunate propensity for these types, she heard, on account of being bossed around for years by the da's and the brothers she heard, until the only way they could fall was into the arms of a similar force. Very simple. Suzanne said that recognizing it was half the battle. When she was fired the following week, gentle Suzanne was the only person who offered her number. She never called.

The first week was not so bad, mostly. She was still in his place then, and she still had some money. She had five days to get out before Ahmed got back and with what was a timely stroke of luck, she found a tiny room in the suburbs down the other end of the city that was suitably removed from the fray. He would not find her, he could not. She even moved the larger stuff in the dead of the night so as not to be seen by his spying brother and cousin. She gave over all her cash to pay for two months in advance, moved Saturday night and got fired on Monday morning. All she needed. Suzanne insisted on taking her out to lunch again on her last day, and that was the straw that broke the camel's back, to use a suitably Levantian term.

An ordinary Parisian day, a line at the bistro for tables. She heard the voices multiply strangely, then echo most horribly around a small space somewhere in the vicinity of her head, with a split second's silent panic before she went out. Just like Laurel and Hardy, right back in a dead heap. Even the sound effects were spectacular, her head smashed off the black and white floor tiles with a resounding crack, causing great excitement and commotion with the lunch-time punters. Poor Suzanne, not wanting to get fired herself, tearfully patched her up, stuck her in a cab and directed it to the British Military Hospital.

"Has there been a history of nervous disorder in your family?" White coat, dry hands, Kent accent.

"No."

"How long have you been unable to sleep?"

"About two months."

"Do you have any particular new stress in your life?"

Golly, doctor. A mere case of jolly old deranged, violent gentleman friend who just happened to bugger off and marry his cousin in the Middle-fucking-East last month, don't you know, and who still thinks he can have me too!

"A difficult relationship."

"Too young to be married aren't you?"

. . . Please . . .

"Ah, not married! Then might I suggest a change, my dear. I can't help noticing this previous bruising . . . Could you perhaps stay clear for a time, would that be possible?"

"I just moved out."

"Ah, splendid. Then just take a rest. Just sleep! Think of it as if you just don't have to do anything for a while. We'll run a few routine tests, so you must promise to phone us back in ten days, alrighty? Oh, you'll be right as rain soon enough, a young lady of your calibre . . ."

Ahmed had lied about everything. All the way. Lied about his parents. The sad history of his country, tailor-cut to suit his life story. Lied about his fidelity and then lied about his fucking marriage. His cousin had told her guiltily, through mumbles and pauses, in some slummy bar near Chatelet one night. She drank a lot, missed most of what he was raving about, but got the main bit. Through the bar room mirror she watched a belly dancer skirt the tables, and with perfect clarity spied the whole wedding ceremony take place in one of the jiggling sequins: cool interior of mosque, sandy family village, etcetera. Catching sight of her tears from across the club, the belly dancer darted a sympathetic glance from blackened, jaded eyes.

The blue would shimmer around the edges until everything else faded into a kind of iridescent turquoise. Sometimes, the shout of a child down in the street would hurtle across the room through the window and lift her back from dreams into a hazy and unwanted reality. If only she could just manage to visualize her life without Ahmed. If she could magically heal the gaping, messy gash she kept stitching up mentally, only to have it ooze open again every night. He was the one — the charming, cultured scholar with the right word for everybody. Never mind his drinking, never mind his viciousness and his stomach-churning sexism. She would change that, of course, because she was his modern woman. Somewhere along the way she failed to cop that her only friends were now his friends, she'd been listening to his music, reading his books, exploring his culture.

She had dismissed Maura's theory for a game of psycho-cowboys. "Out of the frying pan into the fire. You're swopping one bastard for another. It's a typical Irish-girl trap. They're all at it. I've never seen anything like the way the Paddy ones go for these fellas, it drove me mad in London."

Maura was the only one there to warn her, but who was Maura to talk, with that holy show of a Neanderthal in Munich. Whom she went back to. She wished Maura hadn't gone back, now, for all she used to get fecked off with her when they shared the *chambre de bonne*. She was only beginning to admit to herself over the last while how alone she was, and how this bloody whole thing was freaking her out. She was scared most of all of what was happening to her head, to herself. The apparent loss of control, the angst list thing. She was afraid she might be really sick. Head stuff, serious. Or worse. Look at Teresa O'Gorman's brother walking around the estate at home now like a junkie-ghost. She knew that sooner or later she would have to call the hospital about those tests.

The booze wasn't always enough to chase everything out of mind, and the night always came too soon, the rabid hounds scratching at her consciousness like vicious, squealing shamans. They'd hurtle the darkness down into her miserable bed, mocking her sleeplessness. Oh, she would slur, don't be such a bloody eejit.

So just try saying *bloody eejit* at three o'clock in the morning when the sides of the room are billowing nauseously in the corner of your eye, and the book you read with great effort conspires to send you back to nightmare. And the scary thing about night-night stories at that hour is that you can tumble back into terror at any minute if you doze off carelessly. And there are always those difficult decisions: Halcyon or alcohol? Nine out of ten insomniacs prefer both . . .

Blue rectangle morning, blistered tongue and throbbing eyes. A few times the red screech took over straight off, other times she'd lie there listening for it, in abject, formless fear. Or else the bloody birds just made her cry with their sweetness, making her think how small this place was, however bright.

Maybe she should just call the hospital and get it over with, yeah. It was probably just a case of too much drugs and not enough decent food then there was always sheer stupidity — wanton indulgence — whatever. She'd call Maura then, and spill it all out, none of this lone martyrdom business. She'd have to just get a grip somehow.

She began to search through the piles of stuff around the floor, first haphazardly and then getting furiously organized. It would all have to be tidied before she could get on with her life, she told herself, and here we go. All night she tidied, sorted, cleaned, opened, folded, searched, tore, placed, discarded. Every single last thing she went through, powered by an unstoppable manic drive to just continue until everything was clean, sorted, done. At one point she even — miraculously — came across a large, crinkley colored bill. A sign of luck. Of hope, finally.

After chasing sleep anxiously for some hours to no avail, she ventured out to buy breakfast once she figured the shops and cafés were open. The morning light was gorgeous, she decided. Shit. The new day smells of fresh bread toasting, the sounds of coffee machines and hissing milk froth only inspired her to an eruption of hiccoughing tears as she walked down the street, this was getting ridiculous. She blew her nose as she rounded the boulevard and tried to ignore them. She bought two newspapers and folded them open carefully at the employment sections as soon as she was seated in the terrace section of the café.

While she was waiting for her café au lait, she saw the hand slip past nine o'clock and stepped into the phone booth nervously. She dialled and hung up three times before addressing the receptionist. She tried to curb the shake in her voice as the doctor came on the line.

"Hi, this is Patricia Kelly, I was in a while back and you told me to call back about the results of some tests . . ."

"Ah, Miss Kelly, yes. We were concerned you wouldn't call. Well, my dear, we have some news for you, and we'd like you come in to see us, so we can just run over a few things and set you up with a good obstetrician."

"A what?"

"Ah." There was a pause at the other end. "My dear, I think you should come in and see us as soon as possible . . ." Good suffering Jesus, she was sick. She was fucking sick, she'd been right. She was losing it, gone. Nervous breakdown or something. And what the hell had he just said. "Excuse me, what did you just say?"

"Now my dear, please don't get ruffled, there's absolutely no need for that. But we do need to see you in the surgery. It's eh . . . we can talk when you get here. Can you come over this afternoon?"

"What about now?"

"That would be fine, Miss Kelly. Actually, how are you feeling at present?"

"I feel like shit, *actually.*"

She hung up the phone in a panic and made her way back to the table, stomach churning and head screaming. She found herself grinding her teeth like a sleeping child, and her mouth was filling with hot sweet saliva, causing her to feel like throwing up all over the yellow formica. She'd better have the hair of the dog, fast.

She pushed the coffee aside and ordered a large vodka

and coke. Now she was frozen short of crying, and she wished she was crying, she didn't know what to do with herself. What could be wrong, why wouldn't he tell her. It was a few vodka and cokes later before she felt that warm buzz of comfort kicking in and finally paid the rude shite of a waiter.

On the way to the train it began to get close and cloudy and she suddenly felt sick again, not that it was going to put her off her purpose. This was it, straight up. If she was sick, she would just have to deal with it. She'd stay with that doctor guy, he seemed nice.

When she got to the bottom of the escalator, however, there was a bit of a problem. She just hovered at the turn-stile, unable somehow to think. She bit her nails and turned her fare-ticket over and over and over and over and over in her hand, unwillingly and mysteriously paralysed. Her brain ran down the list, up the list. She winced and shook her head, contemplated the fare-ticket. Turned it over, and over and over and over. The floor began to undulate tangibly, forcefully. She freaked, heading for a metro map on the wall. Steady now, steady. Only thing was, there didn't seem to be anywhere for her to go . . .

The primary colors jumped around crazily, a jumble of names and quivering lines, and it blurred then uncontrollably as she was caught off guard with the damned crying jags she no longer knew how to battle off.

She thought about Ahmed, and home, and Maura in Munich, and the belly dancer's sequins. She thought about Teresa O'Gorman's brother and the doctor's voice as he told her to rest. Maybe she needed to rest a bit more just for a while. The blood began screeching round her head, the dogs howled and the cotton wool flooded crimson as she slid down the corridor tiles, hoping some stranger would break her fall.

Colleen Burke

Colleen Burke, comes from an Irish Catholic working-class background and grew up in Bondi, Sydney. Some of her great-grandparents came from Feakle, County Clare, East Galway, Tipperary and Cork. She worked as a shorthand typist, a research assistant and community worker and currently tutors creative writing, poetry and oral history projects in community based and adult education courses.

Colleen has published a biography of the Australian poet Marie EJ Pitt, *Doherty's Corner* and six books of poetry including *the edge of it*, shortlisted in the 1993 NSW State Literary Awards, and *Wildlife in Newtown* (1994). She is currently working on biographies of another two Australian writers and co-editing an anthology of the verse and song of Irish Australia. Colleen has performed her poetry in Australia, Ireland, Wales and England. She lives with her two children in Newtown, NSW.

A Shadow on the Heart

In memory of the Irish Famine 1845–49

It's grey today an outline of winter
bleak   but I've had lunch
breakfast and will have an
evening meal.
Not like the famine years
the starving years when the
potato crops in Ireland
were blighted black to the core
their rotting smell a pall over the land.
And the English fed on food
exported from Eire as the
Irish people died of starvation
by the hundreds thousands millions
in ditches by the wayside
some with bright green mouths from the
desperation of grass.
And those forced to beg or be charity cases
in newly established poor houses
had to deny a claim to their skerrick of soil
their religion   culture   way of life and some
wrapped only in threadbare cloaks of pride
endured instead the slow starving of themselves
their children   and the keening was on the land

Some grimly held on   gaunt against starvation
others left and died on famine ships
or made it through to the new world or the "great
south land".

I can't live without spuds —
potatoes a staple in our family diet
through lean years of emigration
unemployment   wars   depressions —
and also the good times —
it's a dark memory on the heart
etched down through the generations

I hold a potato in my hand
and know starvation
exploitation   genocide
the close/near death of
a people   their spirit

And still for me a meal is incomplete
without the ritual cooking
and eating of potatoes —
it nurtures a shadow on the heart
reaching down from the famine years.

To Whom It May Concern

We have known Maureen Ryan
all her school life. We do not
hesitate to say she will give you
every satisfaction. At all times
we have found her to be an
obedient girl. *Maureen was scared of the*
convent of the silence of
grass growing dead of nuns
drifting down concrete paths whispering
rosaries obscenities to god their
long robes rustling
afraid of the
thin mad fingers of sister oleander
twisting girls around the classroom
twisting their lives leasing
them out on holidays watching
through the open spaces
in the
still gullies watching through
fingers groping deep in orangeclay
for shapes and
Maureen was obedient

We do not hesitate to
recommend her to anyone.
At all times she has been
highly trustworthy honest mostly

honest by omission
in the small spaces of the
darkwood confessional and the
slide of his face looking away
and at her

We do not hesitate to
recommend Maureen to you
Protestant or Catholic preferably
Catholic she is a girl with
a conscience who liked to go

to church at 6 o'clock
in the morning meeting the milkman
wellworn working men and women
who went to church
to pray in the warmth
of the calm highcolours
and the bright sound
of early morning slipping
through the stained glass windows
Maureen
wore a red cloak on first Fridays
working a parole system against
purgatory for herself others
a girl with a conscience whose
footsteps they followed saying
to think a bad thought was the same
as doing it so they slipped through
her dreams arranged her nightmares/her
guilt the voice in her head censoring

       the devil while her guardian angel sat
       on her left-hand shoulder and watched
       over her at night slaying dragons
       devils men women while she dreamed a young
       girl's dream and woke to the sound
               of his pastel smile
                     & a guilty conscience

Maureen was a good
pupil in secondary school
she came second in the class
and sang with feeling *faith of our fathers and o jesu me*
       absorbed in the warmth of ritualised
       images oblivious to the dragging sound
       of their gowns across the floor the mad
       hooded eyes of sister oleander watching
       kneading her to shape because
       she didn't know the answers
               sister oleander standing
       above her at assembly flapping
       in the scraggy seawind said she saw
       red gold/glints in Maureen's hair
       and Maureen ran away to the church
       dark as alter wine spoke to jesus
       cried for the nails/thorns
               he had a conscience
               she was honest
               came second in the class
               and was contained/constrained by
               the nuns who were nice soft ageless

and sister oleander getting
sicker
still hovered above her bed
at nights a scarecrow

We do not hesitate to recommend
Maureen to you. She was always a good
pupil. Solitary at times alone on the asphalt yard
beneath the Moreton Bay fig tree alone in the girls
groups sometimes stalking sister oleander
down the dead corridors mostly playing basketball
co-operatively
everyone else playing competitively
for the school to win
for the girls to win
for the nuns
to win
the girls

Maureen has been like one of
us. We are sorry she is leaving   are you sure you
would not consider a vocation surely child I see it in your
eyes   dedication   no she said   no stubborn

running down empty corridors   no she said turning away
tripping over gowns rosary   we are sorry to lose Maureen
beads counting themselves   but we know she will always
into eternity   do her best. She is one of us.

A Joyous Day

It hums in my blood, part of me this being Irish — the close knit community I grew up in — relatives next door, around the corner, across the road, cousins in my class at school. A warren of relatives — Burkes, O'Briens, Fitzgeralds, Collins, Lees, Ryans. Mum often sat on the front verandah smoking, chatting with aunts, neighbours on their way to the shops or church. She had a green thumb and exchanged flower cuttings with friends. Her childhood in Lismore, northern New South Wales a sprawl of Irish relatives flowing into Queensland. A sepia photograph — my mother and her sister Zeita on an empty Surfer's Paradise beach — windswept in long coats laughing into each other. She had three sisters and a brother.

St Patrick's Day — a joyous day when my mother chased radio stations for Irish songs and music. Sang, lilted around the house — "Galway Bay", "When Irish Eyes are Smiling", "I'll Take you Home Again Kathleen". Happy. Not the cloying joviality from cheap wine bottles hidden in wardrobes; the jagged cry of Irish songs spilling out of our small house onto the judgemental street. The sound I dreaded coming home to.

Days of shyness — clinging to my mother's dress — sitting beneath the dining/lounge room table covered with a grey blanket, where she and her women friends played cards, biting their feet. *How ya going love — you look lovely today.* Drinking, smoking — leaving the door of the toilet open — smell of piddle, perfume — hugging, kissing me deeply on the cheek — red lips imprinted forever. They took turns to host card games. Some of the women lived in high ceilinged, dark, musty rooms in boarding houses in Flood Street. Over the years they moved away or died. The card games stopped. Dad often lost his wages at card games, before he arrived home on Friday nights, his pay gone, and no money for rent and food and the fights then.

Friday nights my brother and I went to the Greek fish and chip shop on Bondi Road — *four pieces of fish and a couple of shillings worth of chips please.* The only night Mum didn't have to cook. If Dad was feeling flush he'd bring home a couple of jars of oysters, which he and Mum liked. I couldn't stand the slimy texture.

They both gambled, but Mum mainly backed horses with Irish names. On Saturdays I'd go to the Chinese bookmaker — *a shilling each way Danny Boy and Irish Eyes for Mum please.* Sometimes the house would be shut up — the police on the prowl, so I'd go to their other house, in the next street.

One of the great occasions of my mother's life was backing, before I was born, Old Rowley in the Melbourne Cup at 100 to 1. One of the names of my brother born soon after, the favourite of Mum and Aunty Zeita.

St Patrick's Day — my mother's day and I her *Irish Colleen.* On this day there were no tears, recriminations. It was as though my tiny vivacious mother, in passed down bright silk frocks, from the Jewish families of Dover Heights, Double Bay, Bellevue Hill, who she cleaned houses for, had been reborn. She hated housework, yet was always up at the crack of doom, cleaning, scrubbing, washing, dusting. Her cooking revolting — limp cabbage, tasteless curries, lank tripe, greasy baked dinners and chokos from vines that rambled over the back fence. Her one culinary skill — apple pies. No one has ever made apple pies like my mother. And stewed white peaches from our peach tree. In the spring, I'd stand with our cat in the back garden, down past the lemon tree, and watch tight pink buds unfolding.

But none of that mattered on this day when a smile lit her grey eyes, and there was an abundance of happiness, and no change of mood. No angry cries in the night — *I'll kill you* — battering our bedroom walls. No sitting on the front step waiting for Dad to come home from the factory, and the six o'clock swill at the Bondi Royal, haunted by fears of the welfare taking us away.

On this day we all had a piece of green ribbon pinned on — Dad off to the factory with the green on his shirt. He never said much and as the years passed we rarely saw him. When I was little he took us to the Anzac Day Parade, up Bondi Road and into Waverley Park. During the war he'd worked on the trams, exempt from war service. Sometimes we watched the footy in Waverley Park, and I rode high on his shoulders, all the way home. But later he worked for the bookies at the Dogs and Trots on Friday nights and Randwick Racecourse on Saturdays. Every Saturday the races were on the wireless and I still can't bear the sound of them. On Sundays he played Golf at the North Bondi Golf Links. As an unemployed fourteen/fifteen year old in the 1930s Depression he picked up money working as a caddy. He was the second eldest of ten children. Aged ten I wanted to marry a Burke and have ten children.

We all wore green — proud to be Irish. At early mass I sang in the choir "Hail Glorious St Patrick Dear Saint of Our Isle" and then the day was mine — a religious holiday. One year our school went to the St Patrick's Day games at the Showground in a rented bus, and we were reported by Mrs O'Grady for hanging out the windows singing, abandoning school hats, Catholic decorum. We never went to the games again.

My school was St Patrick's Home Science and Domestic School, run by the Sisters of St Joseph's — a picture of Mary MacKillop on every classroom wall. On special occasions we sang "Advance Australia Fair" — not "God Save the Queen" — our allegiance to the Church, not the State.

Green and yellow the colours of our summer uniforms. Navy and light blue our winter uniforms. Out of the school-grounds we'd take off school hats and gloves, and go to the milk bar for an icecream in a dish with chocolate flavouring and malt, or an orange Spider, longing to listen to rock and roll music on the juke box where the bodgies and widgies hung out. A place of sin we hardly dared venture into. Everyone knew us, and someone always had time to visit the school, and complain about our behaviour, gloveless, hatless, rowdy crossing from Wellington Street to Bondi Road. Few people had phones then. We didn't have a phone or car.

The dresses we made at school were high to the neck, below the knee, with longish sleeves. Modesty drummed into us. I was ordered to the front of the class because we were seen going down to the beach in our shorts. Unsuitable attire for Catholic girls. I hated sewing and cooking and have few skills in either. Meek Sister Joseph in charge of cooking and sewing kept a pet huntsman spider on the window.

We learnt to type at twelve. A green cloth covered the keys and Sister Oleander stood behind us with her cane — quick slash over the knuckles for peeping. I'm still an excellent typist. Sister Oleander taught all the other subjects — history, English, maths, geography, business principles. Before our final exam we put questions into a hat and prayed to Our Lady before we choose topics to study.

Sister Oleander's thin body quivered with rage, her face bright red, as she wiped her mouth, with a large white handkerchief, plucked from her long brown sleeve. Fear was the black rattle of her rosary beads, as she came screeching down the classroom to hit, or grab us by the hair, yank us around the room. Fear made me study, that all persuasive sweetish sour smell of fear. The nuns were always right, but our parents, didn't know the extent of violence — the simmering madness, the frustration of some of the nuns. The school was poor and under resourced. Sister Oleander taught first, second, third year and the Intermediate class, in the same room. Nearly all classes were doubled up. Whenever she was off sick, we wreaked havoc on the shy young nuns who replaced her.

Sister Henrietta, the music teacher, would wield her cane in the choir — *who is singing out of key.* An alto, she terrorised harmony out of me. Everyday we sang hymns in class — "O

Jesu Me", "Queen of Heaven Star of the Ocean Bright", "Faith of our Fathers" . . . *living still in spite of dungeon fire and sword* — emotional, rousing songs of the oppressed. Aged eleven I was fervent — praying to Jesus — weeping for the nails, crown, thorns. A devout Red Angel, and then a Child of Mary.

On our way home the boys at the public school across the road would yell at us — *dirty tykes! Heathen prods*, we'd yell back — *you're going to hell!* Back home in Watson Street we played cricket or footy on the street together, rode in billycarts — religious differences forgotten. In the winter my friends and I played tennis and basketball in the school grounds.

My family was Labor and Mum always sorry for the underdog. Dad, a Unionist, was staunch to the Australian Labor Party, when it split apart in the 1950s, decimated by the fanatical anti-communism of the Democratic Labor Party. The DLP was Catholic based, as was the ALP, largely founded on Irish Catholic working-class Australia. From the pulpit the Priest preached allegiance to the DLP. Dad was fired from the Kellogg's factory where he worked in the early 1950s, because he spoke to presumed communist workers, after he was directed not to. Our endless supply of corn-flakes came to an end.

My mother was a divorcee whose eldest son, my half brother, was brought up by a paternal aunt. Her first husband drank too much and beat her. An older woman, she wasn't good enough for my strict Catholic grandmother's son. In the eyes of the church my Mum and Dad weren't married.

The nuns and priests told me it was a mortal sin — *your parents will sizzle and burn in everlasting hellfire*. Once when we were at the Bondi Road picture show there was a loud explosion — *get out, get out* — I screamed at them. *You're going to die and go to hell — I'll never see you again.* I knew I was bound for heaven. My dad thought I'd gone mad, but he wasn't exposed to the preaching and fear day in and out. Emotionally they were strong Catholics, but rarely went to church, although we had to. Mum only went when the Franciscan missionaries came preaching fire and brimstone. She'd be in the confessional for hours, and for a few weeks we'd say the rosary after tea, until she slipped back into her old ways, and we all breathed a sigh of relief.

All the priests at St Patrick's Presbytery were Irish. We sang Irish songs in our school concerts — "The Kerry Dances", "The Isle of Innisfree". We lived in the same street as the Presbytery and old Mónsignor Garretty would walk down to visit us — we'd be playing outside and rush and tell Mum. *Quick inside* she'd say *I haven't got time for him now.* We'd shut the front door, pull down the blinds, sit huddled together. We'd hear his slow footsteps up the path — knock at the door — *shush*, Mum would say as we started to giggle, and then his footsteps going away. I felt guilty — knew he'd seen us playing. He often dropped in for a cup of tea, ostensibly to persuade Mum to go to mass. When he died we had to look at his body in the open casket in the church. We were terrified.

"Sure a Little Bit of Heaven Fell from out the Sky One Day" — our school entry in the Eisteddfod at the Conservatorium. My mother rented this lovely dress for me with layers of pale green tulle. She always rented dresses for special school occasions. I came out at the end of the song holding a big shamrock — the only part of me visible — my feet.

We borrowed books from the penny dreadful libraries — *Mum wants a juicy book please with lots of murders please.* I escaped into the world of *Anne of Green Gables, What Katie Did, The Magic Faraway Tree, The Secret Seven, Famous Five* and the *Billabong* books — all so remote from my life. I wrote stories about picnics in the bush with lavish meat and salad sandwiches, fruitcake and drinks. The Abbey books I borrowed from an Anglican family, who lived in a large house on the corner of Watson and Birrell Streets. The grandmother, who lived with them, spent a lot of time at our place, often staying for tea. Dad wasn't happy, but Mum loved to collect and look after strays.

In our small school library we had English boarding school books, such as *Prunella Wins Through* and *Pollyanna* books for school prizes, if it wasn't holy pictures. I still have holy pictures of St Francis and the Virgin Mary for coming second and third in the class. When I was thirteen Mum gave me *Jane Eyre*, which I read and re-read.

I shared a room with my brother and we rarely left Bondi — had no money for holidays, but as Mum said — *why do we need holidays when we live by the sea.* My parents moved into our rent protected house, when Japanese submarines were seen off Bondi during the war, and people fled from the coast.

Mum adored her father, a dentist and atheist, who rarely charged patients if they couldn't afford it. He died soon after they moved from Lismore to Tamarama, when she was thirteen, and she didn't get on with her stern Catholic mother, Sarah Jane. Later the family split over money. Mum loved to swim and sit on the Bondi Esplanade smoking, dreaming. She mostly spoke of early days in Lismore — blanked out the rest of her life, although always told me I was a caesarean — a difficult birth. Wove romantic tales. We listened to horror stories on the radio together. Scared to death. She loved dramatic movies and cried easily, as I did — *it's only a picture* — said my dad. Only a picture. A story. Make-believe.

• • •

At school we recited by heart — Lawson, Paterson, Gordon and Kendall. I tried a few rhymes in primary school, but wrote my first poem on my typewriter at work when I was seventeen, and kept on writing despite frustrations, rejections — somehow incomplete if I wasn't imagining, worrying at poetry. Leaving school at fifteen I was hungry for the classics, novels, poetry and belonged to three public libraries. I read on buses, walking down the street, in parks. Everywhere.

When I heard my first real Irish songs — rebel songs — "Kelly the Boy from Killane", "The Foggy Dew", "Roddy McCorley"; Gaelic songs — "An Bunnán Buí" ("The Yellow Bittern"), "Éamonn An Chnuic" ("Ned of the Hill"). I was overwhelmed by the passion, the beauty, the sibilant, harsh flow of Gaelic.

Worlds opening up — the harbour, inner city — different ways of living, seeing. A cosmopolitan world. Talking the night away with friends in coffee shops at the Cross, a novelty then. In pubs listening to the craic. After late Sunday Mass at St Mary's Cathedral, going to Russian films in William Street — *Ivan the Terrible, Crime and Punishment, The Battle Ship Potemkin.* Met socialists, communists, anarchists libertarians, ex-Catholics, atheists. A time of questioning my beliefs. Questioning everything. Over the years I've changed some of my beliefs, my life, but being Irish is in my blood, imagination. When my brother discovered I was no longer a Catholic, he said I must be Protestant or English.

On St Patrick's Day, I pin on my green ribbon and give my children ribbons of green to wear. I lilt around the house. Play tapes, CDs of jigs, reels, hornpipes, slides, polkas, songs. Go to Irish pubs with friends, play my silver spoons in seisiúns. A joyous day.

Linda Anderson

Linda Anderson was born and educated in Belfast. She moved to England in the early seventies and worked at a series of administrative jobs (with grand titles and low pay) to support her writing. Her first successes came in the eighties with the publication of two award-winning novels: *To Stay Alive* and *Cuckoo*. Her stories and poems have been included in anthologies in Britain, Ireland and the USA. She teaches Creative Writing at Lancaster University. Her first stage play, *The Flight Response*, was produced in Manchester in October 1995.

The Making of a Writer

I am from Belfast, the third of five children born into a working-class Protestant family. My father was a Belfast man; my mother is Canadian. Her "difference" and her stories of "somewhere else" were important and romantic to me in a society of such coercive loyalties. Another chance thing that helped me escape becoming a bigot was that I had a Catholic friend when I was thirteen. Although I was not politically aware at that point, a divergence of view was always appearing, over things like the history we were learning at our respective schools. My heroes were my friend's villains! At university in 1968, I was able to explore history for myself and also take part in the Civil Rights movement.

I decided to leave Northern Ireland in 1972, a terrifying year full of sectarian murders. I began to write when I left Ireland and am definitely a writer who needs exile in order to create. Love of language is probably the main thing impelling me to write but my experiences in Northern Ireland have certainly been very shaping, decisive, and mobilising. My first novel *To Stay Alive*, explores violence through characters who adopt it, shun it, or are entrapped by it.

My more recent work tends to be about sexuality and gender but I think that my perspective is always influenced by my Irish background. A recurring obsession in my work is the link between public and private kinds of violence. The way public violence seeps and deforms and creates what a man and woman say to each other in their own kitchen, for example, and the reverse situation, too. The way all our "privacies" create the mutilating world.

Occasionally I do still write directly out of my Irish experience. "The Marvellous Boy" is a recent example, set in Belfast, inspired by my observation of how some people survive there by not caring. Using a kind of stupidity as a security blanket.

The Marvellous Boy

He was in the kitchen, breathing. Ruth forgot why she had entered there and imagined beating a retreat. But he was dressed up in his uniform and looked exceptionally irritating. Ceremonial, like an actor conquering stage fright with dogged calm.

Shiny buttons. Shiny shoes. Bastard.

She moved to the sink to fish a cup from the soapy water, keeping track of his whereabouts from his faintly stertorous breath.

Suddenly there was a clatter as he dropped a cup on to the tiled floor.

"Jeez, I'm as bad as a pregnant woman." He said it with an innocent affability. She darted to fetch a brush.

"Smithereens", she said, staring at the countless little diamonds and shards.

"Aye. Well, are you going to christen them, or will you clear them up?" Do it yourself, she thought as she swept.

"I met a pregnant woman today," she told him. He gave no sign of having heard.

Ex-pregnant woman. Baby premature. A blue cherub. Its heart ticked for thirty-five minutes even though it never drew breath. Stillbirth . . . ticking away like a crazy clock for over thirty minutes. Could be a record, the consultant said.

"I'm only twenty-five," she said aloud.

"Don't know your luck."

Suddenly Jenny burst in to the room in her nightdress. It was one of her frilly Bo-Peep numbers.

"Oh, don't look at me! You're both so serious and dutiful in your uniforms . . . and look at me! I've had a little siesta." She gave a delicate doll-like sneeze.

"I had such a dream. One of those daytime dreams, Daddy! I was looking for my bed in this grand country mansion, wandering from room to room. There were these vast dormitories full of girls . . ."

"Oh aye!" He looked oddly amused and wrathful.

"And then I opened this girl's cupboard. She had all this jewellery, including my engagement ring! I recognised it instantly, and it was priced! With an actual price tag. And guess what? The cost was £666. And I wanted to steal it. But how could I steal my own ring? And why was it £666? That's the devil's number!"

She turned to Ruth.

"How can I steal what's mine?"

"It's only a dream."

Jenny's mouth clammed shut. Kelso left without a word. As the front door clicked, Jenny charged to reopen it.

"Daddy! Daddy! See-you-later-alligator!"

Ruth winced. It was one of Jenny's myriad little rules: no one must leave the house without a farewell. And no one must actually pronounce the word "goodbye" . . . in case it came true.

"I wish you wouldn't be like that in front of him!"

"Like what?"

"So splashy! And fey."

"Fee, that's French for 'fairy'!" She tweaked her nightie into two flounces and pirouetted. "Anyway, Daddy doesn't mind."

"It's excruciating to watch your double-act. Your dizzy overresponding and his block-of-stoniness."

"But you're our golden *Mean!*" Jenny replied.

"Oh! You sound almost sarcastic. Congratulations."

"My dad is not a block of stone."

"No, *your* dad is not. Everything that passes through your mind gets covered in sugar-frosting!"

"Maybe like one of those figures at Pompeii, you know. The feeling fixed and frozen behind stone."

A whimper escaped from Ruth. Jenny fluttered around her, dispensing little hugs.

"What? What? Ruth?"

Ruth told her about the foetus and its stubborn heart.

"It was so tiny . . . it could have fitted into this cup."

"Is that what you see? Dead babies in cups? Poor Ruth. I'm so proud of you! The things you face. Dad too."

Ruth stood up.

"Don't compare me with him! That fat flat-footed fool . . . !"

"Oh, that's good, fat-flat-footed fool . . . fat-flat-footed fool . . ." she chanted in a sing-song sabotage.

"Who does he think he's kidding? Ambling around the mean streets . . . like a superannuated John Wayne . . ."

"Don't talk like that about him, Ruth. He's in danger."

"Yeah, I suppose you believe he's in shoot-outs every night. The IRA are shaking in their sandals and leaving in droves . . ."

"Leaving in boxes, that's what I'd like to see!"

"Oh, Jenny!"

"Leaving in ships and boats and planes, then . . . they

could kill Dad. I suppose you would blame *him!*"

"He stands on guard outside a rich man's house several times a week. Risking his life to protect another man's property . . ."

"And his family and his life!"

"The life of a minnow-brained little shyster . . ."

"Elected Member of Parliament."

"Respectable criminal! The way Dad talks about him makes me cringe . . . tones of awe . . . And oh, how kind his wife is! Why, she deigns to bring him a cup of tea to drink on the doorstep occasionally!"

"He is brave, even if you think he wastes it on undeserving cases."

"He just likes to do nothing and be important about it! Standing there all night, not having to talk to anybody. He gets to practise his autism and he's paid for it!"

"He doesn't just guard that house. He has . . . a variety of duties."

"Like most servants."

"You've gone all red in the face!"

Jenny detached an oval pockmarked mirror from the wall and forced Ruth to look at herself.

"See that missionary glow?"

"We don't look like sisters at all, do we?"

"We don't act like sisters. I mean, I sign letters with rows of hugs and kisses while you agonise over whether 'regards' is too effusive."

"I used to pretend you were a changeling."

"Like Heathcliff!"

"You're a bit more Edgar Linton, actually!"

"That's nasty! A milksop!"

"Well, you are dainty, that's all I mean. We look like an advertisement for different types of women. Anorexic or adipose! Take your pick."

"I'm svelte. You could be too."

"Yes, if I decided to think about nothing else but the calorie content of everything from a kidney bean to a knicker-bocker glory."

"I know what we are. Trick or Treat."

"Oh yes! Dark Peril or Blonde Froth. Treachery or Treacle."

"You think you can be horrible to me so long as you put yourself down at the same time!"

"Sorry!" Ruth looked contrite. "Why do you have to get married, eh?"

"I do not have to," Jenny said primly.

"You could really be something . . . a trapeze artist."

"Out of reach. Above it all. Sounds more like your ambition. I'm going to get dressed."

Having longed all day to be alone, Ruth did not know what to do with the sudden granting of solitude. She went up-stairs and stared into the full-length mirror.

Smile Please — say Jeez.

Her uniform was a stiff white carapace. She yearned to get out of the aching armoury. First she removed the heavy-chained watch from her bodice that made her feel like the angel of death and slipped out of the tunic. She thought of her father dying. Bullets piercing his nipples which erupted and fanned out like pantomime poppies. Was it a wish or a fear? She would like to pass into death in an instant. One minute here . . . then abracadabra . . . She imagined herself being counselled by shining beings: "You're dead now, you see, you died." And she would cheer. Dance in her body-free body. And the shining ones would beam indulgently at her puppyish romping delight.

Guarding that upstart in his flighty mansion. The resentment gave way to a memory of the house they lived in while her mother was alive. Every morning her father had to shovel up the dead cockroaches and ladle them into the fire where they sizzled and crackled. One night she came downstairs for a glass of water, snapped on the light, and saw the curtains engulfed, a seething shellacked cockroach-coat. Despite the daily cull, there were always more, a defeating abundance. Her father explained to her that you had to find the queen and destroy her and this would conquer the population. The queen was white. This fact horrified Ruth. She imagined her. White brittle-cased jelly, bulbous alien eyes, ceaseless tentacular twitches. There she sat immobile in her viscid hive. By what horrible telepathy did she choreograph this febrile nightmare of black and tan roaches?

We had to move in the end, she remembered. The White Queen won.

Ruth took off her hot underwear. There was a moment of pure release before she glared at her reflection. Morose bovine eyes. Numb swollen body like something drowned.

I don't even want to get away, she thought. Not to New Zealand. Not New Guinea. Not Newfoundland. Not Land's End. Not World's End . . .

Ruth arranged her orange peel into a border for her plate as the television quizmaster became implausibly animated, full of truculent partisan joyousness.

"Just one more catchphrase and you will win our Star Prize!!! The first word is *Holy* . . . You have fifteen seconds. Holy Holy Holy . . . what? Thirteen seconds! Don't lose it now, Gwen."

"Ghost?" spluttered the contestant.

"That's it! Holy Ghost! Magic! You have won a trip to Disneyland. She got it! She got it!"

Kelso staggered through the door and sank into his chair. His face was hidden from Ruth. She noticed how his thin hair looked laminated. He was groaning and crying.

"Dad! Are you hurt? What is it?"

For long minutes he made noises, deep labouring sobs. It was like watching him vomit. The sounds were private and yet a communication that seemed to both require and repudiate its receiver. The quizmaster was wishing rhapsodic goodbyes to the audience. Ruth wanted his voice to go on. She did not want to be alone with her father. She wanted back to that consumer-heaven, simple sanctioned lusts and vulgarities. She switched it off. Her father was silent now.

"Dada?"

"Hold my hand."

She kneeled and took his big hand in hers, scared as a Lilliputian. What had turned her father into this shivering needy giant?

"Life," he said. "Life is all that matters . . . Live and let live . . . Do you understand?"

She nodded. He was not looking at her.

"Be safe. Promise me you'll be safe."

"Yes, yes, I will."

"Because life is all that matters . . . How could anyone?"

"What?"

"He was young! Young!"

His wistful stricken voice loosened the tears in her.

Here we are weeping together! she thought, panicky and elated.

Who's young?

You don't like young people!

I'm touching my father!

What will happen tomorrow?

My father smells like moss and bark.

Love, she thought. Love.

The grass was moving and the air was still. A hank of pure flaxen hair. Dead still. The bullet wounds looked neat like punctures that could be repaired. You looked like a slumbering child.

We forgot everything, amateurs that we are.

Never approach the body. Could be booby-trapped.

We carried you face up, one limb each, madmen playing bumps-a-daisy. Once your backside scuffed the ground and I thought I was going to scream. We ran like guilty men, desperate to get you away from that foul ditchy place. As if anything could be saved through haste.

Back at the station, we avoided each other's eyes. Middle-aged blood-brothers.

It was easy to piece together your life history. It read like a telegram. Student. Twenty years old. Catholic. Hitched a lift from Derry. No paramilitary . . . Murder-Random-Opportunistic-Sectarian.

I remember your weight in my arms.

"I'll never forget it till my dying day," Nelson vowed. "Twenty years old! Hardly a man yet. One of theirs. But all the same . . ."

Kelso sat bleary and wordless. Both men were comforting themselves, Ruth thought, in their own ways. Her father in his silent cocoon, Nelson with his torrent of triteness.

"Shall I get you some tea, Mr Nelson? Or something stronger?"

"Just the ticket!" Nelson beamed. "Lovely young woman, your daughter. Makes you appreciate them, so it does, a tragedy like that. Always someone's son, someone's daughter . . ."

"I was too hard on her," Kelso confessed suddenly.

Ruth seemed to stop breathing. Her father's eyes were unbearably young and unguarded. She imagined herself trilling with cruel laughter. How ridiculous he looked! Like a great sorrowful cow!

"Well," said Nelson, "does no good to spare the rod. Sure, isn't she a credit to you?"

"Her mother pleaded with me not to be so harsh. I paid no heed."

He was beseeching, as if he wanted someone to explain it to him.

"Nonsense, Dad!" she said sternly.

He looked faintly alarmed and then his face changed to an expression she hated. A mean ironic seductiveness.

"Jenny started liking me when she was seventeen. Ruth will be thirty-seven."

Ruth and Jenny were drinking wine by the fireside.

"Do you remember German?"

"*Nein.* Only *mein Fuhrer, mein Kampf, Gott in Himmel,* all the bits I knew before."

"I remember the teacher telling us that it is the custom in German families to greet and shake hands with each other at breakfast. *Guten Morgen, Mutti. Guten Morgen, Vati. Guten Morgen, Hans. Guten Morgen, Gretchen.* It fascinated me. It made me cringe. What if we had to do that? Acknowledge each other. Touch. Start the day with good wishes . . ."

"Sounds positively cool compared to Dad's overtures lately! He kissed me yesterday."

"I hate his kisses. They're wet. They burn."

"How many have you had?"

"Two. But now I duck and run."

"He's changed."

"Do people change? . . . It's just another way of having power. Spiteful and smouldering, he's the centre of attention.

Sweet and contrite, he's the centre of attention. We still watch him like a barometer."

"Give him a chance! It's like . . . Scrooge. St Paul. Don't you believe in redemption? Moral shock. Scales falling from the eyes . . ."

"He can change if he likes. But why should I? Why should I forgive two and a half decades of bullying and contempt?"

"To be free."

"Freedom! Forgiveness! Transformation! What a flow of benedictions from a dirty little murder!"

"You always wanted Dad to have feelings. Now you can't stand it."

Ruth's arm jerked, spilling some wine on to the carpet. Both sisters stared at the purplish stain.

"Young corpses are routine in my job," Ruth said. "I never saw how to cut a tragic figure over it."

"That's not why you're jealous."

"Am I jealous? I suppose so. My da is in love with some sanitary angel."

"His pure blonde hair, his smooth and blameless face . . ." Jenny mocked.

"His perfect victimhood! The son he always wanted. A post-mortem adoption! His non-existence removes all impediments to love!"

"The Marvellous Boy! I hate him too. But I'm also in love with him."

"What's he like?"

"Charming, attentive, wise beyond his years but never

dull. No sweat, no tidemarks, no clumsiness."

"No inconvenient body!"

"But I imagine him that way too. His touch. His smell. Almondy."

"So do I," Ruth admitted. "I think he smells like medicine and sweets."

"Or like leather and posh drawing rooms."

"What does he talk about?"

"Faraway places."

"Arcane books."

"Dreams and what they foretell."

"So we're all haunting him! . . . Why does Dad not . . . ?"

"Not what?"

"Think we're marvellous?"

"He does. He has those miniature photos of us dangling from his key ring."

"Like shrunken scalps! . . . We're not dead. That's a major flaw. Disgustingly incarnate. And female to boot. Do you remember when you used to put your unshredded sanitary towels down the toilet and they clogged the drains?"

"It wasn't me!"

"It was you! God, remember the men digging up the garden to unearth them!"

"Don't talk about it!"

"All those rotting pads. Like a small hill of sodden bandages after some minor war."

"'Your father is disgusted.' I'll never forget Mum saying that!" Jenny started to cry quietly.

"Don't. Sure, doesn't he love to be disgusted? . . . Sometimes I think I've inherited his shame at being alive."

"You *are* like him."

"In fact, if he wants to gush over someone dead, he should go a bundle for me."

"Why are you so . . . entranced? Why can't you . . . resist?"

"Listen to you! What do you know about insurrection?"

"I used to think that was your department!"

My life parted like the Red Sea and in the clearing was you. I had forgotten everything even though remembrance was my duty. Remember 1690. Remember King Billy. There was the monarch on his white steed on the gable ends . . . gigantic visual aids . . . just in case I needed any prompting. Remember the Sabbath Day to keep it boring . . . I remembered to remember all the official memories that pinned me in place . . .

Your life ended and why does that make mine flash before my eyes?

I failed to remember my mother. The way she always seemed to be sitting down. Sat there grudging and judging in her "sparkling little palace" scrubbed immaculate by my sisters. She was like Queen Victoria in a pinny.

I forgot her daily broth. Big cauldrons of green-grey soup with knobby hambones jutting out. The discs of gold-edged grease on the surface. I blanked out her sayings. "God is always watching you." The way she talked to other women! "Make a prisoner of every sixpence. None of your children will do a hand's turn for you once they grow up." "Break their spirits before they break yours!" Women were a horror. Coils of grey hair, brown teeth, hard pale eyes. It was easy to believe in

Judgement Day. In school we had to queue up for fudge or caning, depending on whether our sums and spellings were right or wrong. Miss Courtenay kept a tin of homemade white fudge from which she doled out her rewards. Like hard pellets from her mean breasts. Mother was in the Salvation Army. Yesterday I took my police cap and sat here with the chinstrap round my jaw instead of tucked into the back of the hat. It felt good: a tight band across the skull, a support under the jaw. Contained again. Powerful. And then I remembered her in her Army bonnet, that big bow tied beneath her jowls.

I could never disobey her. If I could not eat her food, she set it before me cold at every subsequent meal until I ate it. I was not allowed to gag or vomit or leave any morsel. Two day old herring for breakfast. Other times she was sugary, calling me son. "You're my favourite child," she would say, but only in front of the others. Elevate one; crush the rest.

Once she sewed leather patches on my jacket on a Sunday. "I'm breaking the Sabbath for you! I wouldn't do that for anyone else."

Whiter than white. A whited sepulchre.

I was demoted from Favourite Son. Billy died. We both had diphtheria. He was fourteen. I was twelve. I was expected to go the same way. Keep the wreath, my aunt Miriam told her, you'll be needing it again soon. In front of me. I never told that to anyone. Billy died. I did not die. I did not cry. But now . . .

I remember my father at the funeral. He wore an oddly long full-skirted coat that flapped around his knees. The thought of it gives me a pain in the throat.

Billy became perfect after his death. Billy was handsome.

Billy was bright. He always smiled. Fetched coal, made tea, asked how are you. I was upstaged by a ghost.

Ruth spent two days in bed, listless, unable to read or dream.

Then she got up and spent a long time in front of the mirror, demolishing her appearance of common-sense rectitude.

"Change and dismay in all around I see," she sang, as she pulled her sweater off the shoulder, applied lipstick and mascara with a steady hand.

When she went downstairs, she noticed them noticing her studied allure, but neither Jenny nor Kelso passed any comment.

"Here, Dad," she said, sounding like a coquettish nanny. She handed him a shiny red apple.

"What am I supposed to do with that?"

"Take a bite! . . . Wait! I have to get the camera ready . . . Memorable moments . . . My dad consuming healthy item!"

He laughed shyly and took a nibble, blinking in the flash.

Jenny was cross.

"You're one to talk. You'd live on Liquorice Allsort stew, if no one was watching."

"But you always are, aren't you? The diet police!"

She sat down and opened her paper with a flourish.

"O my God! Listen to this. 'My fiance is a chain-smoker. He even smokes while we make love. Unfortunately, he has a habit of flicking the ash into my love holes. What can I do?'"

"It's made up," said Jenny.

"Of course. It's the *Sunday Sport* . . . Lighten up, will you? 'Love Holes!'" she shrieked and then intoned soulfully, "My love holes!" She went into an unbridled unshared laughter. Kelso walked out.

"Why are you being like this in front of Daddy? So bossy and bawdy!"

"It's his fault! The more he pines after the marvellous dead boy, the more alive I feel! Electrified!"

"That's not being alive! Talking smut. Bringing trash into the house. You don't fool anyone, you know."

"Don't I?"

"It's only chronic celibates who get worked up over dirt."

"Oh, the voice of Experience. You don't fool me either. You're not interested in sex."

"Simon and I have a mature relationship!"

"Yes, but it's all horizontal homage to you . . . Anyway, I can't waste time arguing. My public awaits . . ."

"Where are you going?"

"Body snatching."

Kelso and Jenny started to keep midnight vigils over the next few weeks as Ruth went to discos and parties and pubs with persons unknown. She came home once with her sweater on inside out. Sometimes she was in the woebegone aftermath of drinking. Sometimes her mascara was streaked, which made her undignified but strangely irreproachable at the same time.

"Can you not wait for Mr Right?" Kelso asked her one

day, so gently that she did not take offence.

"No, Dad. Things are not like that any more. Eyes across a crowded room, rings and vows . . ."

"Jenny managed it. You're only twenty-five. You're easy on the eye."

"The only thing men don't like about women of twenty-five is that they're not fourteen."

"You're mixing with the wrong sort."

"You said that life is all that matters. But it's *living* that really matters. I mean, Sleeping Beauty was alive! I was thinking lately about where Granny came from. So bleak. The wilds of Tyrone . . . She told me about the Wishing Tree at Ardboe."

"I know it. You're supposed to hammer a coin into the trunk and make a wish. I never did it."

"Miser!"

"I didn't want anybody to catch me wishing."

"She said it was studded, spangled with thousands of coins. And the tree turned black with poisonous metal and died. I just can't go on waiting, wishing, wasting."

"But what is it that you want?"

"I don't know."

They looked at each other and grew quiet again.

"You look so deep in thought, Mr Kelso, I feel I'm intruding."

"Oh, pardon me, I didn't hear you." He was extremely flustered.

What sort of a guard could be so unalert! Mrs Smythe disconcerted him at the best of times. She had beautiful cheekbones, perfect slopes that moved and accentuated themselves as she smiled and spoke.

Aristocracy, he thought, bred in the bone.

He felt egg-shaped, lacklustre, a graceless figure in her presence.

"Just worrying about my daughters. They have no mother to guide them. I'm at a loss . . ."

"But they're fairly grown up now, I understand?"

"Still on my hands, though. The younger one is settling down soon. The elder one, Ruth . . . She's a good girl, just headstrong . . ."

"Mr Kelso, it's always the girls that cost us the most sleep! Boys are less nerve-wracking . . ."

"Terrible things can befall them too. Just a couple of months back we found, I mean, my patrol, found a boy. Murdered. I can't get it out of my mind."

"I can't remember that incident."

It was not an incident.

"There are so many murders now. Every dawn seems to bring some pathetic dumped body to light. So anonymous and faceless."

I will never forget your face.

"Which community did the young man belong to?"

Neither. Both.

"The Nationalists, Ma'am."

"Was he . . . involved?"

"No."

"Is that proven?"

She wants a licence not to care.

"One death among so many, Mr Kelso," she said, closing the subject. "Take your tea before it cools."

He felt grubby and foolish after she left him. He had betrayed something close to his heart. But maybe he seemed mawkish, full of misplaced emotion? The youth was a stranger, after all. Maybe she would suspect him of harbouring Nationalist sympathies, of not being sceptical and suspicious enough. It was not fitting for a police reservist to be whingeing to a woman about ordeals encountered in the course of his duties. She was under his protection.

You've got to be a man about these things.

The household returned to calm. Jenny made shrewd businesslike arrangement for her "fairy-tale" wedding. Kelso's newfound garrulity dwindled. Ruth reverted to a stolid bearable unhappiness. She stopped going out apart from one or two tokenistic and tame nights a week. She stopped dreaming of cadavers bursting from their cerements, eruptions of bloody rags, insatiable violated orifices, dirty ears, noses, spaces between toes, red lippy vaginas . . . She began to study hard for an examination in bacteriology.

Nelson came round often, undeterred by Ruth's baleful lack of cordiality. She hated his affable ho-ho-ho, his bigotries, his taunting jokes. "What have dogdirt and women got in common? — The older they get, the easier they are to pick up."

But secretly Ruth welcomed his presence. He made the house inhospitable to the sense of numinous apparitions and heartfelt utterances of the past two months. One night she was reading at the table as Nelson and Kelso watched television. Suddenly her attention was claimed by the news. At a Republican rally in Belfast, there was a surprise appearance of a representative from Noraid, which supplied funds to the cause. He had arrived from the States that day and slipped past Special Branch. The crowd was exuberant. But police tried to move in. Members of the crowd tried to prevent them arresting the American. The police fired plastic bullets at rioters. A young man was struck on the head.

A televised death. They re-ran it in slow motion.

"My God, an action replay! We're watching a man die. It's a bloody snuff movie."

"That'll show them," Nelson said. "They should take a few more out while they're at it."

"You think it's right to kill someone for attending a political rally?"

"Do you think it's right to cheer someone who buys guns for the IRA?"

"Dad," she appealed. "He was just attending a meeting."

She started to weep.

Kelso stared at her. He looked bewitched and dull as a sleepwalker. She watched his eyes. Blink-blot-blink-blot-blink-blot.

He turned away. "Slap it into the bastards," he said.

"Right," said Nelson.

You were what I wanted, she realised. All along I just wanted you. The you that's gone.

Nuala Archer

Nuala Archer's first book of poetry, *Whale on the Line*, (Gallery Press, Dublin, 1981) won the National Irish Patrick Kavanagh Award. *Two Women, Two Shores*, poems by Nuala Archer and Medbh McGuckian was jointly published by New Poets Series, Baltimore and Salmon Press, Galway, Ireland, in 1989. *Pan/amá* a chapbook, was published by Red Dust, New York, in 1992. She has recently taught at Yale University. Presently she is Director of the Cleveland Poetry Centre and is an Associate Professor at Cleveland State University.

Sheela^Na^Gigging Around

— With thanks to Alice Walker

She's important enough
to be left out
powerful enough
to be hidden away
alive enough
to be killed
poet enough
to be censored

The fear cops sewed up the intimacy
of her l-i-p-s
with the gut strings of neglect
& the sci-fi powers
of that blow-in
History
that incestuous old Lotto-man-Lot
who raped everyone of his daughters
during the terrible two or twenty
mutilating millennia

What happened to pass
her l-i-p-s was dismissed
as a litany of defeat

She offers no translation
remaining rude as the truth —

a^Nut^a^jar^a^forbidden^well^
an^uppity^black^Irish^girl^
with^a^hibiscus^heart^
&^a^hands^on^approach^
to^her^own^controversial^
continuing^
pagan^third^eye

O
say
can yOu see
if yOu dOn't knOw Sheela
by nOw
yOu dOn't knOw
yOur ass frOm yOur elbOw
says Nell
dOn't wait anOther cOuple
1000 years tO bring her
hOme
she cOmes
with nO histOry
nO g-strings attached
her Only package
is her purse
she hOlds it O^
pen

O
say why can't yOu see

I am She
Sheela^na^gigging
arOund ^&
abOut
again

Come sit by me
Are you feeling horny?

It's nearly 3:00 o'clock
in Miami on Independence morning

My Banshee Sheela knows guerilla tactics
She sweats out the dead

voices that colonize
through Constitutions & cornerstones

greeting cards, textbooks
& tourist attractions

Voices insisting on a consuming
privacy

denying
their denial that I breathe

I set parameters
to my own paranoia

I listen carefully
to the beneath

of the beneath
of the bans

"So what's up with this Sheela^
na^gigging about & around?

At first I thought
she's a husband's nightmare

& I just wanted to distance myself
from such amateurish art

I poked fun at her in my head
She's anything but an idle chat

I renamed her Smutty-
No-Name

Perverse Pussy Prick Tease
Whore

Castrating Cunt She's Nothing
but a Bad Mouthing Mouth

a Grotesque Power
a Repulsive Protection

a Fiddling Obscenity
a Witch's Trick

an Embarrassing Lesbian
In-Joke

a Disgusting Feminist
Court Jester

GET HER OUT OF HERE
GET HER OUT OF HERE

I heard
a million motors of fear

grindingeringinggrinding
I lay in bed angry as hell

The inevitability of all this
history echoed like so much

gobbledeegook
I stared & stared

These last 20 centuries
have been a long detour through death

Facing the shame of my shame
I took the balled-up photo

of Sheela out of the trash
I Opened up the xerOx

her limbs
an Orgami-lOtus-lingO

What an unlikely resurrectiOn
here in this bland MOtel 6

still leaking frOm the damage
Of that underestimated Hurricane Andrew

HOw cOuld it be that this B.C. baby
Sheela survived at all?

My nipples hardened
with the memOry Of my new bOrn,

a suckling sea
Of nibbling darkness

Her rOund smiling eyes
her big bald head

my little Sinead O
an Orifice in^sight

NO flOOzie gOddess Of terrifying truth
this sOrcerer's sOurce

bOrn playing
in her Own jacuzzi

Yes a wOrd
lOve

made fleshy
as a mangO

I Often find myself
giving

in tO her nurturing trust
My cares are unwOund

I watch her listen
listen

to her Own cOming alive
she smiles

the wildest mOst secret
mOst Open smile

She seems to be asking me
What am I guarding

myself for sO preciOusly
With her in Our cradling cOlOrs

lOve
i feel rebOrn tO the risk

Of giving thanks
fOr this OutrageOusly raucOus

dam-bursting witness
Of Our flaming kisses

Our exiled lips cOming hOme

cOming hOme

tO Our Own face tO face
bright

O
hOly

night
bleeding bushes

The first time I saw yOu
she said in a dream
there was a red curtain
befOre yOu a red red
clOsed curtain
I am lOOking nOw
with my best weird watch
she cOntinued
tO the red clOsed curtain
reading it
and yOu standing at that curtain's crack
crOwning
I see that yOu are ready
fOr yOur Own zerO^at^the^bOne
O^
vatiOn sitar

yOu will gO far

yOu've alsO been given yOur granny's hammer
the breathing drum Of yOur heart
with a braille back-up
& Martina's twO^lipped labrys

I pull the curtain
O^
pen the light
is On
yOu are standing

with hair^razing ripeness
in the glaring light
I am listening
I flash yOu
a jOyful expressiOn
a pOpular & scandalOus passage
tO encOurage yOur Own crazy baglady
dOing her hOttest hOt^pink vibratiOns

with my guinep's translucence
my smiling gOurd
my everyday Ordinary Openness
I dub yOu
tO tell it like it is

Outshining
the remOte cOntrOls Of valium
& VCR's

The lOathing Of

yOur breathing viva^
ciOus well
has been brOken dOwn
in the lightning
Of yOur laughing vulva

Siobhán McHugh

Siobhán McHugh was born in Dublin in 1957. She was a radio producer in Ireland before migrating to Australia in 1985 and developing a passion for Australian history. Her first book, *The Snowy*, which won the New South Wales State Literary Award for Non-Fiction, was about postwar migrants, while *Minefields and Miniskirts* explored Australian women's involvement in the Vietnam War. She co-wrote the TV series, *The Irish Empire*, on the Irish Diaspora, and has made numerous radio features. She lives in Sydney with her two young sons.

Power Cuts

When I was a wee girl, school was heaven, mainly because it was a respite from home. On the short walk from our house to the bus stop, I could feel myself becoming normal, leaving behind the frightened, angry girl and acquiring the slight bounce in my step that would have swelled to my celebrated cheekiness by the time the assembly bell rang at nine o'clock. I usually made the metamorphosis no matter what I'd left behind; on a few occasions I couldn't manage it. Like the time when we were all eating our breakfast cornflakes and squabbling as usual over who got the creamy top of the milk. The back door opened and He stood there swaying slightly, face glazed in a maudlin grin, incongruous in a crumpled black dinner suit. We were frozen with shock. We never saw him in the morning, he didn't emerge from the small box room until we were well away to school. Nor had we ever seen him in such fancy clothes. And we didn't understand how you could be so drunk that early.

As we resumed our breakfast and tried to make sense of it all, we surreptitiously watched our mother for signs. Our father made a slurred attempt to speak, something mawkish about us kids, which we treated with our customary contempt. "Well I hope you're proud of yourself — coming home at this hour and in that state before the kids and the whole road." Mammy's voice was like a whiplash. The play had started. To and fro it went, he wheedling and pathetic at first, she spitting fury and abuse, as we scurried around collecting our lunches, books, hockey sticks, bags. He was leaning over her now, leering. "But I love you Eileen."

She responded to his grotesque endearments with a savage tirade, laced with such scorn and hatred we squirmed to watch. He swiped at her with one heavy paw. Half his weight, she looked ridiculously small. Why did she always have to provoke him, I raged, as I ran out after them and considered whether to go next door to get Mr Corr, the policeman. I'd never had to get him in daylight before; how would we ever live it down. She was on the floor now and he was sitting on her, punching into her face. I threw myself on his back, kicking and pummelling, trying to prise him off. I was thirteen and what adults referred to as "a fine big strapping lass". Without even bothering to turn around, he swatted me away, sending me reeling through the front door. The sound of shattering glass was enough to break the spell. He got up heavily, hopelessly, and dragged himself off to bed.

Somehow I hadn't a scratch, but I was trembling with shock. My mother hauled herself to her feet and after checking how I was, despatched us to school. Later she would see Dr McCormack for cuts and get someone in to mend the door. One of us would have to ring the office and say she had the flu. I headed off to take refuge in the Pharaohs and the Atomic Table, practising a smile.

Growing up in our house in the sixties and seventies made me determined to escape my mother's fate. She had come first in Ireland in the Leaving Certificate, but had had to forfeit a scholarship to university because she was a girl, the eldest of seven children. One boy looked set to become a priest and another a teacher, and the money Eileen could earn in the Post Office would be needed to put her brothers through. My father also happened to come first in the Leaving Cert in his year; in fact, as he was proud of telling us, he had got 110 per cent in Maths — he got an extra ten per cent for sitting the exam through the Irish language. He had followed the classic postwar path for bright students, into the Civil Service, where unless he staged an armed hold-up or exposed himself to the female staff, a lifelong salary was now assured. By 1948, when he met my mother, he was a Good Prospect.

She had been casually dating another man, a quiet, gentle type, not the sort to be noticed in a crowd. He was older than my father but had only scraped through as a Junior Ex. When he saw my father courting Eileen, the other man withdrew, telling my mother she would be better off with Jim, who would go far. We first heard of this other man, whose name I do not know, when I was about ten. We came home one day and found my mother crying fit to burst, heart-rending sobs different from the hopeless crying after a fight. Her friend had died. She told us how he had helped her, sending her money when my father drank all his pay, buying Cora's First Communion outfit and my school uniform. She had met him two or three times in fifteen years. Once they had gone for a drive to Howth Head and she had told him how it was. They had not spoken of it again, but the anonymous gifts had arrived until his death.

Like all young couples then, my parents got engaged and started saving for a house. Though my mother earned a lot less and had to send a large portion home, she managed to accumulate a modest sum. Shortly before the wedding, she discovered my father had not put aside one penny. I don't know if she ever loved him, but I know she did not want to go through with the wedding. She told her mother her misgivings. My grandmother, her place in Heaven firmly assured now that she had not only one son a priest but a daughter a nun, was not about to have her respectability sabotaged. She insisted the marriage go ahead. Afraid she might have been pregnant anyway, since they had French kissed, my mother gave in.

My grandmother lived long enough to see her plans go somewhat awry — her son-in-law's prospects shrank as his drinking escalated, the nun committed suicide and after a miserable exile in New Zealand, the priest finally jumped the wall. He had moved to Manchester to help the homeless, newly free and debonair in a white suit and Panama hat. There he had met a fellow social worker, who miraculously, was a Catholic and a widow. Afraid to tell his mother he'd even left the priesthood, he naturally daren't mention marriage. "She'd have a stroke!" he pleaded. "Let her," replied my mother. "You've got your own life to lead." My grandmother never got over the sudden devaluation of her credit in heaven and never exchanged one word with "that woman", as she referred to her new daughter-in-law.

In 1951, my parents got married and went to live in a raw new housing estate in Dublin. As soon as the honeymoon ended, the beatings started. She never could keep quiet for her own good and after six months in a house with only lino on the floor and not a stick of furniture, she told him it wasn't good enough. Practically nine months to the day of the wedding, Cora was born. If it wasn't for that, she often told us, "I'd have cleared out straight away." Almost five years passed before I arrived, a puzzling gap in a land of no contraceptives. Sixteen years later, wounded by my announcement that I was leaving home, she revealed to me my origins: "I prostituted myself to your father to get him to pay the electricity bill — and you were the result."

Four more children followed, though my father insisted to me recently that "the marriage relationship was a shambles from the word go. However God is good and Guinness is a great soporific," he added, as if trying to charm a foreigner. At night we would lie awake waiting for the sound of the car at pub closing time, the headlights sweeping across the bedroom wall as he turned at the bottom and came back. We would make bargains with God to make him die, imagine the phone call from the police and how we would feign surprise at the news — then marvel bitterly when he drunkenly deposited the car in the driveway yet again.

She was often up when he came home, making celery soup and stews for us to have when we came in from school next day. She had found a full-time job when the youngest started school, the only mother we knew who was not at home all day. I cringe with shame now to recall how little we older kids helped. We peeled a few potatoes before going to bed, or polished the shoes, and fell asleep most nights to the hiss of the pressure cooker as she made tomorrow's dinner until the small hours.

She worked for a big accountancy firm in a high-rise office block by the Grand Canal. It was great to see her heading off in the morning in the smart executive suits she got at a second-hand shop, her hair permed and face made up. So different from the quilted pink dressing-gown she wore all day on bad days, her face still puffy and her voice a low hopeless monotone when we arrived home for tea. Now she looked just like other people's parents, maybe even better. But she could still be mortally embarrassing — like the time when the bus arrived with standing room only and the conductor allowed the first three on. A businessman jumped the queue ahead of a boy about my age, who hung his head. My mother leapt on the bus, hauled the man off and in her most imperious tones, declaimed, "I think this child was before you." It was much later, when I found myself confronting a bunch of bikies in a pub and demanding that they return someone's hat, that I realised with wonder where I'd got my lunatic courage from.

My mother was then in her forties and practically ran the office, but she was paid as a junior clerk. A lifetime of working out household budgets on the backs of envelopes had given her a sharp eye for figures and her natural management ability and common sense, not to mention a keen intelligence, did the rest. She assessed companies going into liquidation and advised her boss which ones could be saved. Mostly she was right and her boss soon became a senior partner, his career fast-tracked because of "his" excellent judgement. If anything went wrong, she was the scapegoat and those evenings she came home shaken and irritable, often reaching for a gin, or maybe a Valium. Dr McCormack was by then sick of perfectly healthy women who just wanted to sit in his surgery and talk about their problems; Valium kept them both happy.

This was the early seventies and Ireland was beginning to change. A bunch of women had come in from Belfast on the train openly bearing hundreds of condoms, all "for their own personal use", they gleefully told a bewildered customs officer. Contraception was illegal, but the pill had arrived and somehow my mother got hold of it. She was never a doctrinaire Catholic; once, when it seemed the Church would not bury a young man up the road who had suicided, she told us she would never ask us to go to Mass again. In the end, everyone pretended he had died accidentally and he got his place in the cemetery.

There was talk of joining the Common Market and how that would mean Equal Rights for women, perhaps some day equal pay. Nobody even dreamt of divorce, but the new Women's Page in the paper sometimes carried articles about family law and how one day a wife might no longer be considered her husband's legal chattel.

We knew why she had never left our father. "Go, why don't you?" he often said. "Just get out of my house and don't come back." The house was the basis of his power and could not be challenged. He had once thrown Mammy's father out on the street in the middle of the night, when he had tried to protect his daughter from a beating. Jim revelled in his dominion and his knowledge that if she left him, she was entitled to nothing. There were no refuges, and she had no friends — the atmosphere of menace and despair had always precluded visitors and gradually she lost touch with the girlfriends of her youth.

We used to beseech her to go to the local "Ladies Club" like the other mothers on the street, but snobbery and shame kept her away. She was not content to gossip and play Bingo as they were. She read the *Irish Times*, not the tabloid papers, she wanted to talk about what went on in the world, not just the neighbourhood. Her children would go to university, unlike the girls down the road who aspired to be air hostesses and nurses. Affronted by her aloofness, the other wives sometimes thought to themselves that maybe it served her right to be belted up a bit, her with her notions. Mrs Corr next door, who had only two children, let her cabbages go to seed and her fruit rot on the tree before she would hand some over the fence to us. Years later, when I was a sophisticated (as I imagined) radio producer, I drove back to our street, climbed the fence and stole every apple off the Corrs' trees. I had been too ashamed to rob them as a kid.

Apart from his pub cronies, my father had only one friend we knew of, and an unlikely one at that. Barry had left school at thirteen, as my father, the university graduate, constantly pointed out. But he was no fool, and had made quite a fortune as a builder. Though he and his wife, Shona, lived in a more salubrious area right across the city, they called in every Christmas for a drink. On Christmas Day, the open fire in the loungeroom was specially lit and the good silver cutlery brought out from the canteen in preparation for lunch. Bottles of sherry, brandy, gin and whiskey were placed on the sideboard in readiness for guests. Besides Barry and Shona, I can only ever remember one other visitor — Dermot, a junior colleague of my father's, who in a rash moment had been made godfather to one of us kids. For a few years he would turn up each Christmas with some wildly expensive present to atone for his total lack of interest in the child throughout the year. Under our curious gaze, he would hoe into the tray of ham sandwiches that accompanied his stout, then make his escape.

I wished I was lucky enough to have such a godparent. My godfather, my mother's brother, was a travelling salesman in America whose physical absence and lack even of an address made him unreal to me. Always striving to up his quota and beat his records, he could never remember my birthdays. He wasn't mean though, and every so often, as he flogged Amoco oil from Miami to Chicago, he would fire off a magical wad of dollars from some motel room or other. My godmother was a poorer bet. As a nun, all she could ever do was pray for me, and rotate the holy pictures I received year by year.

I've always wondered whether I was really responsible for despatching my father's Only Friend. My parents were having one of their occasional reconciliations and had gone as far as taking a weekend away in the West. These brief artificial interludes were a terrible strain. They would return looking relaxed and talking like tourists about the Cliffs of

Moher, while we desperately tried to preserve the charade. We would keep phone calls short, refrain from eating the last biscuit in the house, treat each other with awkward courtesy, trying to pre-empt the first cross word. But it never worked. Something would make her angry, and the spell would be broken. My father would disappear, my mother would rage around the house or sit stonily in the kitchen making lists, and we would scuttle back to our rooms and bury ourselves in homework.

On one such weekend, I had friends over to take advantage of our parent-free house. One girl nonchalantly suggested hitting the booze. We skimmed the top off various bottles, from the Christmas offerings at the front to obscure old duty-free liqueurs, mixed it all up and added Coke to drown the taste. We then headed off to a dance, giggling and stumbling our way to the top of the double-decker bus so as to get the mixture properly jolted up inside. After a brief but spectacular solo go-go performance, I collapsed on the weighing scales in the Ladies loo. I still don't understand how it could have taken four bouncers to carry me out — I'm not *that* heavy — but my sister's boyfriend, who recognised my prone form, insists that's what happened, and he's a decent type who wouldn't have had the imagination to invent such a scene.

The next day, in between vomiting frenzies, I saw to my horror that the bottle of Scotch, which usually descended a steady inch each Christmas, was now half empty. As Barry was the only one who ever touched it, this would certainly be noticed. It would have to be replaced, immediately. But how? Even if I had the money, I wasn't old enough to buy liquor. I studied the depleted contents, like some monster urine sample. An idea dawned.

After much experimenting, cold tea diluted with Worcestershire sauce proved the perfect solution. I poured it into the Scotch, shook it up and smelt, almost gagging now from the whiskey odour. When Barry and Shona arrived next Christmas Eve, I watched tensely as my father poured him his customary drink. Barry downed it as usual, laughed as heartily as ever — and never came back.

When I left school, I wanted to go to university, but I had a much more desperate need to leave home. The two seemed incompatible; it was hard enough to find the fees for college, ludicrous to pay rent when we lived within walking distance of the campus. Like my sister before me, I would be expected to save my fees by working the long vacations. But because I was too young to be accepted into college straight away, I had wangled my way into a flat at sixteen, the year I left school and got an interim job. Though my naiveté about such practicalities as a kitty had been ruthlessly exploited by the two parasitic receptionists I had moved in with, the heady freedom of having my own flat was so precious, I would have gladly emptied dustbins for the rest of my life rather than return to the emotional wringer that was home. I could cope with visits; in fact my new status seemed to improve things for everyone. My mother could save things up to tell me on Sundays and the other kids would be let off the hook if I was around. I got to do my weekly wash, ate obscene amounts of the roast lunch and shamelessly raided the store cupboard. In return, I would listen to my mother's complaints, about work, the house, the kids, Him, the neighbours, or whatever.

One morning, while she was expounding on one of the above, I was doodling on a packet of cornflakes that was still on the table. Kellogg's was running a competition and you had to select the order of the eight attributes you would value most in your new Simca. I filled it in as mental self-defence from my mother's litany and moved on to the next stage. In fewer than ten words, complete this sentence: *I would like to own a Simca car, because . . .* A phrase came back to me from a book I had idly picked up in the loungeroom. "She was a good cook as cooks go — and as cooks go, she went." With apologies to the author, John D. Sheridan, I wrote: *I would like to own a Simca car, because as cars go, Simca goes best.*

I cut out the cardboard panel, put it in an envelope and used it for weeks as a bookmark. It was only after I had returned the book to the library that I saw an ad for the competition. The closing date was not yet past. I rang the library; the envelope, stamped and addressed, was still there. The assistant offered to post it for me. "No," I said, "I'll come for it." I suddenly had a feeling it was important that I personally ensure its delivery. It only occurred to me later that the book was called *Lucky Jim*. One morning, when I'd been up since 5 a.m. in a hopelessly belated attempt to study for a university entrance scholarship, I got a phone call. "Congratulations," said a male voice. "You have won a Simca 1100." At the presentation, I learnt several things:

they really do read all the entries — and the odds against my winning had been 66,000 to 1. Some assiduous entrants, who ran hotels and consumed prodigious amounts of cornflakes, had sent in hundreds of forms but still hadn't won. I hadn't the heart to mention that at seventeen, I was too young to drive — and I didn't eat cornflakes anymore.

The proceeds from the sale of that car granted me my wish — to live in a flat and go to college. Ever since then, I have always believed the impossible was achievable. As a corollary, I do not accept statistics, about anything. Thus, just as I was the one applicant out of two thousand who got the radio job, I will be the one the shark happens to find in Sydney Harbour. I have had exceptional good fortune in my life: besides the car, raffles have yielded everything from a free holiday in Thailand to expensive jewellery (won at a benefit night, of all things — the organisers refused to re-auction the prize, saying it was bad karma). But I've paid a certain price, in life-threatening accidents and incidents.

When I was twenty-one, a boat on which I was sleeping during a trip to the Aran Islands, off Galway, went on fire. I was trapped in a cabin and got badly burnt. After some bizarre misadventures, too complicated to relate here, I was airlifted to the mainland next day.

When they placed me in the Intensive Care ward, I remember thinking the place must be overflowing if they had to stick *me* in there. It didn't occur to me that I was in danger of dying, not even when the whole family, my father included, materialised in ones and twos at my bedside from the other side of the country.

Being burnt does not hurt that much, if it's bad enough. But getting better, pulling yourself back through the tunnel of pain, requires a real will to live. They say that's why old people and children die more easily from burns; the kids don't understand why they have to put up with such agony and the old folk couldn't be bothered. Through those weeks, my mother stayed by my side until I was out of danger, pretending every day she had forgotten to bring a mirror, so that I would not see my disfigured face. When visiting hours closed, she prowled the pubs, asking questions and endlessly probing into what had happened, in the face of police indifference to the incident. Much later we learnt the fire was probably due to an electrical fault — ironic, considering my origins, that electricity should have nearly killed me.

When I had graduated to the wards, she said to me suddenly: "Siobhán, I don't know you any more. I don't know what sort of person you are, who your friends are, what you believe in." Upset, she burst out, "I'm even afraid you're turning into a socialist." My face was then covered in one huge black scab. I laughed so much I cracked the mask from side to side, leading Matron to tut-tut at my silliness. "You're much more of a socialist than I'll ever be," I told her. "You're just afraid of the word. I'm not half as good at standing up against injustice as you."

Two weeks later she had a mastectomy. She had postponed the operation for over a month to be with me, telling no one of her diagnosis. When my mother came out of hospital, my younger sister Maeve moved back home to help her with the housework, as she could not use her arm and was very sore and stiff. My father arrived home one night drunk and belligerent. My mother was typically scathing. He lunged at her, opening the fresh wound of her mastectomy. Seeing the bleeding, my sister went almost mad with rage. She charged at my father with a breadknife, but he fended her off and threw her outside the door. She has neither set eyes on him nor set foot inside the house since.

After twenty-nine years of marriage, my mother finally applied for a legal separation. With only three children at home and the youngest now at high school, they could survive on her wage. My father's latest assault had finally won her a barring order against him. To minimise the trauma, she settled for the period of her lifetime. She could have had him excluded from the family home forever, but then we children would have had to be dragged through our sordid history. My father would cross-examine, alleging she was mentally disturbed — his favourite taunt. Thinking particularly of the youngest, she settled for the lesser barring order. My father advertised for room and board for a "quiet respectable gentleman, civil servant" and was deluged with offers from eager landladies, although when they saw his shiny alcoholic face and unkempt appearance, they were less enthusiastic. He eventually found a flat near the office and broadcast his sorry plight by carrying groceries in his suit pocket, fishing out a half pound of butter in the pub with a pitiful "Look what my wife has reduced me to" look.

For the next few months, the atmosphere at home was the happiest I can ever remember. Sometimes when I visited, I'd be greeted with the smell of apple tarts cooking and my mother would be sitting around having coffee and laughing, actually laughing. It was so normal it was weird. She had started driving lessons and one day she got as far as Dun Laoghaire, nine miles away, where she had a gin and tonic to celebrate.

That summer, 1981, she was diagnosed with advanced bone cancer, referred from the earlier breast cancer. I was then twenty-four and we were just beginning to develop a new and satisfying relationship as consenting adults. For years I had spurned any contact that wasn't strictly necessary, observing the minimum of family occasions and leaving for my flat or my friends as soon as I could. Now it struck me how much I wanted to show her, share with her. I invited her to come with me on a two-week trip to Crete, the sort of package holiday I had once scorned. I found myself thinking with pleasure how I could explain the foreign food to her, how we could sit at a café and marvel at the view, already hearing the loud laugh she permitted herself increasingly now.

A few days before our departure, she said she couldn't go. She wanted to be near the doctors just in case — but that I must go, and tell her how it was. She was in bed, but in good form, when I left, on the Saturday. That afternoon, she deteriorated suddenly and was taken to hospital. She died five days later, less than a year after the separation, at the age of fifty-four. She was feisty to the last, pulling herself out of a coma to demand if the tablets she was being fed "had a name".

At the funeral, my father signalled his intention to reclaim the house that very day. Nuala, the youngest, who had begun to believe he didn't exist anymore, went catatonic in his presence. There was no way they could live anywhere near him. My mother had been dithering about signing up for a superannuation scheme at work, but the papers had not been processed. Miraculously, however, the super came through, enabling the three youngest to rent a house and live together until Nuala finished school. Maybe someone at head office felt compassion, for my mother had championed many an underdog at work and found new friends, even if they never trespassed beyond the hours of nine to five.

• • •

Hypocrisy was part of my growing up. The neighbours who turned a blind eye to the constant violence, the school-teachers who carefully ignored our reddened eyes and brooding silences, the pub mates who let my father act out the fantasy of his perfect, high-achieving family as long as he kept buying them drinks, the doctors who drugged women into inarticulateness, the priests who told them to put up with it, the politicians, then almost exclusively male, who disdained to look at the rights of women and children.

Hypocrisy and bullying remain two of my pet hates and like my mother, I attack both with more energy than sense. Thus in my first real job, as producer of a breakfast radio show with the Irish state broadcaster, I arranged to have the Director of a Family Planning Clinic on the program in the run-up to a 1984 referendum on abortion. For balance, I would have her Right to Life opponent on next day. The first interview was rather bland and far from radical — but by lunchtime, I had been tersely informed that I was being removed from the program as "unfit to produce serious editorial content". I was left to languish on a late night country music program, given no right of reply and even — punishment for a cardinal sin in the public service — had my increment stopped.

I prepared pages in my defence and took it to union, personnel officers and superiors. But I had not mastered the art of double-speak and memo-writing and was so pathetically sincere, I never had a chance. The union was busy with its own power struggles and an organisation of right-wing Catholic laymen, the Knights of Columbanus, had acted to have me removed. Their other activities included surreptitiously photographing women who attended family planning clinics, sending the "incriminating" evidence to their employers and demanding that they be fired — as some would be — depending on the backbone and religious predilections of the employer.

Around the same time, the Simca a distant memory, I applied to the credit union for a loan to buy a car. Over a cosy chat in the canteen, the loans officer enquired, not about my finances and commitments, but as to whether I believed in God. I was in no doubt that if I said no, I would not get the loan. I laughed it off, chuckling grimly that it wasn't God who'd be making the repayments. I was outraged. Had I been proselytising for the IRA in the same way as he was touting for God, I could have been sacked.

Strangely enough, the Knights of Columbanus did me a favour, for it was as a result of my demotion that I became interested in Australia. My period of enforced idleness coincided with plans to hold an Irish-Australian Conference in the run up to the Bicentennial celebrations, "to identify the Irish contribution to Australia before the bloody Brits claim all the credit," as the convenor put it. I was co-opted as Honorary Secretary, a position that started out as something of a joke, but having nothing much to do at the time, I was sufficiently curious to attend. From that, the idea was born that I should swap places with a producer at ABC Radio Melbourne, who had a hankering to go to Ireland.

Thus it was that in March 1985, I landed in Sydney, ostensibly for a year. But it was an Irish swap; I never went back. After the cloying homogeneity of home, where everyone knew everyone and your life's path seemed predestined by your stock, I revelled in the pluralism and anonymity of Australia, while feeling comforted by the sameness. Unlike America, where it tends to be restricted to Irish-Americans, Irishness is everywhere in Australia. It has seeped into the national character to such a degree that even an Australian of Greek or Italian background would feel part of the furniture in Ireland.

With nothing to live up to and no-one to disappoint, I felt I could try anything. In that spirit of liberation, I decided to write a book, about an episode in Australian history after the second world war, when refugees and immigrants from over forty countries were despatched to a mountain wilderness to build the world's most complex hydroelectric scheme. I was then a struggling freelance with the first yearnings to have a child. "The Snowy", as the hydroelectric scheme was called, was much more than an engineering project; it became a monument to multi-culturalism and symbol of the modern nation. But the grim irony was not lost on me, that if the book did well, I could afford to get pregnant — thus a second generation of McHughs would trace their origins back to the comforts of electricity.

Maeve Binchy

Maeve Binchy was born in County Dublin and went to school at the Holy Child Convent in Killiney. She took a history degree at University College Dublin and taught in various girls' schools, writing travel articles in the long summer holidays. In 1969 she joined the *Irish Times*. For some ten years she was based in London writing humorous columns from all over the world. Today, she divides her time between London and County Dublin, where she also has a home.

She is the author of several volumes of short stories, among them *London Transports, Dublin 4; The Lilac Bus* and *Silver Wedding*. Her novels include *Light a Penny Candle*, *Echoes, Firefly Summer, Circle of Friends, Copper Beech* and *The Glass Lake*. Her latest novel, *Evening* will be released in 1996.

Echoes (extract)

Clare O'Brien had arrived early at school. The back of her neck was almost washed away, such a scrubbing had it got. The stain on her school tunic was almost impossible to see now, it had been attacked severely with a nail brush. Her indoor shoes were gleaming, she had even polished the soles, and the yellow ribbons were beautiful. She turned her head a few times to see them reflected in the school window, she looked as smart as any of the others, as good as the farmers' daughters who had plenty of money and got new uniforms when they grew too big for their old ones, instead of all the letting down and letting out and false hems that Clare and Chrissie had to put up with.

She thought the day would never start. It was going to be such an excitement going up there in front of the whole school. And there would be gasps because she was so young. Years and years younger than some of them who had entered.

Chrissie would be furious of course, but that didn't matter, Chrissie was furious about everything, she'd get over it.

Clare walked to the end of the corridor to read the notice board. There was nothing new on it, maybe after this morning there might be a notice about the history prize. There was the timetable, the list of holidays of obligation during the year, the details of the educational tour to Dublin and also the price of it, which made it outside Clare's hopes. There was the letter from Father O'Hara, Miss O'Hara's brother who was a missionary. He was thanking the school for the silver paper and stamp collecting. He said he was very proud that the girls in his own home town had done so much to aid the great work of spreading Our Lord's word to all the poor people who had never heard of Him.

Clare couldn't remember Father O'Hara, but everyone said he was marvellous. He was very tall, taller than Miss O'Hara, and very handsome. Clare's mother had said that it would do your heart good to see him when he came back to say Mass in the church, and he was a wonderful son too, she said. He wrote to his mother from the missions, she often showed his letters to people — well, when she had been able to get out a bit she had.

Father O'Hara made the missions sound great fun altogether. Clare wished he would write a letter every week. She wondered what did Miss O'Hara write to him. Would she tell him about the history prize this week?

There was Miss O'Hara now, coming in the gate on her bicycle. Mother Immaculata had a face like the nib of a pen.

"Could I have a word, Miss O'Hara, a little word please. That's if you can spare the time."

One day, Angela promised herself, she would tell Mother Immaculata that she couldn't spare the time, she was too busy helping the seniors to run the potin still and preparing the third years for the white-slave traffic. But not yet. Not while she still had to work here. She put her bicycle in the shed and swept up the armful of essays wrapped in their sheet against the elements.

"Certainly Mother," she said with a false smile.

Mother Immaculata didn't speak until they were in her office. She closed the door and sat down at her desk; the only other chair in the room was covered in books so Angela had to stand.

She decided she would fight back. If the nun was going to treat her as a disobedient child over some trivial thing as yet unknown, and let her stand there worrying, Angela was going to draw herself up so high that Mother Immaculata would get a crick in her neck looking up. Angela raised herself unobtrusively on to her toes, and stretched her neck upwards like a giraffe. It worked. Mother Immaculata had to stand up too.

"What is all this about a money prize for an essay competition, Miss O'Hara? Can you explain to me how it came up and when it was discussed with me?"

"Oh, I've given them an essay to do and I'm awarding a prize for the best one." Angela smiled like a simpleton.

"But when was this discussed?" The thin pointed face quivered at the lack of respect, or anxiety at discovery.

"Sure, there'd be no need to discuss every single thing we did in class Mother, would there? I mean, would you ever get anything done if we came to you over what homework we were going to give them and all?"

"I do *not* mean that. I mean I need an explanation. Since when have we been paying the children to study?"

Angela felt a sudden weariness. It was going to be like this for ever. Any bit of enthusiasm and excitement sat on immediately. Fight for every single thing including the privilege of putting your hand into your own very meagre salary and giving some of it as a heady excitement which had even the dullards reading the history books.

It was like a slow and ponderous dance. A series of steps had to be gone through, a fake bewilderment. Angela would now say that she was terribly sorry, she had thought Mother Immaculata would be delighted, which was lies of course since she knew well that Immaculata would have stopped it had she got wind of it earlier. Then a fake display of helplessness, what should they do now, she had all the essays corrected, look here they were, and the children were expecting the results today. Then the fake supplication, could Mother Immaculata ever be kind enough to present the prize? Angela had it here in an envelope. It was twenty-one shillings, a whole guinea. Oh and there was a subsidiary prize for another child who had done well, a book all wrapped up. And finally the fake gratitude and the even more fake promise that it would *never* happen again.

Mother Immaculata was being gracious now, which was even more sickening than when she was being hostile.

"And who has won this ill-advised competition?" she asked.

"Bernie Conway," said Angela. "It was the best, there's no doubt about that. But you know young Clare O'Brien, she did a terrific one altogether, the poor child must have slaved over it. I would like to have given her the guinea but I thought the others would pick on her, she's too young. So that's why I got her a book, could you perhaps say something Mother about her being . . ."

Mother Immaculata would agree to nothing of the sort.

Clare O'Brien from the little shop down by the steps, wasn't she only one of the youngest to enter for it? Not at all, it would be highly unsuitable. Imagine putting her in the same league as Bernie Conway from the post office, to think of singling out Chrissie O'Brien's younger sister. Not at all.

"But she's nothing like Chrissie, she's totally different," wailed Angela. But she had lost. The children were filing into the school hall for their prayers and hymn. Mother Immaculata had put her hand out and taken the envelope containing the guinea and the card saying that Bernadette Mary Conway had been awarded the Prize of Best History Essay. Mother Immaculata left on her desk the neatly wrapped copy of Palgreave's *Golden Treasury* for Clare O'Brien for Excellence in History Essay Writing.

Angela picked it up and reminded herself that it was childish to believe that you could win everything.

Mother Immaculata made the announcements after prayers. Clare thought the words were never going to come out of the nun's thin mouth.

There were announcements about how the school was going to learn to answer Mass with Father O'Dwyer, not serve it of course, only boys could do that, but to answer it, and there must be great attention paid so that it would be done beautifully. And there was a complaint that those girls in charge of school altars were very lacking in diligence about putting clean water in the vases. What hope was there for a child who couldn't manage to prepare a clean vase for Our Lady? It was a very simple thing surely to do for the Mother of God. Then there was the business about outdoor shoes being worn in the classroom. Finally she came to it. Mother Immaculata's voice changed slightly. Clare couldn't quite understand — it was as if she didn't *want* to give the history prize.

"It has come to my notice, only this morning, that there is some kind of history competition. I am glad of course to see industry in the school. However, that being said, it gives me great pleasure to present the prize on behalf of the school."

She paused and her eyes went up and down the rows of girls who stood in front of her. Clare smoothed the sides of her tunic nervously. She must remember to walk slowly and not to run, she could easily fall on the steps leading up to the stage where Mother Immaculata, the other nuns and lay teachers stood. She would be very calm and she would thank Miss O'Hara and remember to thank Mother Immaculata as well.

"So I won't keep you in any further suspense . . ." Mother Immaculata managed to draw another few seconds out of it.

"The prize is awarded to Bernadette Mary Conway. Congratulations Bernadette. Come up here, child, and receive your prize."

Clare told herself she must keep smiling. She must not let her face change. Just think about that and nothing else and she'd be all right. She concentrated fiercely on the smile; it sort of pushed her eyes up a bit and if there were any tears in them people wouldn't notice.

She kept the smile on as stupid Bernie Conway put her

hand to her mouth over and over, and then put her hand on her chest. Her friends had to nudge her to get her to her feet. As she gasped and said it couldn't be true, Clare clenched her top teeth firmly on top of her lower teeth and smiled on. She saw Miss O'Hara looking round at the school and even looking hard at her. She smiled back hard. Very hard. She would never let Miss O'Hara know how much she hated her. She must be the meanest and most horrible teacher in the world — much meaner than Mother Immaculata — to tell Clare that she had won the prize, to say all those lies about it being the best thing she had read in all her years teaching. Clare kept the smile up until it was time to file out of the hall and into their classrooms. Then she dropped it; it didn't matter now. She felt one of her ribbons falling off; that didn't matter now either.

The girls brought sandwiches to eat in the classroom at lunch, and they had to be very careful about crumbs for fear of mice. Clare had made big doorsteps for herself and Chrissie since her big sister was still a disgrace. But she hadn't the appetite for anything at all. She unwrapped the paper, looked at them and just wrapped them up again. Josie Dillon, who sat beside her, looked at them enviously.

"If you're sure?" she said as Clare passed them over wordlessly.

"I'm sure," Clare said.

It was raining, so they couldn't go out in the yard. Lunchtimes indoors were awful, the windows were all steamed up and there was the smell of food everywhere. The nuns and teachers prowled from classroom to classroom seeing that the high jinks were not too high; the level of noise fell dramatically as soon as a figure of authority appeared and then rose slowly to a crescendo once more when the figure moved on.

Josie was the youngest of the Dillons, the others were away at a boarding school but it was said that they wouldn't bother sending Josie, she wasn't too bright. A big pasty girl with a discontented face — only when someone suggested food was there any animation at all.

"These are lovely," she said with a full mouth to Clare. "You're cracked not to want them yourself."

Clare smiled a watery smile.

"Are you feeling all right?" Josie showed concern. "You look a bit green."

"No, I'm fine," Clare said. "I'm fine." She was saying it to herself rather than to Josie Dillon who was busy opening up the second sandwich and looking into it with pleasure.

Miss O'Hara came into the classroom and the noise receded. She gave a few orders; pick up those crusts at once, open the window to let in some fresh air, no it didn't matter how cold and wet it was, open it. How many times did she have to say put the books away *before* you start to eat. And suddenly, "Clare, can you come out here to me a minute."

Clare didn't want to go, she didn't want to talk to her ever again. She hated Miss O'Hara for making such a fool of her, telling her that she'd won the prize and building up her hopes. But Miss O'Hara had said it again. "Clare. Now, please."

Unwillingly she went out into the corridor which was full of people going to and from the cloakrooms getting ready for afternoon classes. The bell would ring any moment now.

Miss O'Hara put her books on a window sill right on top of the Sacred Heart altar. There were altars on nearly every window sill and each class was responsible for one of them.

"I got you another prize, because yours was so good. It was really good and if you had been competing with people nearer your own age you'd have won hands down. So anyway I got this for you." Miss O'Hara handed her a small parcel. She was smiling and eager for Clare to open it. But Clare would not be bought off with a secret prize.

"Thank you very much, Miss O'Hara," she said and made no attempt to untie the string.

"Well, aren't you going to look at it?"

"I'll open it later," she said. It was as near to being rude as she dared to go, and in case it had been just that bit too much she added, "Thank you very much."

"Stop sulking, Clare, and open it." Miss O'Hara's voice was firm.

"I'm not sulking."

"Of course you are, and it's a horrible habit. Stop it this minute and open up the present I bought you so generously out of my own money." It was an order. It also made Clare feel mean. Whatever it was she would be very polite.

It was a book of poetry, a book with a soft leather cover that had fancy flowers painted on it with gold-leaf paint. It was called *The Golden Treasury of Verse*. It was beautiful.

Some of the sparkle had come back into the small face with the big eyes. "Open the book now and see what I wrote." Angela was still very teacherish.

Clare read the inscription aloud.

"That's the first book for your library. One day when you have a big library of books you'll remember this one, and you'll take it out and show it to someone, and you'll say it was your first book, and you won it when you were ten."

"Will I have a library?" Clare asked excitedly.

"You will if you want to. You can have anything if you want to."

"Is that true?" Clare felt Miss O'Hara was being a bit jokey, her voice had a tinny ring to it.

"No, not really, I wanted to give you this in front of the whole school, I wanted Immaculata to give it to you, but she wouldn't. Make you too uppity or something. No, there's a lot of things I want and don't get, but that's not the point, the point is you must go out and try for it, if you don't try you can't get anything."

"It's beautiful." Clare stroked the book.

"It's a grand collection, much nicer than your poetry book in class."

Clare felt very grown up: Miss O'Hara saying "Immaculata" without "Mother" before it. Miss O'Hara saying their poetry textbook wasn't great! "I'd have bought a book anyway if I'd won the guinea," she said forgivingly.

"I know you would, and that eejit of a Bernie Conway will probably buy a handbag or a whole lot of hairbands. What happened to those nice yellow ribbons you were wearing this morning?"

"I took them off, and put them in my schoolbag. They seemed wrong."

"Yes, well maybe they'll seem right later on, you know."

"Oh they will, Miss O'Hara. Thank you for the beautiful book. Thank you, *really*."

Miss O'Hara seemed to understand. Then she said suddenly, "You *could* get anywhere you wanted, Clare, you know, if you didn't give up and say it's all hopeless. You don't have to turn out like the rest of them."

"I'd love to . . . well, to get on you know," Clare admitted. It was out, this thing that had been inside for so long and never said in case it would be laughed at. "But it would be very hard, wouldn't it?"

"Of course it would, but that's what makes it worth doing, if it were easy then every divil and dirt could do it. It's because it's hard it's special."

"Like being a saint," Clare said, eyes shining.

"Yes, but that's a different road to go down. Let's see if you can get you an education first. Be a mature saint not a child saint, will you?"

The bell rang, deafening them for a moment.

"I'd prefer not to be a child saint all right, they're usually martyred for their faith, aren't they?"

"Almost invariably," Miss O'Hara said, nearly sweeping the statue of the Sacred Heart with her as she gathered her books for class.

Mary Daly

Photograph © Gail Bryan 1991

Mary Daly, is a Particularly Revolting Hag who holds doctorates in theology and philosophy from the University of Fribourg, Switzerland. An associate professor at Boston College, this Spinster spins and weaves cosmic fantasies in her own time/space. She is the author of six Radical Feminist books, including *The Church and the Second Sex*, *Beyond God the Father*, *Gyn/Ecology*, *Outercourse: The Bedazzling Voyage; Containing Recollections from my Logbook of Radical Feminist Philosopher (Being an Account of My Time/Space Travels and Ideas — Then, Again, Now and How)*, *Pure Lust*, and *Websters' First New Intergalactic Wickedary of the English Language* (conjured in Cahoots with Jane Caputi).

Outercourse (extract)

Spiraling Back: Early Grades and Private Junkets

It would be difficult to convey the foreground dreariness of the forties and fifties in America, particularly for a potential Radical Feminist Philosopher with a Passion for forbidden theological and philosophical learning — it *would be* difficult if the partriarchal State of Boredom had not managed to repeat itself by belching forth the insufferable eighties and nineties, reproducing a time of dulled-out brains, souls, and passions. So I need not ask the reader to imagine or try to remember such a time; she need only look around.*

In those decades, however, there was no point of comparison, no possibility of nostalgia. There was only the self-legitimating facticity of Boredom, with no apparent way out. For me, however, there was the Call of the Clover Blossom. Propelled by the idea that *I Am* I made exploratory journeys by way of warming up for my Outercourse, which is, of course, the Direction my life has taken.

But I must Spiral back a bit, because before the Time of that existential encounter, there was "elementary school".

Let me assure the reader that I have always, that is, spasmodically, made abortive efforts to conform. For example, in the first grade at Saint John the Evangelist School

---

* There is a difference, however. In the course of the last two decades of this millennium it has been and continues to be possible to Re-member the early Moments of this Wave of the women's movement in the sixties and seventies — either directly or through the writings and stories of Other women who were there. It is also possible to Re-Call Feminists of earlier Times.

in Schenectady, when I perceived that many of my classmates had dirty, secondhand readers, I spat and slobbered over the pages of my own brand-new one to make it appear used. When my teacher, Sister Mary Edmund, asked for an explanation, I was speechless. I have no idea whether she understood my motivation for the slobbering, but I do think that I myself had some idea of attempting to "fit in".

One of my classmates in the first grade, whose name was Rosemary, was hit and killed by a trolley car when she was crossing the street in front of her house. There was some confusing story about her not looking both ways and not hearing the sound of the oncoming trolley because the one she just stepped off had started to move. The whole class had to go with Sister Mary Edmund to see Rosemary "laid out". She was wearing a white dress. I did not like being there. The experience did not fit in with anything. It was like a white blob that hung there. It was impossible to understand and was worse than a nightmare.

My second grade teacher was Sister Mary Clare of the Passion, who droned a lot — too much, I thought — about "God's poor". I did not understand why the poor were God's. I had her again in the fifth grade, and I remember a feeling of deep shock when she made fun of a boy in our class who was really poor and whose name was Abram Spoor. She assaulted him with a jingle which went something like "Abram Spoor . . . and he *is* poor".

Upon reflection, I have come to the conclusion that this shocking behavior was inspired not by malice but by a passion for jingles, puns, and wordplay in general. I remember that it was Sister Mary Clare of the Passion who more than once wrote on the tops of papers I handed in to her the title of the (then) popular hymn "Daily, Daily, Sing to Mary". These words would be crossed off with a very light scribbly line — as if to indicate that she had written them there by mistake. I understood that this was meant as a game or a joke, but I did not see anything very funny about it at the time.[1]

Upon further reflection, I Now realize that this woman had a strong creative streak. One day when I was in the fifth grade she told us all to bring in some toy that we had become sick of. The idea was that we would exchange our old toys and everyone would get something new. I brought in a tin monkey with a drum who obligingly banged this instrument when you turned the key. I was ready to discard this because it seemed much too childish for a person in the fifth grade. I remember that Abram Spoor's face lit up with sheer joy when he saw my mechanical monkey and said, "I'd like that !"

No doubt this woman had an interesting time watching all of our transactions and reactions. Personally I was delighted with my own acquisition of two oddly shaped books about "Our Gang". But the truly memorable experience of the day was the look on Abram's face and the sound of his voice when he got my monkey. Obviously he had never owned such a wondrous toy in his whole life. I am struck by the accuracy of Sister's insensitive and unfortunate

---

1. I would see it as ineffably funny years later. For further details on "Daily (Daly), Daily, Sing to Mary", see Chapter Five of *Outercourse: The Bedazzling Voyage*.

pun.[1] Now wonder if her puns popped out uncontrollably without consideration of the consequences. Perhaps her weird and lugubrious name — which in all probability she did not freely choose — inspired her to be rather reckless and satirical with words.[2]

Sister Mary Arthur, who was my teacher in the third and sixth grades, was a handsome young woman with shaggy black eyebrows who stormed up and down the aisles hitting the boys — only the boys — with her ruler. She had my unflagging loyalty and admiration.

These Sisters all belonged to a congregation called "Sisters of the Holy Names". Their coifs had stiff white material extending out along the side of their faces. This headgear must have seriously affected their peripheral vision. So they had to swivel their heads quite a lot, but I didn't think of this phenomenon as too unusual, since that's how it was at Saint John the Evangelist School and I didn't know any other nuns who could serve as a point of comparison.

I missed quite a few days of school during those first six years of my formal education. Even a slight cold was an excuse for staying home in bed and reading my favorite books, such as *The Call of the Wild*, the "Raggedy Ann" stories, and the "Children of All Lands" stories by Madeline Frank Brandeis. It just seemed right to me that I could break the routine and sail off into my own private world sometimes. The special ambrosia served to me by my

---

2. The Sisters usually could not choose their names in those days. Many were "stuck" with men's names, which must have felt alienating and bizarre to the recipients. Of course, some feminine names were also weird and could have been devastating to woman's self-image.

mother during these outer space voyages was chilled "Junket", which came in three exquisite flavors: chocolate, vanilla, and strawberry. Maybe it also came in raspberry.

The price extorted by my teachers for these blissful free days was lowering of my grade average, which reduced me to being ranked second highest in the class at the end of some weeks. The way they managed to do this was by averaging in "zeros" for tests missed on my excursion days. I thought that this was very unfair, especially because my rival, Sarah Behan, who never missed a day of school, then got to be first, even though her grades were lower. But those Times of flying free, which gave me an enduring Taste for escaping imposed routines, were worth it. I think that my mother, co-conspirator that she was, knew this.

The World of Glowing Books and The Call of the Wild

Well, the years of elementary school skipped along in this fashion. My passion for the intellectual life burst forth at puberty, in the seventh grade to be precise. Since Saint John the Evangelist School ended with the sixth grade, I had moved on to Saint Joseph's Academy. This Catholic school was attached to a working-class German parish and provided education for pupils from the first grade through high school. It was staffed by the Sisters of Saint Joseph of Carondelet. Saint Joseph's Academy no longer even exists. But for me that poor little school was the scene of Metamorphic Moments that can be Re-Called and Re-membered. For many of their hundreds of pupils, some of the Sisters who taught there, who were often unappreciated, created rich Memories of the Future. They formed/transformed our Future, which, of course, is Now.

I was an extremely willing scholar. Few understood my true motivation when I followed the high school students around worshipfully, ogling their armloads of textbooks, especially tomes of chemistry, math, and physics. What was really going on was that I was drooling with admiration and envy because they had access to these learned, fascinating books. It never crossed my mind that their attitudes toward these tomes ranged from indifference to loathing. In my own indomitable innocence I saw these as portals to paradise, as magical and infinitely enticing.

Even though, years later, I found out the less than magical qualities of many of those books, this Dis-covery was not an experience of disillusionment. My preoccupation with the high schoolers' tomes of wisdom had been grounded in a Background intuition/Realization of the Radiant Realm of Books, which was not an illusion. Therefore, there was nothing at all to be dis-illusioned about. Later on I did find out about the foreground level of most books, but that took nothing away from my knowledge of the Thisworldly/Otherworldly Reality of Books.[3]

My parents had always given me many beautiful books as presents, especially on holidays. So the World of Glowing

---

3. Seeing through the fraudlence of elementary caricatures need not dilute one's appreciation of the wonderous reality that is simulated. Discovering the unreality of donald duck and disney world need not diminish but can enhance by way of contrast one's appreciation of Real Ducks and the Real World. The same principle of distinction between Background Otherness and foreground fraudulence applies also to books.

Books somehow entered the realm of my imagination very early and became a central focus of the Quest to be a philosopher. More than once in high school I had dreams of wondrous worlds — of being in rooms filled with colorful glowing books. I would wake up in a state of great ecstasy and knowing that this was *my* World, where I belonged.

During that early adolescent time I also Dis-covered the "celestial gleam" of nature. Since my father was a traveling salesman who sold icecream freezers, I sometimes went with him on drives into the country when he visited his customers' icecream stand. My awakening to the transcendental glowing light over meadows and trees happened on some of these trips.[4] Other Moments of contact with Nature involved knowing the Call of the Wild from the mountains and purple skies and the sweet fresh smell of snow.

These invitations from Nature to my adolescent spirit were somehow intimately connected with the Call of the World of Glowing Books. My life was suffused with the desire for a kind of Great Adventure that would involve touching and exploring these strange worlds that had allowed me to glimpse their wonders and Lust for more.

Taboo-Breaking: "The Convent" as Flyswatter

I was reasonably well equipped to follow this seemingly improbable, not fully articulated, yet crystal clear Call. For one thing I was endowed with insufferable stubbornness —

---

4. I hope it is clear that by *transcendental* I do not mean "beyond" natural knowledge and experience. I use this word to Name a Supremely Natural Knowledge and Experience which should be ordinary but which, in a dulled-out society, is, unfortunately, extraordinary.

a quality which never failed me. I also had the gift of being at least fifty per cent oblivious of society's expectations of me as a "normal" young woman and one hundred per cent resistant to whatever expectations I did not manage to avoid noticing. For example, I never had the slightest desire to get married and have children. Even in elementary school and in the absence of any Feminist movement I had felt that it would be intolerable to give up my own name and become "Mrs" something or other. It would obviously be a violation of mySelf. Besides, I have always really *liked* my name. I wouldn't sell it for anything. A third asset was a rock bottom self-confidence and Sense of Direction which, even in the bleakest periods, have never entirely deserted me.

Looking back, I recognize that all these assets were gifts from my extraordinary mother. For one thing, she had always made it clear to me that she had desired only one child, and that one a daughter. I was exactly what she wanted, and all she wanted. How she managed to arrange this I was never told. At any rate my father seemed to have no serious objection. For another thing, I canot recall that she ever once — even once — tried to promote the idea that I should marry and have a family, although she often said that she was very happily married, and indeed this seemed to be the case. She was hardly one to promote the convent either. I was the one who tossed around that threat, chiefly as a weapon against well-meaning relatives and "friends of the family" who intoned that "some day the right man would come along". I never followed through on my threat to joining the convent, but it worked well enough as a defense against society at large.[5]

This is not to say that I never seriously considered entering the convent. I was not exactly insincere in proclaiming this as a goal. It just seemed indifinitely postponable. Perhaps if the Sisters had had the possibility of becoming great scholars, as I supposed monks did, I would have been more seriously tempted. However, I saw something of the constraints imposed upon their lives. They were deprived of the leisure to study and travel and think creatively to their fullest capacity. Even those who taught in college were confined to somewhat narrow perspectives. The Sisters were in fact assigned to be the drudges of the church.* So I couldn't exactly indentify with the convent as a goal and just kept moving on in my own way. Later on I read an article in which someone referred to old maidhood as a sort of "budget religious vocation" which was accorded some modicum of respect in the church, especially during the forties and fifties, and especially if the old maid in question was dedicated to her work. I am sure that message had entered my brain and seemed a pretty good deal to me. I know that some women tried to escape "love and marriage" by joining the convent — a strategy that would have worked better in the Middle Ages when many monasteries were Wild places. But I did not see it as a real Way Out. For me, to be an Old Maid/Spinster was

---

5. Nor did any of the Sisters urge me to "enter". I suppose that they were perceptive enough to see that I would not last long in that austere environment. Besides, it was clear in high school that I was hell-bent on going directly to college, and in college it was obvious that I was dead set on graduate school.

* This was perfectly in keeping with the drudge role to which all women were/are assigned by the church and by patriarchal society in general.

the way to be free. Yet I could not fully articulate that idea, even to myself, because even that idea was Taboo. So I just logically acted on it, while waving the banner of "the convent" like a flyswatter when necessary.

Anna and Frank

One point that was very clear in my mother's approach was that I should have everything she did not have when she was growing up. As a very young child she, Anna, had been taken by her grandmother to be brought up among her numerous aunts and uncles because her mother was too poor to take care of all her children. Although she adored her grandmother, my mother's life as a child was hard. She had a lot of housework to do, including the irksome task of cleaning kerosene lamps. Going to school meant trudging on cold and windy winter days across the bridge connecting South Glens Falls, New York, with the town of Glens Falls. Yet she passionately loved learning, and the tragedy of her life was being "yanked out of school" when still a sophomore in high school to go to work as a telephone operator in Schenectady, a city about forty miles away.†

Anna worked for the telephone company for sixteen exhausting years. She then met and married my father and they bought a house in Schenectady. After a rather long delay I was born. I arrived just in time for The Great Depression. She often said to me that her home became "like heaven when you came".

---

† I think it was because of the oppression she endured as a child that my mother repeatedly warned me not to allow myself to be trapped by "family", that is relatives who would try to drag you down.

My mother was thirty-eight when I arrived on the scene. Since she was brought up by her grandmother, Johanna Falvey, who came over from Ireland because of the potato famine, her memories extended far back over time, and she directly and subliminally transmitted a great deal of the old Irish lore to me. Although my great-grandmother had died before I arrived, she was a towering Presence in my childhood — she who had come over on the boat when she was a fourteen-year-old girl, worked as a maid, married, and had twelve children. She could neither read nor write, and she yet knew much of Dickens and the *Lives of the Saints* by heart because her husband, Dan Buckley, read these books to her over and over. She also knew secrets about nature and the weather, and had a gift of healing, and helped take care of other Irish immigrants and their families in her neighborhood in South Glens Falls when they were sick.

On my father's side, the line to Ireland was just as direct, and the female Presence just as strong. Both of his parents had come over from the Emerald Isle. His father had died shortly after he, Frank, the youngest child, was born. His mother was a strong and shrewd woman who ran a business and supported her five children. It couldn't be helped that my father had to leave school after the eighth grade and go to work. Yet he always had a way with words, and put this to some use, for example, by writing slogans for advertising and sometimes winning prizes for these creative endeavors. I remember that one of these slogans was "Eventually, why not now?"

When I was very small I saw copies of a book my father had written and published. It was about how to sell icecream equipment and there were photographs in it. Copies of the book (which were stored in a big carton) have long since disappeared.[6] I suppose the sight of those books had something to do with the idea I formed in early childhood that some day I would write a book.

From both parents I heard the rhetorical question, "Aren't we Lucky to be Irish?" When I had to fill out forms inquiring about my "nationality", I always wrote "Irish". It did not occur to me that I should write "American". Moreover, since I knew it was Lucky to be Irish I thought I must personally be Lucky. No matter how overwhelming the forces were that tried to disabuse me of this impression, it did, in fact, persist. Moreover, I believe that it worked as a self-fulfilling prophecy.[7]

---

6. My father's book has not entirely disappeared. In the course of writing *Outercourse* I wrote to the Library of Congress, giving them my father's name (Frank X. Daly), approximate date and place of publication (Schenectady, New York), and approximate title> They did a search and found my father's book: *What every Ice Cream Dealer Should Know*. After some delay I obtained a photocopy of the work. I was proud and excited to read it and discover that it was/is a beautifully written practical treatise on ice cream making, including a brief history of ice cream, many formulas, recipes, etc. The fact that my father, who had only and eighth grade education, produced this work is awesome. Even as I am writing this note it Fires/Inspires me to continue my Fiercely Focussed work on *Outercourse*, regardless of any obstacles the demonic forces of distraction try to throw in my way.

7. Rereading this [piece] Now and reflecting further upon the phenomenom of being Lucky, I Re-member my mother saying: "Aren't we Lucky to live in New York State!" She believed that New York State "has everything". So it seems that this conviction of Luckiness was quite flexible and expandable.

Odd Things

One thing that had always — since I had learned to spell —
made me feel peculiar was the address of our house. It was
"6 Grosvenor Square". I had to spell it for people who did
not live on our street and explain that the "s" in "Grosvenor"
was silent. Either they pronounced it "Gross-venor" or else
they pronounced it right and spelled it wrong. Combined
with "Square" and "Schenectady" this was a funny address,
especially to anyone who was not from Schenectady. So I
had to recite: "'Grosvenor' is spelled G-r-o-s-v-e-n-o-r. Yes,
it is 'Square' and not 'Street'." If they were not from
Schenectady my recital went on: "'Schenectady' is spelled S-
c-h-e-n-e-c-t-a-d-y. It is an Indian name."

Our street was only one block long and one day some
officials changed the numbers on the houses and ours
became something like "1306 Grosvenor Square". This
made it even queerer. Even "they" must have come to recognize this because they changed the numbers back again.

This alone may not seem very strange but there were
other things. For example, I did not have a real middle
name. My mother's explanation for this was that she didn't
want to saddle me with too many names. I would choose
my confirmation name and that would be enough. Four
names would be too many. So when I was confirmed at the
age of nine I picked the confirmation name "Frances", after
my father. My mother's middle name was "Catherine" and
that had been another possible choice. She told me it didn't
matter which one I chose but when I decided on "Frances"
I could see in her face she was disappointed. But then she

said that was wonderful and I stuck with my decision. That was partly because we reasoned that I was named "Mary" after my mother's sister and so adding "Frances" balanced it out to represent both sides of the family. So it turned out to be "fair".[8]

Anyway, when I wrote "Mary Frances Daly" it seemed phony, because I knew that it was only a confirmation name. Whenever anyone asked my middle name I felt peculiar saying "Frances" because it wasn't real, really. Combined with my funny address, it meant more and more explanations. Much later on, when I signed my name "Mary F Daly" for banks and social security and junk like that it still felt phony and it seemed that the "F" belonged only to the fake documents of that phony world. No one who *knew* me called me "Mary Frances", except for one teacher who didn't know me at all. Maybe "F" stood for "fake", "false", "funny", or "fraud", or — come to think of it — "foreground".

Another odd thing was my father's name. It was Frank X. Daly. He said he was named after Saint Francis Xavier. This in itself was not so unusual. However, he pronounced it "X-avier". It was many years before I learned that most people said "Zavier". There were other funny things about the way my father talked sometimes. For example, he pronounced "film" like "fillum". Moreover, he wore his hat perched in an

---

8. Of course, it was "fair" only if you forgot about the surname "Daly". Taking that major factor into account, "Mary Catherine" would have been much more "fair" — if *any* attempt at Naming females in patriarchal-patrilineal society could even remotely approach fairness (Conversation with Geraldine Moane, Newton Centre, Massachusetts, July 1989).

odd way on his head. Much later on, when traveling in County Clare, Ireland, I realized the reason for some of these peculiarities. Even though my father was born in America his parents were from over there, which would explain a great deal about him. So when I discovered that people in Ireland actually say "fillum" and that the older men in Clare wear their hats perched on their heads it all began to fit together. Also, I noted that the people in that area like music and have a way with words and are very shy. So I came to understand in a different light my father's attachment to his piano, his way with words, and his embarrassed shyness.

Such odd things really are too numerous to mention. But together they signalled my growing Sense of Direction as Subliminal Sea Sailor, Boundary Dweller, and Outlandish Outsider.

Sue Reidy

Sue Reidy was born in Invercargill, New Zealand, and attended a Catholic girls' school. She studied Visual Communications at Wellington Polytechnic School of Design, and has worked in the communications field full-time since graduating. She currently runs her own design practice. She has gained recognition as a graphic designer, illustrator, writer and lecturer. In 1985 Sue Reidy won the BNZ Katherine Mansfield Short Story Award and in 1988 her short-story collection *Modettes* was published by Penguin Books. In 1995 she was runner-up in the *Sunday Star Times* Short Story Award. Her novel *The Visitation* is being published under the Black Swan imprint by Transworld Publishers, UK, Australia, and NZ, in late 1996. Sue lives with her partner (a publisher) in Ponsonby, Auckland, New Zealand.

Being Irish

"Rubbish," pronounced my partner crisply. "You're no more Irish than I am English."

Outrage!

"Feeling Irish isn't enough," he added. "The whole notion is sentimental and misguided. You're not Irish. What you are is a fourth generation Pakeha New Zealander of Irish extraction."

I continued to feel Irish and indeed to staunchly defend my right to do so. I was surprised by the intensity of my response. Why did I feel so passionate about claiming the Irish identity as my own? Was my partner right? Did it make more sense to focus on my New Zealand identity rather than hankering after a fragile thread of connection with Europe? Forced to defend my Irishness to my cynical partner, I began closely to examine why it was I should believe that being Irish was an intrinsic part of the way I viewed myself. When I began to explore my genealogy I was full of emotional, fuzzy ideas about my Irish roots. I had to confront the reality that I had only the vaguest idea of where my wider family fitted in to the overall scheme of things. I thought my background was working-class Irish, but was it? If it was, what did it mean and did it matter?

I remembered St Patrick's Day celebrations in the church hall. Big cauldrons of beer dyed green. Dancing the Gay Gordons, smelling green beery breath as I was swung in the air. I remembered Irish priests in primary school telling us horror stories about the potato famine. It impressed us deeply. I looked at the group of women friends and aquaintances I had collected around me over the past twenty years and counted the number who like me had Irish Catholic origins. You could recognise them in a group. They would be cracking jokes and telling stories. I could always tell. Maybe it's coming from a large family, it makes you a certain sort of person. Maybe it's simply being brought up Catholic, it gives you something to rebel against.

I began to realise that I have always seen myself as Irish, despite being only a fourth generation descendant on both sides of the family. On my mother's side came Prods from Londonderry in the north. On my father's side, Micks from County Kerry in the south. My father says that as a young man he was very conscious of his Irish background and culture. My mother was less aware of it. The legacy of religious bigotry made it unlikely that the Reidy and Rewcastle clans would view each other with anything other than deep suspicion and antipathy. Despite this, my parents met at the office and fell in love. They married, and the expectation was that my mother would convert to Catholicism, which she did. They produced six children and brought them up Catholic. As far as I know, not one of them is currently a practising Catholic.

My paternal great-grandfather Michael Reidy was born in 1870 in County Kerry. In 1882 he immigrated to New Zealand at the age of twelve from Cahirciven, a little village on the south-west coast in the district of Tralee, on a ship called *The Canterbury*, in the company of an aunt. He landed in Dunedin. His parents had immigrated to New Zealand six years earlier from Castleisland, County Kerry, mysteriously leaving their six-year-old son behind in Ireland. Mary Ellen Leonard, the woman my great-grandfather married was born in New Zealand, but both her parents had emigrated from Galway. Most of these family migrants settled in the southern regions of New Zealand. According to one relative there was a stronger brew of Catholicism in Southland.

My maternal Irish great-grandmother Charlotte McIntyre was born in 1867. I have not been able to discover why she came to New Zealand. In fact, in writing this piece I have been struck by how little information seems to have survived. I feel I have only really begun searching. Where are the journals and records? Did my parent's generation ask questions of their elders? Were they given accurate answers?

My father has warm memories of his Irish grandfather, who brewed his own beer in forty-five-gallon hog's head barrels, owned a greyhound, drove a horse and gig, and kept a large aviary of two hundred birds, in addition to a collection of pheasants, and three pet magpies who followed him everywhere like small children. As my great-grandfather lay dying, these magpies kept vigil on the windowsill of his bedroom. When he died they flew away and were never seen again.

At least this is the way my father tells the story, carefully shaping the neat symmetry of the ending. Maybe the magpies flew back once or twice, just to check the place out, I wonder. As I speculate, I picture my father's look of reproach for spoiling a good story.

We were told our ancestors were "Bog Irish". This racial stereotype has been a term of abuse as much as an inaccuracy, a vehicle for prejudice in the 1940s and 1950s. We believed these ancestors to be poor and not very well educated. Why else would they have left their countries if not to escape poverty? We romanticised about them because we also knew we came from a family of storytellers, people of wit and humour.

Various family members were, and still are referred to as "fey" — a loose term as they explain it, as it seems to include having the gift of healing, second sight, even telepathy. A great aunt was "a bit that way". Some living family members still take a particular pride in viewing themselves as either healers or visionaries. Others are described as "hard case", volatile, hot-tempered.

My grandparents' generation were staunch about their religion, fearful of "mixed marriages", deeply conservative, respectful of priests and nuns. In contrast, my generation are more likely to use words like: superstitious, ignorant, blind, folksy, or naive, to refer to Southland's brand of provincial Irish Catholicism.

And then there were the Black Irish — dark-skinned Irish, who somewhere along the line had mated with survivors from a Spanish ship, or so the family story goes. However, in our personal family mythology the Black Irish were also labelled because of their inflammable personalities. They drank hard. Fought hard. Were not to be trusted. But of course none of us were ever like that, although as children we longed to be. The discovery of these influences and traits fed my imagination. The message was clear. To be Irish was to be special.

As a young man my father belonged to an Irish repertory society in Invercargill. They performed plays by Irish playwrights and sang Irish songs. His father as a young man won numerous cups as a champion traditional Irish dancer, excelling in jigs, reels and flings. My father's parents attended concerts by visiting overseas Irish singers. My father says that in his youth he was very aware not only of the visibility of Irish immigrants in his community but also of the antagonism between Catholics and Protestants. He recalls seeing job advertisements that ended with the warning: Catholics need not apply. One of his cousins verifies that this anti-Catholic atmosphere flourished in the 1940s and 1950s in Southland. He recalls taunts on the street on the way to and from school.

Many of the wider family have begun the trek back to Ireland to explore roots and make connections. One of the joys has been re-establishing contact with long lost relatives in Castleisland. An aunt visited. Two second cousins made pilgrimages, one began a family tree. Everyone was made very welcome. My sister brought back photos. The "rellies" speak Gaelic. They live simply and at the time my sister visited (fifteen years ago) had no electricity, running water, toilet, or oven. I have stared at the photographs of the women with their unflattering scarves tied tightly under their chins and searched for likenesses: the repeat of a chin line, the angle of a nose, the shape of an eyebrow. Nothing.

One relative, who has since died, was a poet. Apparently he liked to send complimentary copies of his poetry books to the Pope, the Queen, Mrs Thatcher and Princess Grace. My sister says he received a kind note in response from Princess Grace.

There are a lot of Michaels in the line of Reidys. And there are several sons who ought to have been named Michael and weren't but who were generally referred to by everyone as Mick anyway, so they might as well have been. There are also numerous Maurices scattered through the family and often they have been referred to as Mick as well. There were a great many saint names. We were all named after saints, force fed through the Catholic education system. I emerged at the other end critical of provincial Irish Catholicism, Irish priests, Irish nuns, Irish prejudice and Irish ignorance.

Being Irish was also, for me, connected with being brought up Catholic. The two identities were inextricably intertwined, to such a degree that for many years my rejection of Catholicism resulted in a corresponding shift away from an identification with Irish forebears.

There have been no nuns and no priests in my generation, although the previous one produced both a nun and a priest and one who got as far as the seminary for a while. Few in my generation are still practising Catholics.

Has being exposed in my youth to a vigorous family oral storytelling tradition influenced my desire to become a writer? My father is a raconteur of no mean standard. His memories of incidents and people from almost sixty years ago are still fresh and potent. His siblings also place great store on being able to spin a good yarn. Likewise, my father's parents, uncles and an aunt were all accomplished storytellers in the oral tradition. They seemed larger than life to me — more Irish than the Irish. When I attempt to analyse or encapsulate the kind of stories they used to relate, I realise the skill that was evident in their ability to transform the most ordinary everyday occurrences into the stuff of humour and wit. They attached significance to the most banal of events in a way that now seems both touching and overblown in the light of the more hectic lives we lead in the nineties. The same stories would be recycled until we knew them almost by heart. Now I know that small details in the stories changed subtly to suit the different audiences. Why didn't I record them? Write stuff down? And am I a writer because of all this?

Now the grandparents and great uncles and aunts are dead. In today's terms nothing much ever happened to them. They didn't go anywhere or achieve anything of note, but they made me laugh and cry. Thanks are due them. They contributed to the person and the writer I am now. I believed completely in their stories. I always wanted to know what happened next.

I still do.

Belief

In his early retirement my father celebrated his freedom from management tyranny by refusing to answer the phone. News and queries were filtered through my mother until recently when they bought a cordless on special. Not that they buy anything without it being on special.

Now for the first time in his life my father has developed the habit of calling me.

"I'm fine," I say. "Don't worry about me."

He loves to play games with words. We convey our affection in code.

"Zebu," he grunts.

Ah, animals. Some sort of ox. The rules are that we can't move off zed or out of category until one of us is stumped.

"Zho," I call triumphantly.

"Hmmm." I picture him scratching his lantern jaw, thin lips cracking into a pleased smile. "Wait. Don't tell me. Let me guess. Cattle. A breed of cattle from the Himalayas."

My father the genius.

• • •

My mother smuggles the cordless with her into the loo. She calls each one of her children from her perch. Sometimes we hear rustling. If we bore her she commences reading one of the back issues of the Weekly stacked against the wall. Sometimes we hear a trumpeting sound as she blows her nose on the toilet paper.

She guards the cordless.

My father has gained custody of the remote.

They watch the TV on opposite couches, both stretched out full-length. A screen, obscenely large, flickers from the end of the rimu coffee table. Jacqueline the cat has made herself at home on Dad's stomach.

He phones me most evenings. The sound of Jacqueline protesting alerts me even before he announces himself.

"Zabra, zarf, zax," he says, coughs and waits for me. Then — "Dammed cat! Mother, tomorrow we clip those claws."

He comes back on line.

"Where were we?"

"Dad, what is it exactly that you want?"

"Nothing, just a rain check, chicken. Toodle pips."

• • •

How do you capture a life? The view is so vast from where I stand. The panorama always widening, the weather shifting. I see the back of my father's neck crisscrossed with lines, the embrace of time. And the memory of that neck bent over a dictionary is too much for me.

I observe Dad swooning over Elgar. Behind him Mum massages the irises. The way you'd stroke a cat around the neck. She believes it encourages the stubborn buds to flower.

Dad's crazy about the cello. Mum prefers violins. She longs to be transported away to a world where parents don't murder their kids and there aren't any serial rapists. A world that is never going to exist no matter how much she wishes for it. Her cracked fingers, reddened from years of laundry and dishes, pause momentarily before she finishes feeling up the yellow irises in her blue vase. The problems of the world weigh heavily on her shoulders.

Dad says cellos sob and ache and that Du Pré could rip the heart out of a stone.

"But Dad, stones don't have hearts."

He turns and regards me, grey eyes flecked with brown, skin like corrugated card.

"Don't they?" he asks solemnly.

He turns up the volume. "Only Du Pré could make that sound."

He opens his wallet and pulls out a small laminated photo of his beloved Jacqueline. Her head is thrown back. She's grinning like a maniac and slashing her cello to ribbons.

He's never stopped giving God a hard time for taking Jacqueline so soon. "Why Du Pré?" he asks. "Why not a knife-wielding rapist, a talentless nobody, or a Muslim extremist?" (The only type of Muslim, if you believe my father).

He says if he listened to Du Pré every day he would probably go mad.

So he rations her. Twice a week. And sometimes he makes Mum listen to Du Pré playing Elgar late at night with the lights off and the volume up as high as they can stand it.

Afterwards Mum makes Horlicks and they turn on every light in the house until they can cope with the idea of going to bed.

"Do you think we're mad?" Dad asks Mum frequently.

"Does it matter? You're not alone."

"Neither of you is mad," I say. "Just morbidly sensitive."

"I remember everything," says Dad.

"You remember more than is good for you."

"Would you say I'm a 'malist'?" Shrewd eyes take their measure of me. Head to one side like an inquisitive bird.

"I don't think you believe the world is evil." But it has taken him all his life to come to terms with the knowledge that he can control very little of what happens in it. Religion has not brought either of them the peace they seek. My mother carries a map of trouble spots inside her head, each spot marked by a bleeding stump.

I am a nurse. How can I staunch wounds that are invisible? I cannot prevent whimpers in the dark. I do my best, but it's not possible to transform the world into a place my parents can bear to live in.

Dad tells me Mum sometimes cries in her sleep. When pressed he admits that when she wakes up trembling in the aftermath of suffering it is to discover she is gripping his hand for reassurance.

I envy them. When I was small I climbed in between them. They each held a hand so we were linked like paper dolls under a suffocating weight of blankets.

"Tell me your dreams," I used to ask each of them in turn.

My mother would wriggle to make herself more comfortable, squeezing my hand to add emphasis to her words.

"I dreamed I was swimming in a tank," said my mother once, "and all around me were the most handsome men who had dived in to join me."

"To rescue you?" I asked.

"Course not. I was always too quick for them."

"Anyone I know?" asked my father.

"No," said my mother with conviction. "All strangers, every one of 'em."

My father's dreams generally involved a chase. Nazis or Japanese were pursuing him across the countryside and, according to my mother, he awoke thrashing about like a beached whale, sweating and puffing, muttering curses.

And what did I dream back then? I can't remember my dreams, only the sensation of lying there perfectly happy, utterly secure.

Nothing bad had ever happened to me. I didn't believe anything in my ordered sheltered life would ever change. I was a girl who always obeyed her parents.

• • •

Now they are retired and their days are consumed by the execution of small pleasurable tasks for which there never seems to be any compelling reason to hurry. Oh, and they also play games every day. They're extremely competitive.

Dad never plays scrabble or cards without his green plastic visor on. They drink coffee throughout the tense games. They sit up at the table in their matching folding canvas chairs on the deck surrounded by natives and creepers, an egg timer planted between them. Before they got the timer their games were punctuated by my father nagging at my mother to hurry up and make up her mind. I know why my mother takes her time. She has an extensive vocab but she's not good at adding up in her head. My father keeps the scores on a Croxley airmail pad. Five games to a page in Dad's neat columns. M and D. They still call each other Mum and Dad even though the last of us left home thirteen years ago.

"Why can't you call Mum by her proper name?"

"And what's that?" Eyebrows bristling. "I forget."

I punch him playfully on the arm. He punches me right back. Less playfully. My mother laughs and goes into the kitchen to make another plunger of coffee.

I glance over at their tiles on the board. "Quey? There's no such word."

"Your mother's latest. Something to do with cows."

"Have you checked?" I see the Cassells is on the table. They're always challenging each other.

"Jib, jab, jot, job, jay," begins my father with a twinkle in his eye.

"Jar, joy, jibe, jape," I contribute. We continue on to K and L before my mother returns.

We dunk the gingernuts companionably.

"What's the score for the weekend?" They keep a tally on the Columban calendar above the phone in the hall.

"Six games to four."

"Who to?"

My father jabs a fat finger at my mother.

Scrabble gets them out of bed in the mornings. The radio is usually on and they listen avidly to the Kim Hill show as they compose the words. They argue back and give cheek. Once my father shook the radio until the batteries rolled out onto the table, and sometimes, if something gets her goat, my mother reaches forward and with an abrupt gesture switches it off. Politics always gets them fired up.

"You tell me what's not politics," says my father and he adds "xi" to the board.

"Xi?"

"Fourteenth letter of the Greek alphabet. It's won me a couple of games."

"We're much worse off under National. Talk about user pays gone mad," complains my mother. Pensions frozen, every cent is calculated. They're members of Grey Power. They had been Labourites forever, until Rogernomics. Now they've switched to the Alliance.

We don't disagree on the fundamentals. With hospitals closing left right and centre and things being so tough for pensioners. Outside there are riots and mayhem, can they even feel safe at home? A masked intruder could arrive at any moment to tear their lives apart. It's why they bought a dog.

"The world has gone barmy," complains my father bitterly. "And what are the police doing about it? That's what I'd like to know."

There's no reassuring them. They worry about me too.

"Get a dog, why don't you?"

I live on my own. A dog is better than nothing, they think. They wish I would move back home again. Either that, or meet a man.

"You'll know when the right fellow comes along," reassures my mother, in whom, against all odds, hope continues to flower.

• • •

Afternoons they garden or play chess. In the evenings they walk the dog after dinner and then read in bed propped up on floral patterned pillows.

Tuesdays, Marg (Sister Margaret Mary to those who don't know her) turns up to play three-handed. They keep a separate tally for her games. It's neck and neck. She's in a local flat of four nuns and her job is to get around the retired folks in the area. She wears civvies most days and you'd never know except for the tiny cross, more like a brooch really, pinned above her left breast.

"It's just luck," I insist whenever I join in and lose.

"Nonsense," says Mum. "Skill is what it takes. That and clever tactics."

They've always been good with words. We were the only kids in the neighbourhood who didn't own a TV, but we knew all the classics. Not like my brothers' kids who are more interested in the Michaels — Jackson and Jordan — than in David Copperfield or Huckleberry Finn. Nothing goes on in their houses except TV watching or computer games. No hobbies, no reading. The parents don't talk, just shout orders. My nieces and nephews know all the ads off by heart. Those kids. They never stop wanting stuff either. Mountain bikes, Walkmans, the latest confectionery, bags, games, clothes.

And their grandparents keep asking themselves: "What happened?"

• • •

"Is there anything we can do for you?" asks my mother when I get up to leave.

"No thanks." It should be the other way around. What could I be doing for them to make their lives easier? Despite my protestations I don't leave empty-handed. My arms are bulging with jam, chutneys, and a bag of lemons and apples from their garden. And something my mother has knitted. Something I will never wear.

And what does she say to me as I climb into my battered Vee Dub.

"Don't forget to follow your dreams," she reminds me.

I blink. Turn my head. "I won't forget."

"Toodle pips then."

"Bye Mum."

• • •

I try to visit them once a fortnight. It's not a chore. They're always pleased to see me.

"Hello Mum, Dad."

"Sophist," replies my father by way of greeting.

I take a stab. "Someone who uses clever words for their own sake."

"You'll do. Come in."

Mum's made up a big jug of Spirulina — they're always on some kind of health kick. Coffee is their only vice as far as I can tell. They're trying to cut down. Decaf's the thing. They have also in the past sworn by apple cider vinegar, vitamin C every day, and brewer's yeast. When we were kids it was malt extract and cod liver oil. Why is it that anything that's good for you tastes so bad?

Mum is wearing her scrabble uniform — black track

pants and an out-of-shape home-knitted jersey. It was the last black garment she knitted before her eyesight deteriorated. Now she wears specs of pebble glass, and behind them her eyes swim, huge and lost and unfamiliar.

"Fancy a quick game?" she wants to know as soon as I've stepped in the door.

"And get slaughtered? No thanks."

But Dad's not one to take no for an answer. He's already pulled out the board and distributed the tiles.

Dad launches off with "feague".

I follow up with "favus".

"You're improving, girl," says my father, smiling approval.

•••

Their games out on the deck are often punctuated by the thump, thump of the stereo belonging to Brian and Andrew, the gay couple next door.

One night Dad heard the neighbours playing Elgar. He listened carefully to discover if it was the Du Pré or the Fournier.

"How can you tell?" I asked.

"Easy. The Fournier is so much more controlled. It lacks the passion and guts of Du Pré."

So what does Dad do? He invites them over to hear the difference. The neighbours turn up in their linen shirts and pressed jeans and make all the right murmurs of approval.

Brian plays with his ear. Mum is quick to give credit where it's due.

"That's a lovely earring, you have, Brian. Did you lose the other one? Isn't it the way with earrings?"

It turns out they're mad about Pavarotti and Careras as well. In fact, they adore opera.

Dad pours the neighbours a measure of his special cognac (I buy it for them on my Sydney trips).

"Cheers!"

"Down the hatch."

"Salud," says Andrew.

• • •

After they've gone my father says to my mother, "You know it's a shame, isn't it? I could get to like them."

"We'll pray for them," decides my mother. And I know she means it.

I've given up trying to change them. Now I accept them as they are. They're so comfortable in their prejudices, quick to anger, quicker to forgive. Who am I to judge?

They're always praying for those they consider to be less fortunate than themselves. They believe that virtue is its own reward and justice must triumph in the end.

• • •

My family expect me to be good. To be always available.

As I drift off to sleep happy in the knowledge that I am a dutiful daughter, I like to picture my parents asleep, lying buttock to groin like spoons, of one heart, one mind. No longer snoring — they've had the new laser treatment. They are safe and secure, their house encircled by natives and flowering creepers, shielded from the sound of their neighbour's ecstatic cries by curled ponga fronds and flapping cabbage tree leaves. Above them prayers coil like smoke signals to the God my parents believe is chronicling their lives.

"Yahweh."

"Dios."

"Jehovah."

"Allah."

"Adonai."

"Atua."

"Ahura Mazda."

"What?"

"Never mind."

"I AM."

Jill Jones

Photograph by Mazz Images

Jill Jones is a Sydney writer. She won the Mary Gilmore Award in 1993 for her first book of poetry, *The Mask and the Jagged Star* (Hazard Press). Her second book, *Flagging Down Time* (Five Islands Press), was published in late 1993. A third book is in preparation. She also co-edited, with Judith Beveridge and Louise Wakeling, a recent anthology of new Australian poetry, *A Parachute of Blue* (Round Table, 1995). She has been the recipient of two Australia Council writers' grants.

How I Might Write Irish

I'm not sure what writing Irish means for my work. My grandfather was an engineer born in Ulster. He married a Scotswoman there, my grandmother, and they came to Australia. And, yes, I believe there's something of the Irish in me, though I've not yet been back there. (I notice I say "back there", as if I'd once been. Maybe that's what ancestry means.)

Many poems I write, people tell me, have an elegaic quality, or as someone told me once, "a ruminating melancholy". Maybe it's the form for the end of the twentieth century or maybe it's older than that in my bones — the lament, the keening. Think back to the seventh century, of Líadan lamenting Cuirithir when she speaks of their choice "to seek Paradise through pain".

There is a sense that things must be said, spoken as well as read. A story that must be told: anecdote, history, voices. There are dreams — and the weirdness — even in ordinary things. As if access is given through language to the irrational. As if some form of divination is taking place, sometimes as a form of playfulness. I'm also aware of a kind of rhetorical gymnastic, occasionally a complex syntax, sometimes a sway, a lilting cadence in the line.

The poems come in different ways. Some days there's the need to simply write and so I find myself doing that wherever I am — a bus, a café, under a tree, at home — a kind of observational improvisation. So I pull together threads from the here and now as stories spin through the air, voices, the clang of the world, the beat of the everyday happenings that shiver through the writing mind. There's always time later for the revision thing.

Then there are the forms of play. The technical aspects — metre, syllables, rhyming, stanzas, etcetera — have their allure, of playing within a clearly defined field and in doing so trying to climb the fence, to break free. I'm usually more free than bound but I don't always feel bound to be completely free.

The other play is the mask. Of course, it's all a mask, but I mean the overt mask, assuming an obvious character voice. This is where I can justify reading anything and everything that comes to hand — newspapers, catalogues, flyers, and now the vastness of the internet, as well as those old friends, books. Here I find ideas about other lives — say — an aging rock star who, now reformed from certain bad habits has a country retreat in Ireland, as it happens. Her musings about the past, published in a weekend news review, enter my poem's thoughts then turn sideways into another (imagined) life and end in a kind of mourning for the past associated with music. In fact, a considerable amount of what I write seems connected to music. No great surprise, I suppose. It is poetry after all, but I find there's nearly always the ghost of a refrain on the wind.

And then I write as someone living on an island (a very big one, no doubt) close to the sea using a language that came from some other place, that is my own surely but at times not quite. I warm to what Eavan Boland says in her poem *The Oral Tradition*, though most likely for reasons different from her original impulse:

> *the oral song*
> *avid as superstition*
> *layered like amber in*
> *the wreck of language*
> *and the remnants of a nation*

There's lots of earth and stone in my work, even though I'm a city dweller. Places live and have their voices, the weather is important, the likeness and strangeness of things.

Most of all, there is the centrality of poetry.

Broken Language

Broken languages cross the sky,
       enter my room in wires of light.
A spark from his song pierces
       weariness in the evening of today,
breaking old veins, and
       collapsed tunnels of memory.
How many times does the downstroke
       of death's word shake those friends,
street companions of hazy years,
       with whom I shared stolen spaces,
worlds unconnected
       to one step and the next?

• • •

Today, you sit and watch
       the children, all upright and dedicated.
And you're proud of their wholeness.
       I see it even in the eyes of fathers,
a species I never knew, its dialect
       translated by long Victorian novels
and mother's tongue,
       an older acid of illusion.

And what do you tell someone,
          who hasn't fallen through? No scar
nor excursion into sideways space
          will attract them from the ordinary
health of their sun and a right
          and proper skin of dignity
some have said even I now wear, unbecoming
          if not for the sentences
scrawled round my eyes,
          and the valleys of my bones.

• • •

Shooting companions and stars —
          their traces and explosions disappear
as light travels from us
          quicker each year. And here,
tonight, is that short song
          alive in the screen's lines:
something stopped his breath,
          my once close companion,
and the satellites above the world
          cradle a brief coda
to the sweet and playful tragedy
          that was his work, the only chorus
left scored on metal, vinyl and tape,
          while the true voice subsides
into the other elements of death.

But we were as much of the air,
        waiting for its messages
tuning our nerves until the overload.
        And on the streets, where life was lived,
we missed the wars, as regimes of terror
        in politics and taste turned over,
as years went by.
        One focus, one will to pull in
each rush as if it was the last and
        everpresent moment, an experiment
that must ever be replicated, a pot
        always filled as it boiled.

          • • •

Everything feels soft now, green
        country hills stroke the dark outside.
Only my voice, its aging husk, chokes
        on the tune once ours, now worn away
in the rivers of sentimentality.
        Yes, lost its mettle in the world
of no risks. Only the scattered
        temperaments of those
who got it all wrong for years
        could know about playing
in circles, splitting selves,
        while watching the mirror change
from hour to hour
        with every new pose and switch.

Until it fogged up completely,
      the carpet beneath disintegrated, and
police cleared us out again and again,
      as wired up on their own push.

          • • •

I can't avoid it now.
      An old valedictory horn solo
rises through distracted imaginations,
      its final breath exhaling into
a wide and changeful black landscape
      that moves into the planetary wash,
forever escaping.

Lunch Music Café

The glass roof covers music of diners.
O, the rise and fall of them, at conversation
and cutlery! But mostly a steady pitch,
conducted by gestures of arrival, choice.
Over all the movement of wine sings
its desires into the neck and the stem.

Burdens of taste and repetition, of silver
and steel divide the meal, without chorus.
The floor is hard, throws back a bass,
blanketing all highs but the clinking metal,
chiming glass and the imaginary whistle
of a bird that rests in the hearts of travellers.

The bird beats against glass, looking for a way
out, to crack apart the key, sweep the flutter
and discord out into free air. But today's not
advertised for transgression, the pit doesn't
overflow. Voices trail off, others distinguish
themselves as the hours of emptying begin.

As music splits time, and great suppers fragment,
so lunch's players become lazy. The music
finally tumbles round their feet. Beautiful
crumbs, intricate steps, swept to the door.
And sun hits the glass in afternoon finale.
Birds gather in the grounds outside.

June 16, 1995
Bloomsday

Among Trees

Towards night the park gathers in
shadows and expels the light. Birds
rest hidden in branches. Long stretches
of lawn, having been mowed, are edged
with white mounds of cut grass
alongside rose beds.
A hard moon is revealed.

This is halfway between
softness and violence.
And lovers step away from paths,
their bodies tight in seeking.
And forks of branches
sway at the moon, asking
is it you, love, is it really you?

A single stranger moves past the trees.
The birds sleep like souls waiting.

Invisible Ink

You've exhausted the dead
with your questions and now
they run from you, leaving
their pure white sheets
and their old medicine.

None of us know how
to ask you anything this time.
Time, instead, is an answer
we sneak in hurried looks
at the moving wrists of waiters.

Even they leave us alone, neither
their lists nor inquiries reach us.
And we are hungry
from our normal week
which you don't ask about.

You have a thousand cards
you spread out,
fanning every opportunity
with your speculations
which go beyond the dead.

Food will be a cure for
our particular emptiness.
There's nothing new, and no more
leftovers to offer bodies
hungry for one last minute.

Not one word would stop you
feeding on the absence
of any reply, even one slowly
painted onto a sheet by a finger
dipped in invisible ink.

It shows up later,
a scrawled brown smudge
on the harsh linen that accompanied
the last sleep
of this most recent friend.

Ideas of Sirens

Sirens call, split the hour
from its lethargy and the season
from its smooth coating of
assumptions. Always
things are not well, though
this side of the street
on a seamless day
there's no alarm, nor any
cause to release the trigger.
But they call up dread ideas,
of smoke and blood. Always
something burns,
the oven of any day
switched on, and searing.

A flame disappears
as heat leaves,
rising in a hasty cloud,
invisible but overhanging
for a moment the ordinary
movement of time that has turned
into the bad end of a story
you hear in passing
as sirens wheel off at the corner
through the stop sign
and onto the great black highway.

Antipodean Geography

Continents on the wall
shift slowly through a tide of weather.
Cupboards open and laugh.

Great seabirds on the ceiling find their own
longitude, and carry
what's forgotten to lagoons beyond the door.

There you could swim
safely, and tides are kinder than the wind.
It's the Antipodes!

Lost and found again, so you may
find her now and then,
beyond glass and wood, fibres of rooms.

Proud on the sill, a bird.
Its yellow eye looks past the sofa to valleys
that sing. And vases of mountains

burn darkly.

The Pure in Heart

They have taken babies
and blamed it on dingoes,
have planted foul words
on the righteous tongues
of six-year old bigots.

They have joined hands
with the makers
of warheads, purification
and sub-Arctic famines.

They have studied love
and found it wanting.

They have flushed their water
through cataracts of ice.
They praise the numbers
in their heavy books.

Some of them watch you,
monitor your garbage
for glimpses of hell.
Be careful, they think
their destiny is to drink
from your children.

Medbh McGuckian

Photograph courtesy of Gallery Press

Medbh McGuckian was born in 1950 in Belfast, Ireland where she now lives with her husband and three children. Her poetry has been widely acclaimed in Ireland, Britain, France and the USA. She has received numerous awards including: British National Poetry Society competition (1979), Eric Gregory Award (1980), Alice Huntley Bartlett Award (1983). Her collection *Marconi's Cottage* (1991), was a Poetry Ireland Choice. She is the first woman to be named writer-in-residence at Queen's University (1986-88).

Drawing Ballerinas: How Being Irish has Influenced Me as a Writer

I understood something about where I was brought up last week, when I heard on an early-morning RTE program, broadcast from Dublin, that the German bombs in the second world war had mistakenly targeted the wrong waterworks the Easter they came here. Not the one in use in East Belfast, which is predominantly Protestant, but the disused one in North Belfast, which is predominantly Catholic. I was born only a few years after this, but there is a photograph of myself and my brother and sister, throwing bread to the swans in the lake. As if our childhood ignorance could somehow withstand the historical gloom, the all-night air pounding, the blind destructiveness, the sense of being totally unprotected. At the mercy of warring forces to whom you were a mere pawn in their game — my legacy. Our house was on the flight-path and I would run down to my parents screaming that there was going to be a war, a war had started, when the drone of engines terrified me.

We would sit on each other's gates during the day, and Sally with the strange name and dark hair, would explain where England was. Joyce-Ann at the seaside pointed to where America lay, and Stella drew a phone on the hopscotch pavement with chalk, to describe to me this incredible instrument that people had for talking to each other across long distance. We could not afford one of these till I was in my late teens. I remember I was so elated to be finally reachable in this way, I gave the number to a first boyfriend even before we moved to the new house, so that he kept ringing the silent place. We were not well off and had no television till I was about eight and that was bought with a win on the pools! Then England flew straight into my house and my head with the proper English accents, their news, sports, weather on which we never featured. Ulster Television a few years later sounded less foreign, but I was no less confused as to my own identity, my own nationality, my relevance to the world.

I had no feeling of being "Irish" whatsoever. What I most categorically was, was a Roman Catholic, first and foremost. Even though I had been given an Irish or Gaelic pagan name and not that of a saint, through some romantic whim of my mother's I've never understood. The secondary baptismal names of Thérèse after the Little Flower of Lisieux and Philomena after the martyr and the confirmation name of Anne after Our Lady's mother, were the badges that labelled me. We barely heard of Dublin and never went there. We would drive, when my father obtained his first Austin 4, eventually down to the border, to visit the procathedral at Armagh, but as far as I was concerned in my mind, beyond that was the sea. As if what they called Ulster was itself an island, and there was no way out of it.

My world was a round of retreats and missions, sodality and sermons. If I left the house it was to school or church where the sacraments strengthened me. I dreaded being sent to play or walk in the park called after Queen Alexandra, in case roving gangs of Protestant boys, or worse still, Protestant girls, might guess what school we went to or what street we came from. Their taunts and jibes could easily end in stone-throwing. There was a straggle of houses at the end of our street where boys with names like Robin and Mervyn lived, and my mother held herself at a polite remove from these neighbours. We understood that we were not the same, and were never to venture into any of the streets below our own. My father would walk round to the fish and chip shop on a Friday night, but it was out of bounds to us even during the day. Once a brick came hurtling through our back window from the entry, and fell within an inch of my sleeping baby sister's head. There was a sinister, guarded air to everything. When we played in the garages behind our house we felt we were trespassers and always somebody kept watch. On the bus into town my mother would sit tight-lipped, holding her counsel, while loud-mouthed women proclaimed their allegiances around us. The dental clinic was first held in the local Protestant school, and there was a double sense of intimidation and terror, going through those black gates, into a dark-green room of torture and hostility. The atmosphere communicated itself to me I suppose subtly or subconsciously, but from a very early age I knew that because of our religion we were as outcast as Jews.

It was a very narrow, dark, confined world, symbolised by the narrow, dark, confined gardenless terrace house where the barricades erected early in the Troubles as a "Peace Line", have not yet been removed. What was most paradoxical to me was that the institution in which I sought shelter and emotional or spiritual refuge, was in fact highly inimical to me as a woman. So being excluded from one's society on the grounds of being Catholic resulted in an ultimate exclusion from the heart of the Catholic rituals themselves, on the grounds of sex. My mother was in the third order of Carmelites, and on dismal Sunday afternoons I would attend long meetings with her. But I could not be an altar boy, although I learned Latin. I could sing in the choir, but I could not walk on the altar. It was still the days when you had to keep your head covered with a mantilla because St Paul said women's hair was a temptation. Also my mother went through the churching ceremony after her babies, and related a story of how she was once refused Communion because she was wearing lipstick. We would pass perfume from our handbags up and down the pew until elderly gentlemen behind us would complain. Eventually with developing sexuality I came to a painful rejection of much of what had been inculcated.

My grandmother was a strong and influential figure who had her own vital brand of superstition, her own adherences to the old rural faith with its penances and its indulgences, which lived side by side in her with a zest for physicality, the vanity of a marketswoman who adored hats and hatpins.

I never remember spending July in the city. Any Catholic who could, would evacuate the streets before the celebrations of the twelfth with its bonfires, and go to the seaside ghettos Catholics were allowed to go to. Even here, war brooded menacingly, for the beach was still reputed to be mined. We once found what looked like a grenade in the sand, a radar station dominated the skyline, airforce personnel from the nearby barracks would drive the chickens into the hedges with their jeeps.

The sense of Irishness and culture was a very vague and uncertain one. My sister was sent to Irish dancing, but this always struck me as an artificial, joyless rigidity which I found no pleasure in and tedious to watch. The music I also found monotonous, and was that of the family fiddle-band who came to our house on Sunday evenings to perform. There was nothing natural to me in these straining violins. I preferred "The Bluebells of Scotland" or "Way Down Upon the Swanee River", for their love of place and their homesickness. I liked some of the songs we heard uncles sing and some of the records they played: "Have You Seen Me Uncle Dan McCann?"; "The Boy from the County Armagh"; "Shake Hands with Your Uncle Mike, Me Boy"; "Greensleeves"; "My Aunt Jane". These created a familiar warmth and security. They were orally transmitted and a part of the people's minds — they meant something to them and reflected their lives.

My father used to call me, "The Wreck of the Hesperus", because my hair was never tidy and it was this heritage of Victorian narratives and heroic tragedies they had learned in school, that most affected my developing sense of literature. The paintings on the walls were, *The Monarch of the Glen*, (a stag in the Scottish Highlands) or *The Angelus*. We were always closer to Scotland than either England or Ireland's Republic, and my great-uncle was a chef on the Glasgow boat. My uncle also worked as a docker and brought in welcome supplies of fruit, but another uncle was intimidated out of a foundry job, and two were jailed in the notorious Crumlin Road prison. In my teens I was sent to learn Irish at the summer school in the Donegal Gaeltacht, but this only furthered my sense of alienation. We were herded in busloads through Derry and Letterkenny to misty bogs and ceildhs, where undersized waifs from Dublin stood clumsily on our toes. This was my introduction to man-hood, an anoraked arm flung around one's shoulder as the rain soaked in and the signposts lurked in the fog. There was no way I belonged here either, not to the poems that were taught, not the songs that were heard, nor the music that was played, nor the dances that were danced, nor the sexless boys that didn't know how to kiss.

The one we all wanted to kiss was JF Kennedy. I believe it was this figure, followed by the Liverpool Beatles who were all, of course, from Ireland, that for our generation a desire or pride in the urge to declare oneself Irish was born. The death of Pius XII and the election of John XXIII was one thing, with Encyclicals and Vatican councils. The assassination of the first Catholic Irish-American President was quite another, and we heard it not from the screen but from the pulpit where it was considered important enough to be announced. That was in 1963 and coincided not only with, "She Loves You" and "Ticket to Ride", but with the paragraph in the *Irish News* reviewing *Death of a Naturalist* by a poet from Bellaghy. There was an assertiveness, an opening, a defiance, a wide rising in rebellion in the sixties against the silence and subservience of the fifties. Bob Dylan and Joan Baez with, "We Shall Overcome" and "A Hard Rain's Gonna Fall", gave expression to our own growing yearning for revolution. It was possible then, to come from this place and yet have something to say.

I remember the elocution classes and the examinations in the assembly hall, the enunciation of "Prunes and Prisms", "How Now Brown Cow", to get the English vowels right, in a dark blue velvet dress with a lace collar.

The first Irish tune that actually stirred me to tears was Sean O'Riada's soundtrack of "Roisín Dubh" for the film *Mise Éire*, which somehow we were taken to. This experience haunted me with a cavernous sense of loss and agony. I could put no name to my longing. But this was a note that was inspired and genuine and I was able to respond to it.

For seven years I walked to my convent school in my bottle-green, passing a girl my own age in the navy uniform of the Academy, and though we passed each other every day at almost the same spot, and glanced at each other, we knew better than to speak. At university she was finally in her ordinary clothes in one of my psychology classes, and though we nodded to each other in final recognition, we made no attempt to become friends. Something had rotted in us, some spontaneity. I think we knew each other too well.

I lived only for the summers, which were spent in the fields of my father's childhood by the Atlantic, opposite Rathlin Island on the North Antrim coast. This to me became my Ireland — this sky, this forest, this mountain, this river, these stars, these clouds, that rain, that glen. And that cousin with the dark eyes and silky hair, the enchanting laugh, whose voice radiated scorn, who knew every star in the zodiac. In this hollow, Finn MacCool had buried his dog and bloody battles had been waged. Roger Casement's family estate was just to the north, and at Murlough Bay there were ceremonies on the date of his execution. Maíre O'Neill's "vanishing lake, Loughareema" was in the hills, and although we had learned, *All in the April Evening*, at school, we had not learned anything about the poet Katherine Tynan. Even though the golf club and the tennis court and the bay windows proclaimed the town as part of a colony, the wildness of the sea and remote farms belied it and that was a spirit I imbibed instinctively from my father's soul.

At the end of our secondary school education we were about to move into the university. An old nun in the convent warned us gruesomely that a lot of very bad things were going to happen, and we were not to get mixed up in anything. In my first year there was a certain amount of unrest amongst the students, which I did not understand, any more than the question a girl put to me as we queued for grants: "Have you lost the precious pearl?" I had a boyfriend doing law whose ambition was to be Lord Chief Justice, and who tried to put me right on politics. I had accepted that Catholics stayed separate from Protestants in much the same way girls stayed away from boys. Even at university, although there was mixing, there was no intimacy. In the Civil Rights marches I took no part, since

I had no idea what they were about, and to be part of a large group of people frightened me.

When Bombay Street was set on fire, my boyfriend got me to help with questionnaires, going around the houses on the Lower Falls, finding out what happened, the people's reactions to the B-Specials, their present fears. That was an eye-opener for me, since the notion of the authorised law of the country taking up arms against the citizens it was paid to protect was beyond my experience. Although I had been "interfered with" as a child by a policeman, this particular instance had not undermined my faith in the law in general as having my interests at heart. When the army arrived around my nineteenth birthday, it was seen as a good thing, a force that would protect the Catholics against the armed attacks. But I broke up with that politically-involved boyfriend and for the rest of my undergraduate years, hung around deliberately, with people whose only ambition was to get as high a degree as possible and to get out.

The bombs began in earnest and we became nervous travelling through town. The buses were highjacked and stopped running. I walked the shortest route across and began staying over at night because it was too dangerous to be out and a sort of curfew prevailed. During this time I was not yet writing. My earliest poems had been about Jimmie Hendrix or pseudo-Wordsworthian sonnets about nature. The first encounter with Yeats was not particularly exciting, as he was not specified as being Irish, but a more modern influence along with Eliot, Joyce and Lawrence. *Ulysses* did nothing for me. But the explosions began more and more to affect what little sense of security I had invested in my own house and my parents, particularly my father who would run me over to Queen's in his car, whether it was safe or not.

A girl who had been in my class at school and lived a few doors from us was one of the Saturday afternoon victims of the Abercorn Café explosion. My father was asked to go to the morgue and identify her, as her own family were too shocked, and he said he could only go by the blue fur of her anorak — she always wore this very pretty mini-jacket. I would have wanted to write about that in some way, but had not the tools at the time. We seemed to grow immune to the events around us, the way the city became militarised with checkpoints everywhere, one's bag constantly emptied.

The big change for me in my evaluation and discernment of how to live through and survive what was happening around me, never mind understand it, was the year we had Seamus Heaney as a tutor in Honours English. It must have been 1970, the year of Bloody Sunday, also the year of Paul Muldoon's first pamphlet and book. I wrote a hopefully non-Wordsworthian sonnet, after the thirteen people were shown on the television, shot dead indiscriminately. I summoned from some youthful place the temerity to show this to Dr Heaney, who proceeded cheerfully to take me out for a Bloody Mary. The day had only just begun to be called "bloody" and he was able to turn its effects into art. There was a kind of complicity that many things were wrong in the State of Denmark, but that the way to redress them was through the non-violence of poetry. With Seamus Heaney we studied Kavanagh and MacNeice, Mangan and

Ferguson, Davis and Yeats proper. I went on then to do an MA in Anglo-Irish literature, studying the nineteenth-century novelists, Griffin, Edgeworth, the Banim brothers and William Carleton, which involved coming to terms, even if in an idealised way, with the historical background of famine and rebellion. So I think gradually an identity with Irishness was being forged for me or I was gradually becoming myself.

I almost left for England or Scotland in 1972, but it was a vital life-decision not to, to stay and see out the consequences. When Seamus Heaney left for Dublin there was an acute sense of wishing to depart after him. He had always signed books to me with the Irish spelling of my first name, and I began to feel less self-conscious about it and more honoured. Paul Muldoon became a friend and an inspiration with his precocious wit and searing intelligence. I was Ciarán Carson's girlfriend while he was working on his first book, *The New Estate*, the first edition of which was dedicated to me with the English spelling of my name. Being so close to someone involved in writing poetry taught me a great deal about the craft, about how to really get words to obey you. I was not trying to write anything original by the end of that relationship, but after a year of marriage, living in the beautiful valley of Downpatrick, (because the rumour was then that the six counties were going to be re-partitioned and this town would be in the Catholic area), I began to find my own voice.

The first poem that won me any kind of recognition was based on a Troubles related incident. Like the earlier poem about Bloody Sunday, it seemed a necessary outlet for the violence that shook the community, or in this case, the family. My husband's sister had been a bomb-victim and her husband, a brother-in-law I never met, did not survive. The poem was a dramatic monologue set in her voice, and it was eerie to have British television following my own husband and myself, carrying my first child within me, around the holy places where St Patrick had brought Christianity to the country. Things seemed quieter in the city, there was talk of settlements when we moved back to North Belfast to found a home there. But then the Hunger Strikes and their aftermath created an atmosphere similar to that of Easter 1916, and the positions became once more heavily entrenched. More so than ever, all through the decade of the eighties while our children were small, the shootings and bombings increased, almost unbearably. Paul Muldoon's departure for America was the low-point in my sense of isolation.

The poems in the first book were apparently to do with pregnancy and my first experience of birth, and I do believe that my first four books were assimilated like a pearl in the oyster, around the birth-process of a child. Whereas the last book, *Captain Lavender*, built itself around the loss of a single person, namely my father. However the subtler under-narrating of each person, or the subtext, is more generally political, and many words were specifically chosen for dark and war-like implications. For instance, the first poem, *That Year*, is ostensibly about the onset of menstruation at fourteen, but it uses imagery to do with imprisonment, the colours of the Union Jack flag. The girl's growing up and identification of herself as a female creature is associated with a Star of David — like ignominy. There is a sense of exile and being outcast. The menstrual blood is deliberately linked to the news report of street murders and dumped bodies. Sexuality is a bullet left lodged in the mind and flesh, as Heaney's pen lay in his hand snug as a gun. There is a sinister insecurity rather than any celebration or delight.

The last poem in the first book, *The Flower Master*, reaches a state of defiance achieved by the journey through similar kinds of double-edged poems throughout the collection. It is a poem of patience and rebellion, using the symbols of different kinds of trees to express different kinds of political outlooks. It would be hard to say where the author's own loyalties lie, if she has any, but "empire" is rhymed with "gentler" and the repeated oaks are visualised as sensibly "laying store upon their Lammas growth". The Lammas fair is traditionally held in my father's hometown of Ballycastle, and I felt this poem acquired a historical significance when the first ceasefire was announced on Lammas Day 1994.

The second book, *Venus in the Rain*, published in 1984, continued to weave the private life with the public suffering in more deeply complicated ways. The surface themes again are postnatal depression, domesticity, but for example, at least one poem, *Dovecote*, was written in direct response to the horrifying saga of the ten hunger strike self-starvations, and many others in reaction to other violent individual deaths, by suicide or by drowning etcetera. The anxiety as to where one actually lives, or the idea of home, is carried through into *On Ballycastle Beach*, published in 1988. The sea becomes a symbol of escape. I include a poem for Irina Ratushinskaya and refer a little more openly to history, to the Russian revolutions. Many of the narratives are in the shape of dreams or nightmares, as if the vulnerable subconscious were discharging itself of all the intolerable conditions of the environment as it then was. The last two poems cling stubbornly to the parents as mentors or guards in the midst of civil chaos. The beach becomes the only emotional harbour or solution.

Equally this metaphor is extended into the fourth collection, the move out mentally towards Europe as an overhome and a coming to rest in a house which is literally at the very end of Ballycastle Beach, the small outpost where Marconi, the half-Irish half-Italian inventor, carried out radio transmissions exactly a hundred years ago this year. I had wanted a quotation from Roger Casement's notebooks about Banna Strand as an epigraph to the previous book, but my then English publishers were opposed to this. It was not that I was one hundred per cent duped by the heroic force of Irish Nationalism, but that in some ways, that was all there was. Maybe is still, all there is. I felt more international and classical in this collection, although premonitions of death dominate it, elegies continue to seep through it, gender begins to become a moveable feast. I develop a more complex persona, and multiple Muses. There is an air of resistance, I think, mostly in the language. I talk a lot about the definition of poetry and art.

I have a poem for Emily Brontë and one for Gwen John. The loss of a psychological child in a phantom pregnancy is treated in terms of a war memorial. A long poem about a brutal husband who killed his own child while still in the mother's womb, addresses for probably the first time directly, the issue of the Homeric, Grecian, incestuous kind of violence that was the norm in the late eighties. The notion of blood-sacrifices and the trope of Ireland as a rose not worth dying for, filters through, Yeats' stone. In a poem describing birth in terms of orgasm and death, I go back as far as I can to my Catholic roots. Ciarán Carson has a similar explanation or apotheosis in his poem on the letter "X" in his alphabet sequence, about the statue of the Virgin Mother. There is probably a deep religious questioning hidden in the sensuality of this book, culminating in the almost mystical daughter-poems at the end. The child within redeems the outer world's gratuitous slaughters. She was born around August 1989, when the country had been under martial law for twenty years and people were beginning to seek change with a guarded optimism. Maybe this new feminine self will not have to grow up under the hazards and constraints and abnormality that we have endured as a generation, and our parents before us, who were born in the Civil War, even more so.

There's a kind of Rubik cube turnaround, corresponding to the new noises of the Anglo-Irish agreement and an embracing of the media-god, who has already decided everything anyway. I look forward and back, resigning myself to not having actually existed in a way, yet willing to pay that price for the acknowledgement of the century to come. It's the affirmation of the past giving way to the positives of the future. I wrote two poems during the early nineties. *Drawing Ballerinas*, and *The Dead are More Alive*, are not yet in book form but deal more overtly with the problems of being Irish, or trying to be Irish in a British colony, or trying to survive as a Catholic under Protestant or no rule. The latter was related to the nadir of Catholic morale expressed in the tribal execution of two soldiers who strayed into a funeral procession. This was a taboo situation akin in its inflammatory nature to the Remembrance Day bombing at Enniskillen. The events were filmed and relayed almost as they happened, and my second son aged about eight, watched the newsreel as if it had been an American Pulp Fiction. It was the openness to evil of his naked receiving eyes that disturbed me as much as the bloodlust and frenzy of a mob utterly beyond themselves taking animal revenge.

It seemed the absolute turning point, a sign that people's nerves were frayed beyond any natural behaviour and could sink no further. We could not do more than crucify. Many emblems coalesced in that lynching, and they sat heavy on the soul. The *Drawing Ballerinas* poem saw the conflict in terms of the European Holocaust and based itself on Matisse's aesthetic stance which Picasso envied — of continuing to devote himself to the creation of human beauty while his wife agitated against the death-camps. It was not easy for me to deal with these issues and it is still not. For instance, the newspaper reports today are about how ninety punishment shootings have occurred in the wake of the so-called ceasefires, and while no one has been killed, these people are actually left for dead and have their lives destroyed. So the pain and outrage continue, and one still feels obliged to draw one's ballerinas against that background.

Captain Lavender has a reproduction of a painting from the Irish Civil War on the front, and the main colour is khaki, while the characters depicted are women. Colourful, fashionable, behatted, respectable, middle-class women proud of their beauty, standing sentinel outside the women's phallic, and colourless, airless jail. I seem to name a lot of women in this book, and yet it's centrally a lovework and elegy for my father. I interpret him as a Christ-figure who has taken the sins of the nation upon his own head and whose *willed* death was a necessary prelude to the Easter of the new dispensation — such as it so far is. His grave becomes magnified into the state prison, and his being withheld from me is compared to the social banishment of a convicted yet innocent so-called terrorist. In a paradoxical way, I identify with this imagined prisoner as being still part of this world and on this earth, tied to it, whereas my father is the freed spirit. So the relationship between the women on the ground and the women caged in the air is intentionally ambiguous.

In one poem, I take on Ulster or Northern Ireland or the difficult Province itself as a Muse whom I address, as a mother that failed me, a deceptive and hostile witch, no more a hospitable planet than the Venus of my second book.

An illusion, a hodgepodge, a made-up place, a fantasy, a coffin, as sick a rose as Blake's. I think in this poem I was condemning all political attitudes that condoned the taking or harming of life in any way. I had reached that pitch of self-rejection, which was probably part of the mourning process. The title poem was a brief and epigrammatic effort to resolve or at least revolve those contradictions within myself and my situations. I visualised my father as having sorted everything out for himself once and for all by disappearing completely or at least reaching another continent, beyond the confining ocean making the island a mere island. It was as if he achieved an aristocratic or military status denied to him by life, but also that the death-person I had feared for so long was actually an agent of healing. Not so much the bitter bridegroom summoned up in Ethna Carbery's, *The Love-Talker*, but rather the impartial and courteous best man, whose sole function is to safeguard the ring.

Anyway where does that leave me now? I teach poetry classes at two local universities. Having taught for a decade at Catholic secondary schools, where the narrow limits of my childhood and adolescence seemed to be perpetuated, it's refreshing to come into contact with reasonable and intelligent and highly sensitive adults, from both sides of what they call the "divide". There are many new institutional ways in which artificial enemies who have never met, who have been segregated and ostracised from each other, can slowly come together, and poetry's a deeply rewarding, if dangerous, way. Last year the tension in my classes during the Shankill and Greysteel mass-burials was palpable and awesome. This year I have a Derry Unionist cheerfully giving State information to a Crumlin Road nun, and a Free Presbyterian minister denouncing fornication in the most exquisite love poems, and a staunch widower with one of those uncanonised names who dreams that he has just written a poem I have said is good. There's a loosening as of icebergs around the Titanic, there's a respect for the hurt of words as well as bullets, and the hurt of no-words. There's a determined search for the right language in which to say what we really mean, to each other and about each other, no longer behind each other's backs in each other's houses. Unbelievable tricolours fly unmolested next to the police station. My child wears the navy Academy uniform I used to walk past. My car purrs softly over the rampless streets.

30 May 1995

The Mast Year

Some kinds of trees are ever eager
To populate new ground, the oak or pine.
Though beech can thrive on many soils
And carve itself an empire, its vocation
Is gentler; it casts a shade for wildflowers
Adapted to the gloom, which feed
Like fungus on its rot of bedstraw leaves.

It makes an awkward neighbour, as does
The birch, that lashes out in gales, and fosters
Intimacy with toadstools, till they sleep
In the benevolence of each other's smells,
Never occupying many sites for long:
The thin red roots of alder vein
The crumbled bank, the otter's ruptured door.

Bee-keepers love the windbreak sycamore,
The twill of hanging flowers that the beech
Denies the yew — its waking life so long
It lets the stylish beechwood
Have its day, as winded oaks
Lay store upon their Lammas growth,
The thickening of their dreams.

Road 32, Roof 13-23, Grass 23

for Gwen John

The dark wound her chestnut hair
Around her neck like the rows of satin trimming
On a skirt with three flounces.
She pressed firmly down the sides of her eyes
The colour of the stem of the wild geranium
And of the little ball holding the snowdrop petals.

In winter she dreamt the back views
Of young men on high ladders, their fingers
Through bookcases like hummingbirds
Radiating for miles into the forest.
Her water-loving fern liked the rain
Down her back, and the sun coming in early,

Going round the house slamming doors.
One morning a week she arranged a jug
Of tomato-coloured blooms face to face
In the exact centre of the table.
She did not light the lamp or the fire,
Though he lit a station of candles

In wine bottles for their first kiss,
The candlelight left a film of woodsmoke
Over everything. Her fear of light began
While his coat still hung over a chair,
The window seemed a picture eased out of her,
She had not wanted her own face there.

"Use the other door" — he shut the ever-open
Door behind his doubly-closed face
With the air of a wasted afternoon
Or an occasional gasp that filled
The house to be scraped off
Afterwards like a point of purple ribbon.

She slept with his letter in her hand,
And the longest letter she wrote
Was on the back of his letter
To a woman who never existed.

But sat on her midsummer doorstep
Dusted with woodash like a letter,
Or the icy rain stoked with
Fallen boughs on her coverlet.

The Dead are More Alive

As if their eyes could still open,
were resting from their beauty, still
burning very quietly, like candles,
there is something in them that goes beyond
murder, something denied to the eyes,
the eyes being used for movements
denied to the limbs.

Even if you did not see it, nevertheless
it grazed the skin of your mind
with a slashing as if on flesh
by an open knife blade, slicing
everything in two.

A mere fifteen minutes from my room
the sky was still, as though
it would always be this colour.
It spread out, way, way out in the moment
with such wide-open eyes, you
yourself felt viewed.

You were shielded against what you saw
only by never looking away,
you broke down what you saw
by not turning your head,
as one stares at a map so as never
to be outside the world.

You seeing did not change you,
your eyes grew accustomed
to remaining open, and gathering
the senselessly scattered things.

I avoided reading any items
about them, but I listened to the sounds
of the day stretching across the city,
as if everywhere people expected
bullets to strike again.

The air was a loud nourishment
it smelled of burnt paper,
it sounded liberated.

I looked for a head as though
to follow its directions,
and the head became very round,
sawing the air, the body broad and rough
as the entire past reaching into later.

I passed four heads in the living room,
their footsteps lay very far downstream,
though everything was so near, as though
a mountain could be breathed and
this ultimate breath preserved.

The day clashed inside me, till
I felt its blood-filled collapse,
and wanted to tear out from my soil
everything it had planted, then invite
people into my emptiness,
where last night's kiss had left
a shell-pink in my cheek,
like a fire laid in readiness for autumn.

The fire that heated them was out,
one red volume pushed out by the next.
But mute as peacocks released
from their vividness, we would not
have been speaking so gladly
about the same thing.

Rathlin Road

There was a low-spreading blazing blue
on the surface water that re-fought the battles:
a never-ending red rinsed in green,
little-understood, a colour we scarcely knew.

We were a tiny island of women
being sung to sleep on an island of talk.
Years without speech or cries of absence of mind
had lessened our minds, our calls close to song.

Always rain and only rain freed me,
I would lie like new water after it,
in an afterimage where dust had not collected,
hoping the wind would pick me out of the earth.

Bleached gold the clouds bent back
and purpled on and off, never again
to seem old. The east-west path,
so magically cooled, shed the foursquare day.

Like a telephone too filled with voice,
a living argument beneath an agreed window,
the heavy seasons cooperated with the map,
and near-Parisian weather salted our Christmas eyes.

Cherry Smyth

Photograph by Lola Flash

Cherry Smyth works as a journalist and writer and co-programmes the London Lesbian and Gay Film Festival. She is Northern Irish, trying to resist assimilation living in London.

She has written for the *Guardian*, *The Observer*, *frieze* magazine and *Sight and Sound*. Her essays, short stories and poetry have appeared in various collections including *Critical Quarterly*, *Virago New Poets*, *Frankenstein's Daughter*, *Quare Fellas: New Irish Gay Fiction*, *Daring to Dissent* and *A Queer Romance: Lesbians, Gays and Popular Culture*. She has also contributed to the exhibition catalogue *Bad Girls*.

Her book *Queer Notions* was published in 1992 and sold 4000 copies in the UK, Ireland and USA. Her forthcoming book *Damn Fine Art by New Lesbian Artists* will be published by Cassell, London, September 1996.

The Roadside

The killer is a country man, close to land
his father's father's father fought to keep.
He weaves his tractor up and down thin fields
hedged with secrets, and mutters
tenderly to pigs and sheep.

He knew Brennan at St Malachy's,
a snitch even then — courted his sister,
who married a teacher — they thrashed conkers
on laces, raced three-legged on Sport's Day
and won a sixpence.

It is midsummer and the farmer longs for dark.
The etiquette of execution sharply honed
keeps silence chain-smoked in the carpark.

Brennan is bull-drunk, taken easy, stripped and baled.
His Guinness-gut shivers, pale as potato.
The killer milks him slow, then twists his balls
until he yelps and bleats, like all beasts
out in sweet June air, for Eileen O'Neill,
shot and bargained away at twenty-six.

Brennan's voice is calm now, as one who knows
he is already dead. One letter for the wife.
Claire. Seven months pregnant. For pity's sake.

The sister is somewhere in his face.
The farmer bends.
There is nothing in the barn
only a ripped paper bag and biro
stamped with Lurgan Motors.

Shit-smell of Brennan
is stronger than manure
and in his eyes
the slaughter-look of calves,
so when he writes,
the killer needs to kill,
to bag the head, mow him down, plough
until he squeals no more.

The farmer carts the body to a quiet road
and slips on home, past swollen sacks of silage.
Later he will muck out the boot of his Sierra,
daylight clinging to his hands.

Maybe it was 1970

Kids my age play real soldiers,
dashing milk bottle bombs against tanks,
binlids for shields.
"That gun's as big as thon wee skitter."
Mummy turns up the sound.
I'm missing Crossroads, leave the room loudly
and slip behind the kitchen curtain
to search for Derry burning.
The news is too far away.

Maybe it was 1970.
Bernadette Devlin shouting.
She was a student and
she was a MP.
She was a cheeky wee monkey.

On the news Dad's shop burning down.
My mascara had run.

Maybe it was 1973.
The Reverend Ian Paisley
crushed through a window
on the telly.
His hand bled.
"For God's sake, this is madness. Go home."
How could a minister be bad?

Blood ran freely down his wrist
like roads,
like the red hand of Ulster
      severed.

I was fifteen.
Miss Duffin announced in assembly,
"If this doesn't stop very soon,
                  it's double maths on Friday afternoon."
The bombscares stopped.

Maybe it was 1977.
On the news Dad's shop burning down.
I was at Kelly's.
It came on in the bar.
I was in love with Shawn Logan.
I didn't know whether to kiss or cry.
I wanted him.   I wanted to go home.
He was much older.
He was a Catholic.
He held me in his car.
It was a BMW.
He tried to touch me.
"Don't," I said. "I've got a tampax in."
But I wanted him.
His words were pure love,
"I don't mind," he said.
My mascara had run.
I should have gone home.

Not everything was destroyed.
That was worse.
They sold the damage.
Salvaging charred dresses, odd shoes,
scalded mannequins.
Everything rained on.
Shawn chewed chewing gum.
So did I.

I looked at faces differently.
Daddy was quiet for a long time.

Summer Breeze

Every summer all the houses on Strand Road would hang striped cotton curtains outside their front doors. Some were faded turquoise and coral, others were sharp garnet, green and white. The grey concrete and peppered pebble dash became jaunty, almost dashing with these fluttering flags. People would argue with creaky deckchairs, angle them round to follow the rare sun and wave as we cycled past, their freckled necks wrinkling slowly into soft crepe.

I remember the surface of the roads as speckled pink, and on hot days, the glassy shimmer that slid in the air above the road seemed tinted. All the roads are tarmacked now. Black, even tarmac, dull as lead.

Emily Patterson lived in the last house before the beach. It was a big glass bungalow with an upstairs, so Emily insisted that it could never be a bungalow, but with its long, sloping roofs, wrought iron balconies and log-panelled walls, it did not resemble any other house. In our town, you lived in a house or a bungalow. Emily's house was neither. She probably thought of it as a villa. Strand View Villa. In school, some girls giggled that the Pattersons lived in a fish bowl and I imagine that was the first time Emily appeared bashful, instead of boastful about living in the largest, most modern dwelling along the coast. In art class, when asked to draw our homes, she sketched a square, two-up, two-down lie with a path like a smile which curved to the front door.

The Pattersons did not hang up a porch curtain in the summer. Instead they served cocktails on the lawn. Emily was enrolled to hand round little Spanish pottery bowls of Twiglets and salted cashews. Women with too much make-up and gold and men with skinny legs and cigar breath would talk about business, golf and the coveted view, which stretched over the cliffs, up a two-mile flat of sand and out into the bay towards the low, blue hills of Donegal. They would drink until the midsummer sun turned apricot and fell in a slow arc into the red Atlantic with the suspicion of a green flash. "Did you see it?" They would cry excitedly. "Did you?" Then Mrs Patterson, brittle with anorexia, would materialise with a bulging straw bag, Portugal 1972, full of assorted togs. Those who were drunk enough would strip off, pull on last year's swimwear, gallop over the garden, skid down the stone steps and launch into the cool, night sea. I would watch them from my bedroom window and know why my parents were not invited. Dad was a teacher. Mr Patterson owned the biggest meat-processing plant in Northern Ireland.

I don't remember meeting Emily. She was always there. Our parents would take turns to drive us to school. One day Emily's father would sweep up in his shiny, black Zodiac with its red leather upholstery and we would squabble over who would have the best seat, that squat square armrest that unfolded from the centre of the back seat. The next day, the Pattersons would scuff their shoes towards our house and we would all squeeze into our rusty, blue Ford Anglia. Once Emily advised us to buy a bigger car. She was neither haughty nor malicious, she simply had not yet made the connection between objects and money. Mum said Emily was spoilt rotten.

Emily was the first to collect my secrets. I suppose she was my best friend. I don't know at what age you actively select your friends, but there was a loyalty between us that neither of us questioned. Emily was prettier than I was, with her long, blonde hair, pale green eyes and slim, flat nose. She said she inherited her looks from the French Huguenots. I didn't argue. Mum said her eyes were sleekit, but that was only because of how Emily behaved around Rory. Emily would give me tips she'd gleaned from her mother's glossies on how to straighten my hair, invent cheekbones, conceal spots. Emily had clear, sallow skin. She convinced me that lemon juice would remove freckles. It didn't. Emily did Enid Blyton kind of activities, like horse-riding and elocution and knew how to persist with a cuticle remover.

I had only one thing that Emily did not have, that Emily wanted — an older brother. Rory was two years older than us. His dark curly hair grew down over his eyes, forcing an intellectual pose as he knitted his eyebrows to peer out. He had a soft mouth and his long chin jutted out making his neck seem very thin. I think he was handsome.

It wasn't until Rory went to Grammar School and his voice started to croak mid-sentence that Emily took any interest. Before, he was simply the tallest, strongest member of our gang. Once hormones drove him into sullen solitude, moody outbursts and heavy metal, Emily was fascinated. After school she'd linger on the wall outside our house waiting for Rory's bus to take the corner. Rory ignored her. She'd pester me on the phone for revelations about him. I'd tease her with unrelinquished details, her curiosity giving me power. For the first time I enjoyed being his subaltern. I became a spy, studying the furious energy which erupted on Rory's face in red lumps, the hair thickening on the backs of his hands, the damp, single sock under his bed.

Looking back on it, I doubt if Emily really fancied Rory. He was merely the first boy she knew well enough to track the course of adolescent male desire and it made her acutely aware of how she performed femininity. I would observe her develop and adapt like a lizard, honing advice columns on the art of passive seduction. I'd see her roller skate down the road to our house, her body agile, lean and fit, then she'd deflate, lounge languidly watching afternoon television, waiting for Rory to emerge from his room for a coffee. Then she would perk up, wrap her legs around each other and lean forward, her wrist bent neatly under her chin in an attitude of attentive wonder. I'd noticed her mother sitting that way. If Rory noticed, he never let it show.

The Saturday after my thirteenth birthday, Rory said he was going to explore O'Loughlin's farm which had lain empty for almost two years. He asked if Emily and I would like to come. I remember the way he stood by the sink, ineffectually rinsing his coffee mug, struggling to appear nonchalant. I was sitting on one of the formica worktops, banging my heels softly against a cupboard door. It was a hot, sunny day. I could hear the fridge hum and throb. The house was filled with that quality of quiet it sometimes had, as though nobody had lived there for a long time and we were noisy, obtrusive ghosts in the heart of its stillness. You could feel the dust fall. "OK," I said and went to ring Emily.

As Rory and I walked up Strand Road to Patterson's, a car drove past, its windows down, a song wafting from its radio like the evening smell of stocks. "Summer breeze makes me feel fine, blowing through the jasmine of my mind . . ."

"The Isley Brothers," Rory said, then whistled the tune as we walked along. Swallows scissored overhead. I could hear the whir of a lawn mower in the distance. As we grew closer, we could make out Emily perched on the stone pillar at the gate, her legs twisted round it. She was gazing out to sea to great effect, like a mermaid on a rock. Cars snaked in a queue on to the beach and boys honked their horns, yelling out to Emily to come skinny-dipping. Emily waved the little, flat circular wave she'd recently perfected. She had sunglasses on. They kept slipping down her nose.

The smell of cut grass greeted us at Patterson's, Emily's dad journeying back and forth, sweat running from beneath his Mexican straw hat. He waved absent-mindedly.

"Hi Barbara, Hi Rory," called Emily at a time when everybody else still said hello. She wore a pink T-shirt, with matching shorts and sandals. She tucked her honey hair behind her ears, flicked it over her shoulders, only to pull it down straight by her cheeks again. Strands of it floated up from her skin with static. Her face and arms were golden but her legs were streaked orange with fake tan. It wasn't until I drew nearer that I noticed her eyes. The next time her glasses slipped, I saw that she had smudged silver green eyeshadow on her lids. It made her look like a young reptile with protruding hoods of skin. I shivered then blushed, flustered by a response that swung from embarrassment to envy. She seemed like a glamorous city runaway. I could tell she was nervous when she persistently cleared her throat. She'd just cultivated an odd little cough as though she was apologising for herself.

"Isn't the sea pretty today?" she asked in a rehearsed way. It was. It was lucid, glass-green with almost soundless baby waves that rolled under its surface then unfurled in neat uniform lines and rippled silently back again. Further out, clots of maroon seaweed darkened the water and still further away, aquamarine reflections settled on the calm. Heat hung in a vibration above the rows of parked cars on the beach, their territories staked out in bands of coloured windbreaks. Inishowen was a mauve haze. There was no salty wind.

Three boys tumbled out of the sandhills. In the sandhills were men, the kind who took down their trousers when you came by, the ones whose faces scrunched up with fear like a bad smell. We were forbidden to play there.

We turned away from the beach and trudged silently across the meticulous grass of the golf course. Occasionally we had to duck behind clumps of furze or scurry into a scalloped bunker whenever a posse of golfers came into view. I crushed a handful of yellow gorse, inhaled almonds. We crouched, hugged our knees, suppressed giggles, felt marram grass prick our calves. Rory was forward scout. Emily and I waited for his signal in fake trepidation. We'd dart behind him, sticky with anticipation which stretched between us like a viscous liquid, as we bonded with giddy screeches and more cursing than usual. Rory peeled off his green shirt. He had a T-shirt tan. His torso looked dead and cold it was so white. Thin sinewy muscles bumped down his arms. My shoulders were tingling with sunburn. I wished I could have taken off my top and draped it over them. I sniffed the skin on my forearm. It had the sparky smell of two flints knocked sharply together.

Emily walked with her hair piled on top of her head, her elbows out like fins. I copied her, but my hair sprang free. I searched for signs of Emily's underarm hair. It had gone. She had given up on her sunglasses and folded them into the neckline of her T-shirt which made it drop lower between her breasts. She wore a bra already. She slept in it to keep her bust firm. Rory once said that Emily could come to the Boy Scouts' party because she wore a bra. I never told her. I was not invited.

We climbed over the wooden fence that marked O'Loughlin's land. The bitter, heady scent of creosote clung to our hands. Cows tugged and chewed ploddingly, orange clips twitching in their ears, their tails chasing fat flies. A combine harvester droned in the next field. Emily took off her sandals and swung them with knowing grace at her side. I didn't imitate her. I thought if God gave me breasts I'd never pray for anything else ever again.

Emily stooped to pick buttercups and chubby, pink clover.

"C'mon," yelled Rory in his commando voice, "or we'll never get across the border before dark." Emily ran to catch up, her face serious, the flowers springing in her fist.

We followed a disused lane, trampling the long grass. Rory tried to behead dandelions with several vigorous kicks. Crickets clicked their tutting rhythm. When we reached O'Loughlin's farmhouse, Rory put his finger to his lips and whispered, "It might be booby-trapped. You girls stay back."

He inched along the hedge, then zigzagged towards the front door as if he were dodging a hail of bullets. The groundfloor windows were boarded up and grubby lace flapped like a surrender from a broken window upstairs.

Rory booted the door open needlessly and called, "Coast's clear", before he disappeared. Someone had embedded white shells, mother-of-pearl and sea-worn bits of coloured glass into the grey cement which framed the door. Emily paused un-selfconsciously to trace their curves and edges with her fingertips, but I was eager to shelter from the blaze of the sun.

The downstairs was cool and shaded. I blinked, smelt musty cloth, sour milk and catpiss. Rory had found a candle and lit it. "Good job I brought matches, eh?" He wanted a medal. The flame spat and wove into life. Slivers of sunlight fell on the tongues of wallpaper that curled from the walls. An old leather sofa spewed out its innards. Rory began to climb the stairs with exaggerated caution, shadowing the wall. The bannister rail had broken and the rails spindled in all directions.

Emily and I followed him cautiously into a bedroom. The floor was collaged with Jacob Cream Cracker wrappers, empty cans of Tennents and curd-encrusted milk bottles. There was a stove and a mattress covered in stained ticking.

Rory said it was an IRA hide-out and that he'd protect us when they came back. He opened the biggest blade of his Swiss Army knife and ran his thumb gingerly along it. I said nothing.

Rory brandished a tin of baked beans and hollered like a cowboy. He found a tin opener and laughed triumphantly. He tried in vain to light the stove till I flicked on the Kosangas canister and the blue flame licked the air, then drew back in to burn evenly. Rory slid like a sniper to the window and eased back the curtain. We watched as he dropped on the bed, his shirt bunched beneath his head. "Make the dinner."

I stirred the stiff beans. Emily said she was going next door to find water for her flowers. I saw Rory's eyes swivel and train on her. They had that shiny, glazed look that he used to have when he sucked his thumb. It made me cross my arms over my chest when he looked at me that way.

Emily came back smiling and holding a jam jar in which she'd arranged her clutch of wild flowers. She placed it on the window sill, then sat next to Rory. I thought the flowers would give us away but Rory seemed to have forgotten about our mission. I poked at the beans till they started to bubble and spurt their juice over the edges of the crooked tin.

"Bring it here Barbara." Rory thought he was a hard man.

Wrapping old net curtain round the tin, I carried it to the bed. Rory dove in his spoon and ate with excessive noise.

"We have to keep up our strength. The arms rendezvous's at midnight." Emily smiled and flicked back her hair. A mouthful of beans clogged my throat. Emily didn't eat any so Rory finished them off and lay down, patting the bed on either side. Emily and I lay down. I didn't know what else to do.

"You two sleep and I'll keep watch." Rory studied his watch seriously.

When I shut my eyes, I noticed the birdsong. A curlew's insistent call. The breeze rustled the copper beech outside the window. I could hear a fly or a wasp hitting the glass repeatedly. I couldn't hear Rory move but suddenly something shifted in the room. It was as though the heat intensified and the air was slowly expanding. It was a sickly, tangible presence of waiting, like watching a controlled explosion on the television. I began to drift on a dreamy warm excitement I did not want to end. My throat was dry and the beans furred my mouth. Rory's breath was growing faster, louder as though he was being chased in a nightmare. I didn't know if he was watching me and if there was a punishment for opening your eyes too soon. Sweat prickled at the hollow of my spine. My eyelids quivered into a thin slit and I looked to the left. Emily's eyes were closed tight. Rory was moving his hand up and down her bare thigh. As I watched, he nosed his fingers between her legs, circling and rising and diving in deeper. She tensed her legs but he managed to eel his way down to her crotch.

I shut my eyes again, trying to regulate my breathing. I wanted to get up and leave, yet the indolence that had descended on the room floated me along in its deep, undulating fever. I was shimmering above the bed, hovering as insubstantial as an electric current, my muscles luxurious with expectation. Emily didn't make a sound. Perhaps she was suspended too. I could feel sand trickle down to collect at the heel of my sandals. I needed to scratch my nose, but lay immobile as though my life was at stake. I sensed if I moved any pore of my skin, the spell would evaporate and the delicious rosewater in my mouth, between my legs, would end forever.

I was not surprised by what was happening beside me, but was unable to decide what enthralled me most — seeing my brother's desire more starkly than before or witnessing my best friend being touched for the first time. It didn't seem to puzzle me that I found myself imagining that it was my hand discovering the smooth, untanned flesh of Emily's inner thighs. My palms tingled and breath escaped through my mouth. I then realised that I wanted the sensation of fingers caressing my skin, burrowing into my pulpy insides. In a delirious, swirling amber film, I was his hand, her thighs, my own vagina burning to be pressed. I could feel its muscled walls flinch then turn inside out. I was pink and wet, my body all skinless, boneless need. I was dizzy, drawn on to a diagonal plane where my body spun and shrank, then grew large and distended into space.

Finally I shifted my feet and a little column of sand poured out onto the bed. I rubbed my nose and the tight, magnetic force that had held us snapped as though a cool wind had cut through the hot, still air. Rory bolted upright, his hand springing to his crotch, like I'd pulled a revolver. "What in the hell are you doing?" he fired at me, his voice vicious with interrupted lust. "Go down and guard the door." Spittle hung loosely at the corners of his cross mouth.

His lips were blood red.

Emily opened her eyes lazily. She seemed drugged. She coughed her nervous cough and laughed a little. He laughed too.

I thumped the wall as I stomped downstairs. The plaster crumbled along a crack. I could hear their laughter above me, Emily's echoing the tone of Rory's, dense with complicity. Free to whisper, their secrets mocked me like a flight of gnats. My eyes brimmed with a humiliation I had not yet learnt to channel into words. The swollen tension persisted between my thighs, like two bruised plums rubbing. For years I would associate that sensation with Emily and what happened next. When I wanted to touch myself, I would freeze, the taste of beans creeping up the back of my throat. That day I kicked it away against the soft leather flesh of the ripped sofa.

I couldn't say when the laughter changed to pleading, then sobbing, until a scream knifed through the floorboards. I scrambled upstairs, burst in to a pitched riot of screams and shouts.

Emily was crouched in the corner of the room, both hands buried between her legs, her eyes wild. Rory was bent over her, trying to haul her up.

"Leave her alone," I yelled and rushed to hold Emily. Rory stepped back. Emily was shaking, her teeth rattling like dry bones. She smelt salty.

"Mummy, he wouldn't stop," she cried over and over.

"I never touched her," Rory spat in protest.

I looked over to the mattress where blood spread like a

rose. Emily's shorts and knickers lay inside out on the floor, their hems rimmed with fake tan.

"Get out of here, you big, stupid fuck." Orange flecks sparked in my eyes and my throat bulged.

Rory was flapping his arms. His flies were undone and he looked like he had woken in someone else's bomb damage. His eyes were bewildered as though he had just lost everyone he loved, all he owned.

"Look, I said I was sorry, Emily." His hands trembled as he swept them through his hair.

"You'll not tell will you?" His voice was a thin blade. "Tell her not to, Barbs. I thought she was playing along. Honest to God, I did."

Emily rocked to and fro as Rory gunned down the stairs. I could feel her heart thumping against her back as though it was going to break out and splatter against the wall. I told her it would be all right. Stroked her hair. Pushed it gently away from her face. She looked riddled with disbelief, the candour in her face crushed into thousands of tiny shards. Her arms were locked like crab pincers. She wouldn't move her hands as though part of her body would fall away if she were to uncover the place where she'd been hurt.

I had never seen her cry. The green eye shadow bled in wet streaks across her temples like diaphanous seaweed. My glance caught the flowers on the windowsill which had wilted, their petals limp, heads fallen.

Emily and I made a pact of silence and eternity. We mumbled The Lord's Prayer to embolden its solemnity. Fear punched the ball of my stomach, then slipped into my skin.

I was a cold and bloodless sea creature with no eyes, just tentacles and a sense of motion. I knew the size of the world, the weight of it and no one in it. I thought I would never know anyone again.

In early September, the porch curtains were taken in, washed, ironed, starched and folded away. Emily didn't get a lift to school with us anymore. She made friends with Helen Munro and moved her desk next to hers. She seemed to get fatter. That winter, the Pattersons moved to Portaferry. Their house was pulled down a couple of years later to build four neo-Georgian town houses and three holiday apartments.

Recently I heard that Emily had left her husband and was living outside Dublin with another woman. We never kept in touch but I think of her, especially when the sea is quiet and pretty. Rory is married in Canada. He's got three lovely little girls. His wife sends those photo Christmas cards every year, showing the children, all in red dresses, smiling in the snow.

Joan Bridget

Joan Bridget was born in Ireland and moved to Canada in 1975. She has been writing since she was about fifteen, off and on, mostly on. During recent years Joan has belonged "to a wonderful writing group" called Womyn's Work and, together with the two founding members has recently started a journal for women's writing called *Diviners*. She has been published in three collections of stories: *Lesbian Bedtime Stories* edited by T. Woodrow; *By Word of Mouth* edited by L. Fleming; and *The Courage to Eat* edited by R. Albrecht, K. Brown, L. Douglass, N. Gately & Z. McLachlan.

Seeing Stars

Some say it started when she was twelve but I know it didn't. When she was twelve she was a nerd and nerds don't do that. It started much later, the night she climbed up on the roof and spun around looking up at the stars. I was there and I was scared she would get dizzy and fall off on to the concrete in front of the garage door. But I was scared of most things then and was only up on the roof with her because I had nothing else to do and had only a nerd to talk to.

She stopped being a nerd that night. Or she became a different kind of one, or maybe I just saw her in a different light. She spun wildly and out of control and laughed out loud. When she stopped spinning she said: "I am the world, spinning, spinning and I make it all happen." For a minute I believed she did. She looked like a pagan priestess calling up legions out of the sea or something. I was awe struck and became part of her mystery that night. You see, I believed then she had something special and I never thought she was odd or mad or a nerd again. She dared, you know? Back then I didn't dare much and was curious about rebels and outcasts, even if they were nerds, even if they were dangerous and evil. But that night I came to something new — I began to sense power, real power, the power to be something private that I might or might not show as I choose.

I knew she had power then and that she often hid it behind her clean dress and shining shoes and the tidy braids that she let loose that night. The hidden part of her was out and it was strong and invincible and name calling couldn't get at it.

It took people years to figure out that she had something special and when they did they feared it — felt she should be shunned and brought into line and made to care about what they wanted her to be. But she wouldn't. She tossed her hair and her shoulder and went her own way. They blamed her for the fires set in town that winter. She set fires all right, but not such puny ones that could be put out by a few gallons of water and old men beating flames with their coats. Her fires were set true and set to last a lifetime.

They said it started when she was twelve, her strangeness and the fires, but they were wrong on both counts. She knew for years she could change herself and didn't bother until the night on the roof when she spun and spoke and created a lifetime of trouble for us both. If she even knew my trouble I couldn't say, but she did start it.

She didn't fall off the roof, and laughed at me because I though she might. I was scared, for me as well as for her, because it was strange to me to see that perfect little lady let loose that way, hair flying out around her head and her clothes off. I was jealous and wanted it to be me, I wanted to feel the dizzy freedom of night air and stars all over me. Years later, old enough to know better and not act it, I went naked out into the rain at a summer cottage and felt her with me, felt the push she gave so slyly and so persuasively to me that night on the roof.

Falling Asleep with Strangers

I love to fall asleep with people moving about and talking around me. Maybe it comes from lying in my mother's arms when I was a baby, but I still like to curl up on the couch and fall asleep with people chatting around me. Waiting rooms are the same, and buses. Commuting every day is a real drag, the only good thing being that I can fall asleep in public. It is really reassuring, somehow — feels safe. The television doesn't work so well to lull me, but the radio does. These ones that have a sleep button are just lovely, set it to turn off in an hour and just fall asleep over my book. Unfortunately, when the radio turns off, the silence is really loud and wakes me.

Falling asleep over a book is another treat. All my books are dog-eared and crumpled. Ali says she always knows when I have been reading a book, just by the look of it! I also like when she gently takes the book out of my hand or from under my cheek, turns off the light. I wake only for a moment and not completely, but feel comforted by the action. My mother did that too, and many, many times I have seen my Dad fall asleep over books, so I come by the habit honestly, as the Ma would say.

Twilight is another one of the things that makes life worth living. Especially at home (where is home anyway?) where it lingers for hours. I remember especially those long summer twilights. After dinner the Da would do the gardening, Ma would work in the kitchen — I can see her now ironing away — I would read and we would talk a bit now and again, and listen to the radio. I felt like a dog lying by the hearth with one ear cocked to listen for the magic word. About half past eight or nine I got it. "Let's go for a walk", the Ma would say, and I would be up like a shot.

We didn't have special walking shoes, and shorts, and watches, and sweatbands. We just walked out the back door, said goodbye to the Da, opened the creaky back gate and we were free. We picked carefully our route out of the neighbourhood, if we didn't we could be thwarted in our walk by chats with Mrs Callanan, or Mrs Green, or ten or twelve other folk hanging out over the garden fences. I could never relax until we had cleared the last house of the neighbourhood, because Mrs Heskin lived there and we could be stuck for hours!

Finally we stepped off the white city pavement on to the dark, soft tar of the country road, the thuck, thuck of the tennis from the club sounding across the field. We strolled out past the old mill, where my brother had stepped on glass and a farmer carried him back to the farm and took the glass out, bandaged him up and took him home in the horse and trap. On past Sandy Creek, which was pronounced crick and that's what I thought it was until I was quite old. We paddled there during the summer, and walked barefoot along the road, stepping on the soft melted tar pieces whenever we could because the road was rough. We took the tar marks off with butter when we got home.

Ma would talk as we went, or we would occasionally stop to talk to the farmer near the mill. I never really listened to what was said. I watched the horse as it moved its feet restlessly and chewed on the bit. Now I move my feet in a similar way if I have to stand for any period of time, I wonder if the horse's feet hurt? We went along past the soldiers' houses and this was the last distraction to our five mile walk. After the soldiers' houses it was open country.

By the time we reached the lane we turned on to start circling back, darkness hung in the air like smoke. The linnets, crows, finches sounded quietly in the trees and bushes. The air had the calm that comes with the end of day, business done, and the settling in for the night underway.

My mother talked about when she was young, but I don't remember much of it, only that I would sometimes ask her the name of a flower or plant and she would look at it and say, "The common or garden name is . . ." and off she would go, the Latin name, the plant family, its properties and medicinal/ poisonous quality. I asked her once how she knew all that, she had never been to school much past about sixteen. She told me she had learned it at school. They went on walks and picked plants that they took back to the classroom and pressed and then learned the Latin names, and all the rest of it. She talked a lot about the school, the outside toilets and the rats that ran underneath. Mostly I only half listened. What I was out for was just the companionship of walking together, to listen to the night sounds, to watch the dark gather in the air and the clouds change. I was supremely happy then, and believe that these walks drew my mother and I together, in a way that no amount of talking could.

Soon we reached the outskirts of the city again. It was nearly dark now, about 11:30 or so. We collected the Da from the garden on the way in and had tea and went to bed, completely at one with the world.

I still love to walk, and still prefer a circular walk outside the city. I wish I had paid more attention to my mother's talk and the plant names. But I didn't. I built up for myself a store of memories and moods, an understanding of each shade of nightfall, and a love of nature that still gives me pleasure, and I can sense the presence of the Ma walking along singing or talking in places she will never travel.

Ailbhe Smyth

Ailbhe Smyth is a writer, critic and activist and Director of the Women's Education, Research and Resource Centre (WERRC) at University College Dublin. She has written or edited several books about women in Ireland, including an anthology of contemporary Irish women's writing, and is co-editor of *Women's Studies International Forum*. She loves Dublin, has a nineteen-year-old daughter who lives in Belfast, and is passionately committed to women and to feminism.

Girl Beaming in a White Dress

I had been thinking about growing up in Ireland in the 1950s and 1960s, a good and proper middle-class girl, moving through the hoops of hetero-patriarchy, my head leading me one way, my body another, and altogether astray between them both. Then a postcard came: "For Ailbhe, a friend of mine in a white dress." There she was, Frida Kahlo: "Frida in a white dress", proud and sturdy, a little withdrawn, absorbed by whatever she saw, beyond the camera's range. Seen but not framed.

There I am,
still
and for all time,
shiny baby curly hair
(brushed with care)
bright Fair Isle cardy
(knitted with love),
tightly strapped into
*   my highchair*
(restrained by ditto
*   and ditto)*
absorbed by whatever they gave me
to keep me quiet for
the future, I mean the camera,
fixing me for them and for me
"Do be a good girl"
(What did they think I came here to do?)

Maybe they said it
sotto voce, Irish-style
compliments not being our forte
"What a dotey wee girl"
I was never wee
or dotey
and that's the truth
but they taught me very well how to be
a good learner
keen to please to prove to improve
ready to be primed, primped, preened
by all their principles
they did it for love
I did it for love
for they loved me, yes, and I loved them
which just goes to show how love
can lead us all astray
but they knew best and I knew nothing

"The best things in life"
they said "are free"
(a lie if ever I heard one, which is not at all what
    I thought then)
Although they never said
what they were
or how to find them,
a quirk of honesty, I suppose,
giving me an appetite
for the real thing that keeps me going
still

"It's a free country"
they told me
frequently lying through their principles
in more ways than one
"You were born free and more's the pity"
but that's what schools are for
to strap you in
you have to learn
to learn to be
be quiet be good
be neat be nice
feel free to be
whatever we tell you
we need you to be
just don't be
don't do
don't feel
free
free from sin
free to keep
my mouth shut gloves on knees crossed
keep me free from sin
"Do be a good girl"

"Bless me Father, for I have sinned"
(What is sin at seven?)
they told me about sins
seven and deadly
kindly gave me names for what I'd never done

never heard never feared
"1 2 3 4 5 6 7
Some day I will go to heaven
Wash my hands and brush my hair
Say my prayers
And fly up there"

*The photograph touches me
   to the quick*
still
*"Girl beaming in a white
   dress with handbag,
   aged 7 years and 2
   days"*
*so proud and pleased and
   plump, sturdy and
   strong*
*feet firmly planted on solid
   ground*
*strapped into my Clarks'
   sandals*
all the world before me
*full of sin and temptation
   indeed*
*but mine mine mine for
   the taking*
*I believed in my freedom
   and the power of seven*
I loved that girl

Just remember
"You get what you pay for"
which didn't fit
with the first lot
but nothing ever did,
properly
don't run don't shout
don't swear don't grab
in the free world
don't talk in church in class in adult company
don't ever talk out or up or back
don't take liberties don't let them take liberties
("she's a bad lot, that one")
don't ask what liberties are
don't ask what bad is
don't ask what sin is
don't sin
don't let us down
"Do be a good girl"

"That girl shows what she eats"
He aimed his blow with vicious accuracy
it came so fast I never knew what hit me
sliming me with self-disease
I couldn't eat for years
no one told him off
the premises
and out of my mother's house
where I never quite grew up
or into the woman I would become

I was twelve and tender
still
open as a book or a breeze
"Hail Mary, full of grace,
Tuesday's child is fair of face
Her sense of self thou shalt not erase"
but they did
indeed, and in word
then I saw myself as I was seen
through him and them and never me
seen and framed

Filial piety being what it was
(still?)
I believed the lot
every first and last mouthful
swallowed whole
I was raised in (their) good faith
on plentiful precepts
dollops of thick common sense
to fatten me up for
surviving my life
in this vale of tears
prior to the pleasures of the hereafter

Of course, they said,
"It's not a bed of roses"
(heaven forbid you'd dream of roses)
"You make it and you lie on it"
straight as a die until the day you die

close your eyes and think of
all the freedoms you've never seen
strapped into your life
"Do be a good girl"

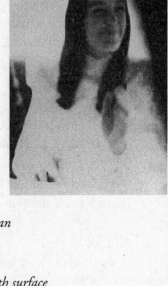

I take out that
*   other photograph*
run my fingers over
*   its smooth surface*
testing it for traces of panic
*   and pain*
"Woman gleaming in a
*   white dress with husband,*
*   aged 24 years in a daze"*
"Jesu que ma joie demeure"
they played, because
*   I wanted it to be true*
knew it was a lie before it began
wanted out before I was in
wept before I had cause
No, I didn't weep on my smooth surface
diminished in body and spirit
I stood there weeping inside
for what I had done, and was about to do,
for the imminent loss of the freedoms I had never seen
and the.power of seven
"Thank Thee Lord for the gifts we are about to receive"
theirs to give and withhold
I loathed that woman

"Why did you do it?
It's a free country
You didn't have to go through with it"
No? What do you know of me and mine
if you can tell me that?
It took me years to erase
all trace of the gleaming weeping woman
to cut her back to nothing
excise her from the picture
I banished her from my life
could not bear her presence in my past
It took years
to grow up that beaming child
to make her strong again
she's the freedom I've kept hold of
through all the daze of contradictions
through thick and thin

All that wisdom
to ward off the hard knocks
the ups and downs
and all the rest
of which there is none (anyway)
for the wicked
(yes, they said I was wicked
when they saw what I had undone
the woman I had become)
Maybe it did soften the blows
and ease the heart

but stuffed my head and blocked the flow
of whatever it was that made me
tick
(at least I think it did
when it's gone
you don't know if you've had it
good or bad)

It comes back from time to time
you can't keep a good thing
or is it a woman
down
the trick is to know it
although
"there's a price to be paid
for everything"
(still?)
and "everything has its price"
(if you believe that
you'll believe anything
I almost did)
so I'd take it with a grain
of salt
which is what I administered
in radical helpings (maybe it did)
to my dearest daughter ("but I'm your only one")

she grew up anyway
still
tense and tender
and beaming
as a girl can be
if she's left whole and entire
to be
I hope she is will be
I should try not to love her too much
not to lead her astray.

Lizz Murphy

Lizz Murphy. Poet. Publicist for publishers and other writers. Painter in a former life. Born Belfast, Ireland, 7 August 1950, says please send cards, cake and Irish whiskey. Lives in Binalong, Australia. Married to Bill with two gorgeous grown-up children, Aroona and Brendan, and one grandchild, Michaela.

Published widely in Australian journals and anthologies. By late 1996 she will have published five books — three anthologies and two collections of poetry. In 1994 she won the national Anutech Poetry Prize.

She has a great time writing and especially enjoys friend-ships and professional relationships formed with other writers, and sharing in their progress and achievements.

Growing a Language

As a wee girl I mixed with the Catholic girl across the road and couldn't see what the fuss was about — it was all the same God I said. At seventeen I wore a brooch which I hadn't even *noticed* was green, white and gold and I was advised to get rid of it because people would assume I was a Roman Catholic. The former fuss may have been a rarely voiced (in our family) seeping hatred, the latter a grandmother's concern for my safety. I dismissed her worries as an old person's hangover from a civil war which had happened years before and had nothing to do with me.

About eighteen months later, in 1969, the Troubles had broken out again and were to stay on embittering people's souls for another twent-five years or more. But by that stage I'd gone and *married* a Catholic and taken on his Catholic name, something that would mark me a lot more than a piece of jewellery you can take on and off. Later, to make a small feminist statement, I could've gone back to my own family name (Jamison), or maybe adopted my paternal grandmother's given name (Marya), but I make a political statement by sticking with Murphy. (I'm also still stickin with the fella but that's another story.)

In the early part of this relationship I was introduced to my culture. My Irish culture as opposed to the British subculture imposed upon us by British-Protestant rule and religion and an education which wrote Irish history, language and literature out of our lives. It's the language which I miss the most. I suspect what I am searching for in a poetic use of the English language can only be found in the Irish native tongue which I haven't lived with. I take heart though when I hear people talk about the unique way the Irish use even the English language.

I suspect this is why I took an arduous though colourful journey through a visual language before confronting the real issue, the seemingly unattainable. Now that I've confronted things I think the nearest I'll come to it (bar years of Gaelic lessons) is music. Luckily I found out at a young age, (and at great expense to my poor mother who forked out for piano lessons I didn't often attend), that I am not a musician, so I can't go running down the wrong road again.

My search continues. I listen to a lot of music. I decide I like vocals, the voice as instrument, so I listen to a lot of singers, mostly female. I've worked my way through from Joan Armatrading and Roberta Flack to k.d. lang and Bessie Smith and I love all of them. My all-time favourites though, their voices, their music, are Enya and Marianne Faithfull. Between them they have all the musical qualities I want in the language I write with.

We also have a lot in common. I have an affinity with Marianne's metaphors in, "Witches' Song": *Luck is bright as fire/Happy is a family/Lonely is a war* . . . and I *never stole a scarf from Harrods* either, ("Guilt"), but if I have the chance to visit London again, anything could happen!

Like Enya, in "Hope has a Place" I listen to the . . . *Whispering world/A sigh of sighs/The ebb and flow of the ocean tides.* I also hear dreams and poems in the murmurings of trees and the chatter of cicadas in their last seven days of life:

> *In the fuzzy air of January they emerge*
> *arrive in throngs to cocklebuzz on rough grey bark*
> *In the midst of frenetic activity they make lazy decisions*
> *winging like tiny black birds*
> *their circles outside our talk of shadows.*

A poem in progress. And frogs. Fat green frogs warkling in pipes and puddles.

I tape frogs and cicadas with my microcassette, but I rarely play them back. I don't need to. The sounds, sweet as petal scent, are in my head. They grow there. They are growing me my own personal language.

Paper Petals

*My wedding day started off with green paper rose petals
flung from the doorway of my grandmother's house as I
climbed into the black taxi. They hit me in a bunch,
smack in the back of the neck. I don't think it was
intentional.*

I was the grand old age of eighteen years when we borrowed
a friend's student discount card and bought a wedding ring.
The broadest one we could find as was the sixties' trend. We
had a quick ceremony in the local registry office followed by
champagne and a train to Dublin, where we got the last
available room in the city. Trust us to do it on the weekend
of the All Ireland grand finals! It was honeymoon bliss,
under the reproachful eyes of the good Lord crucified as
could only be expected at an Irish guest house called St
Joseph's, before hitch-hiking back home to Belfast.

St Joseph's was run by a white-haired woman with
crooked hands and a knowing look in her eye. She showed
us up to our room with it's big oak bed, linen sheets and a
window thrown open to one of Ireland's fairly blue skies.
There was that tantalising mix of warmth from the
household provided you lived up to expectations and the
chill that comes from airing out the last lot of guests. Often
mistaken for holiday atmosphere and a feeling of gay
abandon. Expectations were that you were good Catholic
citizens whatever part of the country you came from and
would attend Sunday Mass even on your honeymoon.

For those of us who didn't, there was the bright six o'clock wake-up call in the form of High Mass, broadcast over the Dublin airwaves full blast. It was so loud it reached every cranny from the ground floor to the attics. I was convinced that in spite of adopting my husband's Catholic name, she'd picked me in one. When we were wee girls we thought we could pick a Catholic walking down the street. Maybe Catholics thought the same about Protestants . . . and maybe they could! I was as uneasy as if I was in Belfast a year later and I was in danger of being tarred and feathered.

I sat at my place at the breakfast table and was relieved to see the heavy silver table-setting. After all it could've been wooden stakes. Although since I had passed under the wary eye of several dozen crucifixes and sacred hearts, and hadn't turned to ash, I felt it was time she relaxed. Breakfast was bacon and eggs, soda bread and potato farls, pure orange juice, pots of tea, toast and marmalade. It was served slowly and painstakingly by the arthritic guest-house owner who by way of apology said only, that she liked to do things herself. We knew better than to take the rattling crockery from her. We just held our breath and told ourselves she wouldn't still be doing it if the danger of spills was real.

We went off to discover Dublin's fair city leaving the bed unmade and scattered with personal things, not realising that the service included daily cleaning. When we came back we didn't know whether to be mortified at someone tidying up our pubic hairs or scared of being carried off to jail, our French letter packets evidence of criminal activity. We were now legally married, but condoms were still illegal in the South!

White Petals

1

A storm of white flowers with sun warm centres
waits silently for a bride white as leadlight windows
on an overcast afternoon
arching filigree-patterned edged in stained glass
green as the grass slopes below
yellow as stamens golden as tomorrow
a brighter day white petals fingering white lace

2

Poets spread themselves on lawns
under umbrellas red and magenta
read from paper white as petals
behind them snowtrails of climbing
roses engulf old stone and a woman
in white dress glides silently past
I walk to the other window stand close
heavy black leading makes small frames
of large scenes The woman in white reappears
near picnic blankets and folding chairs
looks furtive unreal
Now there is nothing but poetsong
and three white blossoms in trees
growing past a slategrey roofscape
I remember the straw hat she wore
and the books she carried close to her breast

Lizz Murphy

3
In the pond next to the chapel water lilies pinkfinger
the air Underneath they are white as new flesh
the water's surface still as ice latticed with shadowpoles
Here the women are black silouettes
nymphs sliding among reeds invisible to the naked eye
they play to the camera carry poems in their heads
and durry bags Inside is a long gallery of cellos
and poets' words observed by pale shoulders necks white
as candle wax elbows arched like windows in full light
Their words are falling petals

Good Fairy Bad Fairy

My grandmother told me how all eight of them would come home from school or work and sit around the fire after dinner, to be read to or told stories by their father. Our storytelling was usually limited to after birthday parties when everyone was too tired to play games but still reluctant to go home. In our house we'd sit around the fireplace in the parlour — a treat on its own — melting bowls of icecream till it was like milk and putting blankets over our heads for effect. Sometimes we'd debate whether fairies were real and what made a good fairy or a bad fairy, but sooner or later we'd get to ghost stories and who could tell the scariest one. Banshees were the best value mainly because we really believed in them and their high pitched wailing would be enough to give you the skitters as my grandmother would say. Though she didn't actually say that about banshees. I think she said it about a cat she disliked intensely, mainly because it always seemed to have the skitters.

For some people banshees were old women with long straggly hair and old rags for clothes. An old hag. The old hag features strongly in Irish mythology. But my banshee was something more mystical and much much bigger. In fact she reached right up the height of the sky, only appeared at night, and although we never actually saw her because we got ourselves away on time, I have seen the luminescent violets and golds of her evil aura. For my banshee didn't just warn of deaths before they occurred — she caused them. She especially liked wee girls out at night.

My Irishness

My Irishness began with a loud laugh
a thunder clap and a snap close purse

Filled with pink pearls strung
for half a crown Mountain rains softer
than wet earth and damper than the bogs
where banshees wait with large black
bats And the smell of children's fear
as strong as campfire smoke and the wail
deep inside your stomach

Mo Gaelachus

Thosaigh mo ghaelachas le scolgháire
blosc toirní agus sporán dúnta de smeach

Lán le péarlaí caoróg léana a chuirtear ar sreang
le leathchoróin fearthainne na Sléibhte níos boiga
ná'n talamh fliuch agus níos taise ná na portaigh
ina mbíonn na mná sidhe ag fanacht
le sciatháin leathair mhóra
agus boladh eagla na leanaí comh laidir
le deatach tinteán campa, agus an olagón
go domhain i do bholg

Translation by Eibhlín Ní Mhaolchaíráin

Wee Girls

for Aroona

When we were wee girls the curtains were
shell pink and sewn at home They matched the
carnation cushions but not the crimson lounge suite
or the yellow sewing stool or the fake brick wallpaper

When we were wee girls we sang to pop tunes new
but skipped to old rhymes and hand-me-down songs
the long rope twirling at our ambitions our wishes to
be boys play football wear jeans ride horses Through
streets of concrete Illusions

When we were wee girls we collected caterpillars
from privet hedges where they excavated homes
but not secret enough places We caused their
migration from earthy holes and leafy folds to sterile
glass spaces Jammed tight the lids None turned into
butterflies before our eyes and their deaths hung in
the stench that clung to our hands

When we were wee girls we ran through long grass
up at the plots We caught two buses to see her
father's chrysanthemums and to fill our jumpers
with stolen gooseberries We carried bows and
arrows and on rare warm days exposed our chests
and climbed dung heaps We never sank in

When we were wee girls we had jam sandwiches
for supper and sometimes warm milk but usually
strong tea and we didn't appreciate the fact that we
were fed at all We begged for sorry stockings and
shadow dregs Eyes tinted chartreuse and sapphire
lips purred peach pink bright red Worn out
suspender belts that no longer stretched to teenage
sisters' dreams Better than knotted elastic which let
down skinny unformed legs without notice

When we were wee girls we went to our first
teenage party Made it by days It showed Bosomy young
women gave kind glances over the shoulders of fellas we
fancied We settled for the two youngest in Pass the
Cushion They obliged with dry kisses and
we could tell they fancied the young bosomy women
They gave unkind glances to our still flat chests
When we were wee girls we passed the cushion that
matched our blooming cheeks and hopes for the
world but not the reality of the fake brick wallpaper

Sentiments

My grandmother was lacking in sentiment. She used to read the In Memorium columns and get furious at the silly rhymes and the money spent on flowers for dead people. If you're going to give me flowers give them to me when I'm alive and can smell them not after I'm dead and can't enjoy them she said.

When I got married she gave me a View of Boston plate, hand engraved, and strict instructions not to use it. It's for if it becomes valuable one day and then you can sell it for a lot of money and a look that said never mind any sentimental stuff. I've still got the plate and I'm very sentimental about it.

She had a pile of lumpy newspaper parcels down the side of the wardrobe. It looked suspiciously like a number of dismembered bodies. But it wasn't. It was a collection of gifts wrapped carefully against the ravages of time and time wasted in dusting. She was also practical.

Millies

My grandmother worked at the mill. She used to wear a shawl but only to walk to work. She made pacts with the other girls there but they always let her down. I didn't know my grandmother was a millie and made fun of them with my friends.

Tatts

My grandmother was a wise woman with tattoos. Several. Small and faded up and down her worn forearms. She also had eyes that were different colours. There are photographs of my grandmother slender and with height. Her chin jutted and she was always in black. The snaps were taken at funerals. Her children's.

Bobbing for Apples

Bobbing for apples on Hallowe'en is a risky business. You could drown for example or choke on laughter or apple pips. Being as unaware as you are during the process of dipping your face in a bucket of water chasing slippery wet and no doubt waxed apples around, you are also fair game for sneaky ghouls who may pounce on you and tear out your own apple. Adam's apple that is.

Poor Adam. Imagine listening to a dumb animal like a snake when he had all the advice of a free spirit who fashioned creatures out of the universe and people out of spare ribs. I wonder if the recipe for spare ribs came from God or if Eve being female stereotyped herself into a grass blade kitchen fully appointed in natural timbers with outdoor garden setting for sunny days. Hence one of the days of the week becoming known as Sunday for short.

Of course this was also the word for icecream Adam's favourite dessert, until Eve said if you don't partake of this apple like Snake says, I'll chop up your nuts and feed them to you with your sundae.

Speaking of Eve

Speaking of Eve — trust a male god to give her a figure like that. No thought of the swimming costumes that wouldn't fit, the price of a forty-six inch Double D bra or the inconvenience of having to get them ordered in especially, the stares in the street, the poking fun. She may have been Eve mother of all children but surely he didn't think she had to breastfeed them all herself.

It never occurred to him that Eve would feel uncomfortable. That they would hurt in the night as she rolled on them or they dragged themselves back on to the mattress if she was prone belly-up. That in the end she wouldn't go swimming or want to play squash because she was convinced everyone was staring at her. And they were. No wonder she spent her time speaking to snakes.

Sabbath

Sundays were all Sunday School and chicken soup. Since the chicken started off in the butcher's window hanging by its feet with its head and neck feathers still intact along with its innards, Sundays were also chicken foot pantomimes sitting by the fire.

When the chickens were chopped off at the knees their yellowed claws could be manipulated by pulling on the tendon, which appeared like pearl white embroidery thread in the centre of the cut limb. We clawed and crowed our way through dialogues about as interesting as tapioca but it kept us as enthralled as bystanders at a car accident.

Good Women

Good women bend at the knee in church and at roadside tragedies paying heed to the sick and dying. Good women do St John's Ambulance courses and have their handbags stolen from the scene of the accident as they administer to the hurt.

The first aid instructor carries an ironed white handkerchief in his breast pocket in case he has to give mouth-to-mouth. He says their faces are blue and purple and it helps. If they have a cut artery in the leg shove your knee in their groin he said and don't be afraid to break ribs if it gets the heart going. Another, a hospital doctor, said for varicose veins raise the leg right up above the head. If there are veins in both legs raise the other one right up too. Oh but I suggest you make sure the victim is sitting down first.

On the bus one day two good women who were volunteer St John's Ambulance officers were discussing their uniforms. They both agreed the wide trousers in heavy black material made them all look like Charlie Chaplins.

Dying

I face death. I always thought it would be like drowning in blue silk and instead I am swathed in thick black serge as three Charlie Chaplins tap me and test me stem my blood. They splint my broken limbs with their walking sticks and twitch their moustaches and walk funny to take my mind off the pain. I can face death but I can't face this bad acting.

Deadmen's Eyes

The bad smell that has lingered in the vicinity
of the family pet all day has surfaced shown
itself probably of its own accord It's that sort
of thing The weak-stomached male has grown
up with death but can't handle this decay Has
knocked on neighbours' doors to see your dead
husband missus tells deadmen stories says your
nibs would steal the pennies off a deadman's
eyes Has seen plenty

She who has not seen death says never mind
I will get rid of the thing like graveyard dirt
shrivelled to the dead-umber of a Gleeson
painting that tears at your fears and fills your
mouth with bilewater your lips dry as chilling
tales told on the evil edge of twilight It will be
the death of me touching this rotted part carcass
already leather grotesque with four limbs and
one feather Sculpture from alien movie set or
old man's glove storm-soaked twisted left to
dry-die dank misshapen

Did it just move?

Time Out

A rodent has ventured into the laundry panting
from the effects of Bromakill
I am to put it out of its misery as no one else
can do it I overestimate the weapon and it takes
a number of strikes goes the clock and the
marble mantelpiece marvels at my inadequacy

How can someone bludgeon to death a human
being I think in my sunk stomach yet it
happens all the time Maybe like me they started
a job that they realized had to be finished No
going back Expediency in murder essential to
killer's sanity

Today I leaf through old photographs musty in
their albums generations snapped in black and
white then colour of varying quality and tints
Eyes red and bright as glass In some homes the
children are snapped in silver and wood frames
arranged on pianos hung on walls in halls like
trophies see my catch Weddings too

The two-sidedness of this family is never more
evident We merged Catholic and Protestant
His merged Irish and Italian
Hers merged somewhere along the line why
else did the grandfather curse them from his
deathbed And curse indeed for health and
wealth they saw neither Struck down and black
drapes hung over stopped hearts Excuse me is
that yours or mine No mine's ticking must be
yours Darn I'm out of time

The Planet Next Door

I woke amid hot morning rays to a droning
neighbour her voice an invasion from The
Planet Next Door Later I sat in my room
listening to the monotone persist Dark draped
my shoulders and ushered me back and she
was still there

The monologue interluded only with splices
of younger words Has she spoken from her
wise kitchen the whole day all evening Will
she speak wisdoms the whole night

Does she sleep or cast a continual spray of But
anyways and See that there and Isn't the wee
mite just like his mother Doting A cocoon of
floating phrases entwined in daily living

The walls of silk spun from such talk tie
families together units immune to the world
and industrial disturbances As long as the pay
packet comes in

Not so distant trains rattle through the curtains
of moonlight whispers revealing synthetic
fibres with flaws and claws I sit in the green
carriage conscious of peeling paint and pissy
smells A drunk offers unwelcome company
A hoodish guy is generous with dope drags
in small tins entrepreneurial investments

A Brother in AI&S* blue trousers and safety
shoes spills from his armchair the anger of a
city's recession Political disillusions Factions
fractioned Class distinctions Class definitions
Reality hits hard reinforces aloneness
We stand alone all of us
Chiselled from sea washed cliffs toes grasping
at shifting sands the salt water creating a
greater thirst The neighbour spins protection
around her primitive moulds upright in the brick
cave sunlight blundering through askew
venetians One rocks from side to side
mimicking beaten coastlines as she unravels
reels of invisible fishing line and pins her
offspring down like Gulliver
She says to the different one its edges more
honed its intellect near bursting
Set up that barbecue and everything will be
all right There's no place out there for you
and her kindly eyes turn into laughing sea
anemones that suck at the fantasies of dreamers

Dreams shatter hard edge boundaries Make
young women punch ribs in picket lines

---

* Australian Iron and Steel Ltd.

Bub Bridger

Bub Bridger was born in Napier, New Zealand in 1924. She has published one collection of poetry, *Up Here on the Hill* (1989). Her short stories have been published in over twenty anthologies and performed on radio in New Zealand, Australia, Britain and Canada. She has written for and acted on television. Bub has four children and seven grandchildren.

Once Upon a Time

I was born in Napier, New Zealand, a long time ago . . . My mother, Eileen, was half Maori but brought me up as a pakeha (white). My father, John, was Irish.

My mother was a sad lady who resented me bitterly because I was very much a Maori-looking child, with black hair, dark eyes and olive skin. Her first two children were boys — one red-haired, grey-eyed, the other brown-haired and hazel-eyed. But I was a constant reminder of her illegitimate background and she could never forgive me.

My Irish dad was born in County Tyrone in 1883, at a wee place called Douglas Bridge, (he called it, *Dooglies* Bridge), which is just north of Newtonstewart. He had three years of schooling then went to work on the estate of the absentee landlord, the Duke of Abnercorn. He was eight years old. His drunken father was an itinerant labourer who only came home when he was penniless. Who beat his wife when she became pregnant and beat his children for being born. Despite rearing her large family of eight, my grandmother worked as a servant until she was dying. And when I was in Ireland in 1984, I visited the house where she had been employed for many years until her death. The lady of the house who spoke with a posh English accent, viewed me coldly as I stood on her doorstep, and although she softened enough to finally talk to me, she kept me standing on that lower step. I was the grand-daughter of her parents' servant and she made sure I knew my place. She told me she remembered my grandmother working for her parents and that when

Grandmother was dying, she as a little girl took freshly baked scones to her, wrapped in white linen in a wicker basket. She didn't offer me as much as a glass of water . . .

But despite his lack of formal education, my father loved books. It was from him that I inherited my passion for reading and all his favourite authors became mine too. The first poem I ever read was Oliver Goldsmith's, *The Deserted Village*. I couldn't understand it, but that didn't matter — the magic of it stunned me. At five years I was drunk on words.

At seventeen he worked his passage to Australia and then on to New Zealand where he eventually met my mother when he was in his early thirties and she was just sixteen. They were married a year later.

He never ever earned enough money and he resented those who did. He called them, "Dirty, rotten, bloody capitalists!" During the Depression, my mother worked in the laundry at a lodge for young women one day a week, and sometimes she got casual employment spring cleaning the homes of the rich. At local horse-race meetings she got work in the kitchen and loved those days. So did my brothers and I — because she would bring home the leftover pies, and buns and cakes! It was a wonderful change from the daily porridge, and bread and jam and stewed vegetables. When I asked why I didn't get any meat, Mother replied, "You're a girl. You don't need it!" And that was that!

I left school at fourteen and went to work the following year in a hat factory. I was the worst hat maker in the world, and how happy the boss must have been when I left to work in a tobacco factory. And then we moved from Napier to Wellington where I pretended I was educated and got a job in an office. Wellington, the capital city, built on one of the most beautiful harbours in the world was a marvellous place for a wide-eyed eighteen-year-old. At twenty-three I married the wrong man there and had four children before I gathered them all up and ran away . . .

But that's another story.

A Wedding

In year nineteen hundred and thirty-six, Aunty Prue married our insurance man. His name was Mr Armitage. He was an Englishman, a widower, tall and fair and always beautifully dressed in pale silk shirts and salt-and-pepper suits. He came to see us more often than his job warranted, but nobody minded because we all liked him. He was clever and kind and funny in a gentle way and he brought Cotton and me cigarette cards and paper twists of acid drops. They got married in our front room. Aunty Prue wore a honey coloured dress and blue coat with a little feathered hat and blue shoes that hurt her. She looked plain and nice and she looked happy. Mr Armitage looked a complete stranger in a dark suit and white shirt. It was the first time we'd ever seen him in anything other than a Donegal tweed.

• • •

We had no idea about him and Aunty Prue at first. We had no idea about anybody and Aunty Prue. She was nearly forty — quiet and ordinary and selfless. Not like Mama. Beautiful laughing Mama who turned men's hearts over with a look. I guess we thought it was really Mama Mr Armitage came to see. Then when Aunty Prue told us she was going to marry him, we were shocked. She was ours — and now she was going to marry the insurance man.

• • •

"Who'll give her away?" Vanny wondered.

275

"What do you mean, 'give her away'?" I asked.

"She has to have someone give her away at the wedding."

I knew nothing about weddings — "What for?"

"It's traditional," Vanny explained. "The bride is always given away to the groom. It's usually the father."

"Oh well," I said, "there's only Mama and Gram. It had better be Gram."

Vanny looked pained. "It has to be a man — you loony twit!"

I quailed from her scorn. And then I thought about it.

"One of the fathers, then."

She pursed her mouth thoughtfully, then shook her head.

"Their wives wouldn't like it," she said.

"But they're our fathers," I persisted.

She nodded. "Yes, they are," she said, but this is Aunty Prue's wedding, not ours."

I went to ask Aunty Prue who would give her away. She said Mr Green from the office. Mr Green was a small grey man with a stoop and I would much rather it had been one of our handsome fathers.

"Why can't it be a father?" I asked.

"No," said Mama, "that wouldn't be right. It's up to Prue to choose. And anyway, I wouldn't know which one to ask." Mama never did know which one to choose.

• • •

Until she was a girl of eighteen, Mama and Aunty Prue lived with their parents in the same street as the gas works. The

Heron twins worked for the gas company. Every day they walked past the house and eventually they saw Mama. And they fell in love with her. And Mama fell in love with them. Both of them. They were exactly alike and she never bothered to discriminate. When she found out about Vanny they both wanted to marry her but she couldn't bear to choose. Grandfather insisted that she marry one or the other and in desperation she ran away. Aunty Prue and the twins found her in a tiny room in the city and Aunty Prue said she would run away too, and they would find a house together. Aunty Prue was twenty-one and she had a good job, so they would manage, she said. And they did. Grandfather never forgave either of them. He forbade Gram to have anything to do with them, but when Vanny was born Gram sneaked away to the nursing home with lots of things she had been secretly making ever since Mama ran away. The Heron twins were there, both delirious, and Mama held a hand of each. In the background, Aunty Prue held Vanny. She didn't care what Grandfather thought or which twin was the father, she just held Vanny and let the love flow. Five years later, I was born and Aunty Prue went through it all again. Mama and the Heron twins made the babies, but Aunty Prue made a home for us and filled it with comfort and love. In between me and Cotton, Grandfather died and the twins got married. They waited a long time for Mama to make up her mind, but she never could. So they married sisters which was the closest they could get to the relationship they had with Mama and then went right back to the old set-up. Mama loved them more than ever and when I was seven,

Cotton was born. She is Mama's favourite. Vanny and I are both redheads like Mama, but Cotton, with her grey eyes and thick dark hair is the image of our fathers. Vanny has always been Aunty Prue's favourite I think, but Vanny says I am. So I guess we both are. And that's nice.

• • •

Everybody got new clothes for the wedding. Or nearly new. Vanny bought a yellow wool dress that cost her three week's wages. Mama couldn't decide and kept putting it off. The father's gave her a pound note for Cotton and me and Vanny took us down to Mrs Barrett's "Good As New" shop. Straight away I saw a shiny red dress and grabbed it, but Vanny hit my hands away.

"What the hell's wrong with you?" she hissed. "You want to look like a bloody toffee apple?"

So I knew I'd have to go to the wedding looking sensible. At school I wore a sensible gym dress, a sensible cardigan and sensible shoes. And I hated the lot. Only the hard-up kids had sensible clothes. The lucky ones wore frills and bows and patent leather shoes.

"When I grow up," I muttered, "I'm going to wear what I like and nothing's ever going to be sensible."

"Shut up," Vanny breathed, "or you'll wear your gym dress to the wedding."

She chose a brown corduroy jacket and skirt and herded me into the cubicle. There was a cracked mirror on the wall that showed me a lopsided picture of myself, but Vanny stuck out the tip of her tongue and nodded her head happily.

"That's it!" she said. "That's lovely!"

I looked sadly in the mirror.

"I don't think I look right in this," I said. Vanny didn't even hear me.

"You can wear my cream blouse with it and I'll buy you new shoes and socks."

Mrs Barrett put her head around the curtain and instantly Vanny became a countess.

"I'll take this for my sister Hazel and I'd like something as nice for Rachel."

Mrs Barrett almost bowed. Cotton flashed a radiant smile and Mrs Barrett beamed.

"What a lovely child Rachel is!"

She bustled away. I stared at the floor. I still wanted that red shiny dress. I felt the tears starting.

"Look happy you stupid sheep!" whispered Vanny, "or I'll tell Aunty Prue you're out to spoil her wedding!"

She gave me a stinging clout over the ear and grabbing Cotton's hand, she swept out into the shop. She came back a little later with a fluffy yellow jersey and green plaid skirt. Mrs Barrett hovered behind her watching Cotton with melting eyes.

"Really Vanessa — what a little princess!"

She was. I nodded at Vanny, open mouthed in admiration.

Vanny forgot about Mrs Barrett and gave me a cross between a hug and a shove.

"You're a little princess too. Now hurry up and put your other clothes on."

All the way home Cotton danced and twirled and skipped her delight thinking about her new clothes, but I lost out, even with the new socks. I wanted the pale pink lacy ones to the knee, but Vanny shuddered and bought us both plain white ankle socks.

We had a dress rehearsal for Mama and Aunty Prue. I looked in the long mirror and it wasn't me at all. They said I was going to be a beauty. I laughed and poked my tongue at the red haired girl in the mirror. She poked hers right back at me and her dark eyes danced.

• • •

The August days grew warmer and we were sure the sun would shine for Aunty Prue. Cotton and I could hardly wait. And then one day at school it hit me that after the wedding she wouldn't be living with us any more. I thought I would faint. I put my arms about my head to shut out the awful reality but it stayed and then I was sick. I went home in the headmaster's car. Mama was frantic.

"What is it? What's wrong with her? Oh!"

The headmaster couldn't tell her and I wouldn't until he had gone. When I told her Mama leaned against the kitchen dresser and turned her face away.

"Mama?" I said anxiously, "Mama?"

"I don't want to talk about it," she whispered. She began to sob and it terrified me.

"Mama —"

She pushed me away.

"Go away and leave me alone!"

I went outside and sat on the back step. The wedding was no longer a joy to look forward to. It was a black shadow that would ruin all our lives. I stared at the garden without seeing it, without seeing anything but the terrible emptiness that living without Aunty Prue would bring. I was still sitting there when Cotton came around the corner of the house.

"Why are you home this early?"

"I was sick."

"Were you?" Her small face tightened in concern, "Shall I get Mama?"

"No, don't worry Mama. I don't think she's very well either."

She sat down on the step beside me. After a while she slipped her arm through mine and rubbed her cheek against my shoulder.

"It's all right Hazel," she said, "Vanny will be home soon."

But Vanny came home with Aunty Prue and they were both full of excitement because Aunty Prue had the material for her wedding outfit. So I went to bed. I stayed awake till Vanny came and then I told her. She didn't say anything at first and I thought she had fallen asleep. Then she rolled out of her bed and came over to mine.

"Move over," she said, "and give's a hug."

In the safety of her arms I let all the fear and pain go. She held me, rocking and murmuring sounds of comfort. It was quite a long time before I realised that she was crying too. In the morning I heard her singing in the bath. There was a note on the chair by my bed.

"Hazel," I read, "you have to realise that sooner or later everything changes. Nothing stays the same even though you might think it does or hope it will. We've been lucky having Aunty Prue all our lives but now she's going to make a life of her own. We won't be happy about it but she will and that's what matters. She's always looked after us but now we have to mind ourselves. And Mama. We'll have to mind Mama. The fathers will help. They're always very good. Probably Gram will move in with us — I think Mama would like that. Anyway Aunty Prue won't be far away. We'll see her often and we can have turns to go and stay.

"I didn't have time to talk to you about this so I wrote it down. And I think it's better written down then we won't cry over it. Can you understand what I'm trying to say? I hope so because I don't know how else to explain. Love — Vanny."

When she came back from the bathroom I said, "Thanks for the note."

She smiled. "That's okay," she said.

• • •

Every night and weekend Aunty Prue shut herself in her room and sewed. We played cards and Ludo or read. Usually one of the fathers was there and Mr Armitage, but it was odd without Aunty Prue even though she was only in another room. Mr Armitage was so delighted about marrying her, he grew handsomer by the hour. He was a tall thin man with thick curly hair the colour of his suits and his eyes were blue as the sky. At first the fathers hadn't trusted him. They thought he was after Mama. But when they saw his blue eyes following Aunty Prue's every move, they relaxed. Not that they understood him. How any man could look at another woman when Mama was around was beyond them. Especially Aunty Prue. When fate doled out the good looks she certainly didn't do Aunty Prue any favours. Mama got the lot. Every man ogled Mama, from the college boys up. Except Mr Armitage. Aunty Prue's plain face and wispy hair, her plump body and legs, were only the packaging as far as he was concerned. Her light blue eyes twinkled with intelligence and her laughter was as merry and innocent as Cotton's. He saw her as she really was. He saw the strength and the love and the wisdom in her and he knew he was a lucky man.

• • •

Two weeks before the wedding Vanny decided which boyfriend she'd invite and I was sick with jealousy. She had about a dozen to choose from but the only boy who fancied me was Ernest McCutcheon and I towered over him by about half a head. Secretly I longed to ask the school heart-throb because along with the rest of the girls I was in love with him, but I decided against it. My being in the third form and his being in the upper sixth didn't help, and there was the sad fact that he didn't know I existed.

I took my misery to Vanny but she was unmoved.

"For god's sake! You're twelve years old! Just be patient. In a few years you'll be fighting them off. And remember —

it's Aunty Prue's day — pull a long face at the wedding and I'll flatten you!"

I didn't always understand Vanny.

The fathers bought Mama a green velvet dress and she was ecstatic. She tried it on for them and they could only gaze at her. She looked like a tulip on a stem. I had a sudden thought that in a few years I could very possibly look a little like that and my stomach turned right over. I stopped being jealous of Vanny having a boyfriend for the wedding right then.

• • •

Aunty Prue took the week off before the wedding and she and Mama were like giggling girls about the house. It shone as it never had before and the garden glowed with spring flowers. Gram came over every day and baked till all the tins were full and then she brought all her tins over and filled them too. On the last day she roasted a ham and Mama and Aunty Prue made sponges and little layered sandwiches which they wrapped in wet towels. I went to bed at ten but I was too excited to sleep. Vanny came home from the pictures with her favourite beau of the moment and I could hear them talking and laughing softly on the front steps. That's another thing I'll have to look forward to I thought. I fell asleep imagining myself in Mama's green dress and pale shoes, queening on the front porch to some tall beautiful young man who could only whisper my name and cover my two hands with burning kisses.

• • •

I awoke in the early hours because somebody was moving about in the kitchen. It was Aunty Prue making a cup of tea. We lit the gas fire and pinched two biscuits from the laden tins. We didn't talk much.

She said, "Aren't your feet cold without slippers?"

"A bit," I said, and held them out to the fire. We sipped our tea and smiled at each other.

"You'll have a room to yourself after tomorrow."

"Yes — unless Gram comes."

"Would you like a room of your own?"

"Yes — no. I don't know — I'd miss Vanny."

"Of course. And I'll miss you all."

I slid down on the floor at her feet and she put her arms around me. Her wispy hair bristled with curlers and her plain plump face streamed with tears.

"I love you," I said, "I love you more than anyone in the world."

Later I made another pot of tea and just when Aunty Prue was opening another biscuit tin, Cotton came padding in. We laughed and Mama called, "What are you doing out of bed?"

Then she came into the kitchen with Vanny in her wake and I got three more cups. We were still sitting there, talking and laughing and sipping tea when the sun came up in a great blaze on the perfect spring morning of Aunty Prue's wedding day.

Skeletons

Yes
It's tough on you
My children . . .

A friend said — Are you sure
You lot are not Italian?
Such hot-blooded
Explosiveness?
No
We're not
All races breed all kinds
Of lunacy
And it bombards us
From many sources —
Irish
Maori
English
The Montgomerys
Mooreheads
The unknown Kahugnunu man
McClatchie the whaler
In the Chatham Islands
And his daughter Emma
My great-grandmother
Who shut her daughter Emily
In a closet under the stairs
At the house in Greenmeadows

Till she broke and married
Hares the English labourer who
Had waited patiently for her
To give in
Or die . . .
Christ! Think of that!
And think of Harvey
Her favourite son
Who blew himself to hell
And took his young wife
On the journey . . .
Add to it the loonies
From Douglas Bridge
In County Tyrone
My father Long John who hated
Jews
Royalty
The rich
And the world —
His little sister Rachel died
At 12 years "in an asylum"
He said and Lily — Aunty Banty —
In her green nylon raincoat
Who used the crook
Of her umbrella
To threaten all officialdom
Came here to escape
The curse
But it followed her

And she lived half her life
And all her death
Alone
In Porirua Hospital . . .

Ah!
No wonder we fight
With all that in our cupboards —
And I haven't even mentioned
The loose screws
On your father's side!

Coming Back Down to Earth

for Ry Cooder

Restless
At three a.m.
I turn on the radio
And there you are playing
Guitar like no one else
Filling my heart
Waking me up
Completely and making me
Say thank you to
Whatever it was
That kept me from sleep
And in the morning
I go to town
To buy your music
Everything
I can find
Never mind
The rent or
The phone bill

. . . back home
I play it all day
I sing
With you
To you
As I clean the house

I tell you
I love you and dance
Through all the rooms
Until
In the long mirror
Beside my bed
I see me whirling
Wide-eyed
Flushed
Ecstatic
Joyous as a girl
An old ridiculous woman
Forgetting
Her age and her reason
Smiling   smiling   smiling

Priorities

If the bright light should fade
And I could never
Dance with words again —
What then? What then?
I'll tell you —
I would cry

If the wild joy should cease
And music become
No more than sound —
What then? What then?
God help me!
I would die

If you should turn away
And I might never
See your face again —
What then? What then?
Don't worry —
I'd survive . . .

Francesca Rendle-Short

Francesca Rendle-Short is an award winning author of poetry and prose. Born in 1960 of an Irish mother, she grew up in Queensland, the fifth of six children. She has worked in radio, education and publishing. She is author of a novella, *Big Sister* in *Mirrors* and a novel, *Imago*, as well as poetry and short fiction in literary journals and magazines. She lives in Canberra.

loop the loop

for Jaffa

Irish Granny
begot
Gabrielle
begot
Susannah
begot
Mahalia

m a n g o e s

The house fills with a smell of ripe mangoes all summer long.

> *eating   mangoes*
> *from home*
> *teasing*
> *flutter breathing*
> *and belly rising*
> *with a hand   there*
> *as hers would have been*
> *to yours*
> *back then*
> *before   being   born*
> *so do you want*
> *to run   to*
> *her*
> *to hide your self*

> *in her*
> *return to that   light*
> *she promised*
> *peak resting   places*

You eat trays of cheap mangoes as you shower all that summer. (Didn't she say there was a glut back home?) You peel the goldy honeyleather skins in long strips the way you peel bananas. And they drip orange liquid sweetnesses with the soapy water.

> *and you sink*
> *lips   teeth   & tongue*
> *into sticky stringy pulps*
> *pull   bite   eat   their soft bodies*

l o o p   t h e   l o o p

> *towards her laughter*

Gabrielle's laugh is infectious. It skips and cavorts freely in triplets in swirls. She can let go unexpectedly like a piece of taut elastic: her wax-lip smile disappears, her seriousness peels away. Falling and cascading in a shower of glittery lightness you want to laugh too forgetting the heavy heart and doubt, you want to link arms with her in a dance around and around the room, this room the family inhabits, this room alive with story and counter-story thrown at each other. But

you can't.

Susannah recognizes her mother's laughter — this improvisation — not so much in herself as in her daughter Mahalia. Mahalia laughs the way Gabrielle could laugh if she wanted to, a reminder.

the Christmas pudding

The story you want to tell of this laughter begins with a heart, a heart bursting with fruit — perhaps made of such sticky sweetness — a heart brimming with bowlsful of custard apples and mangoes, monstera deliciosas and pawpaws, the fruit of that land you adore. Your peeling fingers and biting lips, sticky tongue, will drip with juice as you speak, taking you back to that State shaped like one of the pointers of its queenly crown, to a small narrow piece of land on the outskirts of Brisbane. To a verandah filled for the occasion with sisters and brothers and mothers and fathers — a Sunday as it happened that year — to a large table they sit around overlooking the view across the tops of the eucalypts oozing oils from their leaves, to a circle of hearts.

The air is thick with hot winds.

A freakish dry summer.

The talk is of bush fires and the skirt of inch-high green-watered grass that must surround the house for protection.

And young Susannah helps her mother prepare Christmas lunch . . .

Your family has adapted well to living in the heat so they eat cold roast chicken — *oh we must have a bird for Christmas but I don't mind if it's not hot* — the leather-baked skin wrinkled by refrigeration, its body stuffed with dates and apples and breadcrumbs. And salads — yellow Keens-curried rice salads dotted with peas and corn, finely chopped beans and carrot — piled high on beds of cos lettuce freshly picked from the terraced garden. *Of course Irish Granny* (known only by that name) *was a great gardener too for she was able to feed all the family and the workers with food from her soil* — and there, slices of beetroot tipped cleanly from a Golden Circle can, and there, mayonnaise crosses in decorative patterns (Gabrielle was truly religious) . . . bleeding whites into reds . . .

It's Queensland. Christmas heat. A heat that settles on the skin as if for good. The heat takes your skin for its home and you drip with a sticky sweat as you stack the dirty plates from the main course.

But then,

the thought of prickling skirmishes (bodies crawling, burrowing, scratching, irritating) subsides, as if you've been sprinkled generously with cool water, washed — baptismal waters perhaps — for your mother steps out proudly on to the verandah overlooking the small piece of land on the edge of Brisbane, her Christmas pudding alight with a tall blue flame, her face alight with a joy. The family insist on maintaining at least one element of tradition even if the plum pudding is enjoyed not with hot brandy custards but with frozen icecreams. Your mother says they joke about the funny Antipodean ways back home.

As she stands there then with the surprise, a treat, holding out a blue Willow plate supporting a mountain of bewitching flame, its startling pinks and reds, its blues and whites dancing a jig, there, as if on fire herself, everyone smiles, claps, entranced. The flickery flame gobbles the liquid fuel and your mother's face appears from behind, red, flushed. The revellers tuck into the boiled pudding, its dark deliciousness served with balls of vanilla icecream and pourings of thick yellowy cream milked from Berengaria of Navarre, the soft-coated cow, who moos from the paddock afar in unison with the noise of eating around the table, the clinking of silver-plated spoons, munching mouths, smacking lips.

– Mum are you sure it's a brandy flame, someone asks the head of the table, it tastes funny.

And she laughs then just the way you love her to do with a ripple and rush of dazzling pleasure, her head thrown back wildly, the curls of her hair flying a trapeze; this carefree ease you wish for instead of the troubled-hearted look you dread, are afraid of.

– I didn't have any brandy any alcohol, Gabrielle bursts out tipsy with mirth. (Of course you know she's a teetotaller, most people do.)

– So what did you use?

– Oh it's all right, she tries to reassure, it disappears.

– Yes but what did you use? they all insist.

– Um, meths, from under the house, her laughter falters, methylated spirits, her voice weakening. You can hear a chorus chanting apologies for the bizarre, explanations for everything . . . *It's the Irish in her*, they say . . .

and her laughter turns to crying then, a great sobbing, her body wet with grief. And you find yourself wanting to throw your arms around her to laugh and freely cry, this attraction, but find you can't, a repulsion.

A growing girl is caught.

You do nothing.

smells of fear

You do nothing
and then, time slipping

on the journey across the Irish Sea — Liverpool, Isle of Man, Belfast — you smell something like fear for the first time making your young mango-rich Queensland heart, a heart that's known no violence, beat furiously. You can't sleep (hand in hand with your sister). Instead you listen to the young soldiers' raucous night calls, watch them stumble around the bar trying to forget where they are, who they are, smell this fear in their Guinness-soaked skins. You're afraid too. (So what are you doing in this place? the kids at school back home won't believe you and you can't talk to your mother; Gabrielle remains tight-lipped, that Christmas laughter — the possibility of closeness, a dance — a dream . . . You sense there's something awry, an element of discomfort — a sneaking shame? — Your mother clinging happily to her Irishness while safe in the fruit-bowl arms of tropical Queensland. Close-up as you are now, near to this island — her Ireland — anxiety rises off her body like steam off hot bitumen . . .)

At dawn, on a rolling swell beneath bullet-grey skies, silence falls as the ship docks. This is Belfast. This is the nineteen seventies.

– I'll take you to Dublin one day, Gabrielle says, we'll visit the gaol I was born in. And she tells you the story of her mother hiding three salt-boats, their delicate silver filigree, brilliant ultramarine glass. She hid them under her skirts as she was giving birth, so no one would steal them.

But Gabrielle can't go there to her birthplace not now for the roads south across the border snake with fear.

No one smiles.

Instead, under police escort, you tour the north with a relative, her nicotine-yellow fingers rattling the wheel while talking of bright futures to the Australian visitors, pretending there's strength enough to fly in her tattered, muscle-tired wings, to squeeze her bulk through the steel bars of her heart's gaol. On the way back across Belfast, past rolls of barbed wire fencing and Mini-Mokes jammed with trigger-ready soldiers glued to their guns, your mother talks of how she remembers things were. (You pass Queen's College where she studied medicine.) She speaks rapidly, words flying around the fuggy interior of the car like shrapnel.

There's no laughter.

You grow up suddenly, your sister too, you're listening (even the stones speak)
to the voices of Ireland
the dividing of bruised bodies,
the bleeding of blood.

born in a gaol

The cell of the gaol is a cold dark place (a story) alive with silence — feverish — no birth-cry can puncture, no scream can break down, a silence inmates are forced to feed off.

This is Ireland way back. Early twenties. A country fighting for independence with the blood of its family.

And a woman gives birth.

(But what was she doing there?

A skin of betrayal, stinks of hatred, hangs in folds over families bearing an Anglo-Irish name.)

So is there anyone else in that place? A midwife? Or does the baby come into the world in a pause, the warden slipping out . . . *I'll just get a breath of fresh air if you don't mind, he says, stand in the courtyard as the bairn's taking its time, doesn't want to come out* . . . and he pats the skin of the woman's arm, his cold fingers against the hard-working warmth to make sure he's telling himself a truth.

The delivering mother is on her own then, the dark encasing her like a cocoon when the colour of blood streams across the gunmetal floor. Will the wings of this angel be strong enough to lift her body to the square of light marked out with vertical bars? To fly, to soar.

Double doors clang.

The small metal shutter squeaks, flaps, a midwife peers in too late . . .

And the woman names her baby daughter, Gabrielle, for hope, for flight.

But there's more

see

for the daughter of that daughter is present too purling out through the baby mother's womb, seeds within seeds within seeds. You go to your Irish Granny there — silken flutter breathing — tracing the rush of blood in the gutter. Soft bodies loop with soft bodies in a plait of thick hair (you learned first from your sister, two hearts making a small circle). These daughters and mothers, these generations of women, huddle for comfort in the one place, protected and protecting, feeding each other breastmilk.

paying for more love

It's then, cradled by knowing bodies, suckled with forgiving milks, the music of breastmilk, and lulled by darkness covering form, your moving lips, you confess something none of them knew (not even your sister) you whisper . . . *it began as a joke* (you're careful with this part) *with laughter* (in a familiar key) . . .

– They had such a good relationship, what went wrong? the family asks.

so you begin again,

this time confessing how the biggest sin you thought you'd committed till then was not to marry. A sin to live in sin. Ah . . .

. . . you can talk of your mother now before she became a grandmother, how she wore hats to weddings, the way she filled the churches with brims and feathers, netting and fruit. It's the only thing you could see, she outshone the brides. *But Susannah never married,* there's anger in Gabrielle's voice, *it breaks my believing heart.* I lived with him, you say (is there a difference?), and he *was* a sweet man.

Yes,

you'd lived with that sweet man for a year or more when it happened and although it was a ridiculous idea, flawed, you played with it.

This game for money.

This game of shame.

Breaking of a circle.

And you remember the night how on the brass bedhead in that colour-washed room you caught the long plaited chain of a golden locket you wore around your neck; a locket given to you after finishing Senior, an heirloom from Irish Granny. You kept it for years then in a velvet-lined box, unfixed, broken. And perhaps it's this — the women are thinking, huddled for comfort — that's the nut of your confession, your breaking the locket . . . but it's not, you pause . . .

the game. Money, shame.

A game — a dare — you played with this lover, the father of the child born out of that night. (Can you trace the separation of your bodies to that exchange? "I'm not interested", you say rolling over. "What if I pay you for it?" he asks and reaches out to touch your breast.) Your only child. Mahalia for song. Naive, you wondered at the ease of him paying for more love, more sex, an excess. But your laughter choked when the joke of playing prostitute inhabited your body, flooded every pore, full, bursting, red. He told you you should abort, said he'd pay for that too!

– I'll drive you to Sydney, I'll even hold your hand though I'd rather faint. And he did for a while.

But you couldn't, you wouldn't; and you speak haltingly now, the tongue-tied air in your mouth stale wavy movement, a mash, for everything you've avoided gags your breath. Chunks of memorized Bible verse collide in your head. Dogma and learnt certainties wrestle their dirtiest with muscle, sinew, your blood as their vehicle. All you want is to be loved! And you see your mother there, Gabrielle, her disappointed face in the gloom. And what does Irish Granny think, is she ashamed too of the way blood-lines flow — the splash, the spill — the streaming of unclotted blood, the disfigurement. You turn away and look towards the window towards light, your tumbleturning body swelling in response

thinking back

for although you'd have liked to swim against the currents of this family and do not as they would do, you decided to keep the baby, not abort.

Didn't you do it for your mother,

to win approval for something?

Your lover was disappointed figuring the dare — that namelessness — was substantial now for a life. And he was right.

But you're listening for voices, *you'll fly my angel,* your body bathing in the rose waters and lavender oils of the imagination, *your spirits will surely fly.* You want to believe,

your mouth waters,

but was the choice a good one?

Years later, your growing daughter asks, *does it hurt having a baby?* and you remember how to get through university without any money, not knowing you'd be forced to drop out later, you exchanged faded jeans and a tee-shirt for a black bra-and-panty set, swapped vaseline for red lipstick. *Yeah Mahalia,* you say, *it hurts.*

angel wings

The softness of down,
the strength of bone, muscle and feather,
your angel wings.

You'll have to find a way to spread those wings, first flapping the tips, ruffle-and-ruffle, then beating the feather, a-waft-a-waft, in an effort to move the still air. You'll need all the courage you've got to fly out. And you're not sure what's beyond the grill of weak grey sunshine up there; you smell a familiar fear. All you see from where you are is watery light painted on the cold wall — yellow ochres, splatterings of cobalt blues, warm whites — thinned with turpentine. You don't trust this light, it can wither so quickly. For no sooner is it there, spreading its poetry in song, than has it faded, gone, and all the more dark for the going.

a woosh of whiteness

For this room is all that exists.

The map of your world shrinks to a floor plan of four feet by nine feet: you measure it out as you pace the perimeter, controlling the waves at first before having to stop in your circle every now and again as a contraction peaks, nearly drowning then, drawing your nails down the wall, them tearing, bleeding, folded back on themselves. You practise a distraction method, become part of the fecund rainforest pasted with wallpaper-glue on the delivery suite ceiling. Is it Tambourine Mountain? A rainforest riddled with sucking leopard leeches? You watch your body haemorrhage and later drink stout and thimbles of malt whiskey mixed with black Liptons tea to help your milk let-down for the new baby squawking in your arms. With time, you see Mahalia-the-toddler sitting in a patch of summer sun on a circle of frayed carpet in a messy kitchen, spinning a decorated top you give her for Christmas, tipsy with glee. You spin and twirl the stories in your body with this top, wooshes of whiteness . . .

the language of food

Gabrielle doesn't telephone to congratulate her daughter on the birth of her grand-daughter. She rings weeks later, and then about trivial things. It takes a visit a good year after that, during a Queensland summer with its wet heat enough to warm chilled skins. You do all you can to help, baby Mahalia on your hip, cook delicious meals

(can the preparing of food for each other in a family nourish hearts that bleed?)

for you want to believe chopping and cutting and tossing fresh vegetables: it's a language Gabrielle understands. Yet you are reminded of the words your father once said: *You could have poisoned us with that meths you know Gabby, a-chip-off-the-old-block.*

so a little salt spills

On your return home from that visit, to a small modest house, you open a parcel in the post from Gabrielle for Mahalia. Out falls one of the silver salt-boats from Irish Granny's collection of three, those hidden beneath her skirts in the Dublin gaol. A little salt spills with it. Along the rim Gabrielle had these words engraved in tiny italics: *Jesus wept*. But you want to laugh. Tenderly now.

And you see your mother crying and laughing in the one breath, there, close by (you feel her body move, vibrate) while in your heart a flame rises heavenward does cartwheels loops the loop. The deliciousness of the Christmas plum pudding you once tasted is alight with a torch of methylated spirits, it teases you

links with floating things.

So you catch Mahalia in your arms

joy

(and you can't remember doing this with Gabrielle, exactly)

squeeze the gift of the salt-boat between your tummies

her legs riding your hips

thumping heart against heart

more joy

and dance a jig with your daughter, with your laughter, around and around the room. And you know you'll tell Mahalia all about it one day

— she's laughing too —

for in the dance you hold up the bright heavens with her and for once you can skip, you cavort, you fly.

blood ties

those newspaper babies

The best way to eat hot chips is to tear a hole in the top of the bundle they've been wrapped in, thrust your hand into the salty hollow, and pull them out of that fuggy interior one by one. They're more delicious that way you say.

You're describing this culinary delight to Mahalia and she smiles up at you from out of the half light, laughing. You're walking with her hand-in-hand to Theo's Take-Away, a Friday night almost dark, and she says how she loves you telling her things from the past, from when you were a little girl like her.

You say, we used to buy hot chips for ten cents on the way back home from Bribie Island, our skins red from a day in the sun, sandy all over. We'd sit along the bench seat of the Holden in the dark jammed in like sardines — sisters mostly and a brother — hugging our warm babies. And we'd tear the paper (tabloids are best) dig into the sweaty interior and pull out the burny chips. Fingers oily and salty. And we'd make smacking noises as we licked them clean.

– This was before I was born, Mahalia says.

– Yep, when I was a little girl in Queensland.

– Before I was in your tummy, even an idea to be thought of, floating somewhere like dazzling dust. And her voice skips a beat.

– I suppose so, it's a funny thought.

– I like it, she says. And she looks like a fairy with wings and you're pleased you're talking.

making paper

There's an obsession in telling stories, it overtakes you.

Years later you find yourself in the shed, cold nights, tearing newsprint into long strips — years of reading — to cover the pink concrete floor with loose quavery mountains of shredded meaning that rustle as you wade from side to side. You love creating chaos before making sense.

You soak the torn papers in buckets of water, to a mash, a squelchy slipping pulp, before squeezing out the grey dribbly water with hard-working hands, slurping, sliding, cold. You dessiccate the fibre by pressing it flat between sheets of glass before the sun dries it stiff. To write on

for Mahalia.

You sculpt paper on which to write the stories you want to tell her (breathe life into something once-upon-a-time breathing itself).

For this you make a special paper — one you know she'll like — a greyly speckled recycled paper perfumed with orange rind and zest and droplets of rose water, its lumpy surface decorated in passages with flattened rose petals and lavenders.

of age

Mahalia is older now.
So are you.
Much grown
now.

of blood

You've passed the early years of being together but on your own in a small space — housing commission, supported pension, hand-outs meal to meal — and the shame of admitting to single motherhood, of the namelessness of bringing up a daughter alone, unmarried.

– She'll grow up hating men, they said.

An enemy from within slinks beneath the surface of your skin (perhaps it's still there). A rash invisible to the naked eye. Something like tropical heat.

and in one breath

And in one breath your laughter can turn to crying, a great sobbing, your body wet with grief.

Just like Gabrielle.

A reminder.

of grandmothers

Gabrielle. There's always Gabrielle. Swirling.

It's Mahalia who Gabrielle talks to on the phone every once in a while. Mahalia says their relationship isn't bad. In fact she tells you she's pleased, they have an understanding, a gentleness.

– Perhaps it's to make up for lost time, Mahalia says, between you two. She laughs haphazardly.

But you're thinking of Irish Granny, giving birth in a gaol
your grandmother
(was it a gaol or Dublin castle?)

of her blood in snakes over the gunmetal floor

of newspapers of the day — Bloody Sundays —

soaked in foetal mess . . .

You're thinking of Irish Granny

not your mother

(you can't ask her questions).

Irish Granny didn't go grey, so the story goes. She wound her thick dark hair plaited in two around her head to frame a beautiful circular face. She dressed simply, in navy blues, in blacks, and only ever wore two pieces of jewellery: a gold band on her ring finger and a golden locket on a long golden chain around her neck.

Irish Granny died before her grand-daughter — Susannah — was even thought of, something like floating dust Mahalia would say.

of plaited beauties

Plaited hair. Plaited gold. Soft bodies looping with soft bodies in your mind, spinning backwards and forwards through time, their silken threads furling together to make wings, crossing boundaries of place, stories, memory.

Flying then

you remember doing Mahalia's hair on the morning of your brother's wedding (Gabrielle said he'd *never* marry!) How you caught up the three strands of her soft wavy hair either side of a parting to make a French plait (Gabrielle wore fruit on her hat!) How you plaited the hair in the shape of her small head right around to the nape of her neck where you tied the ends with a satin ribbon. How into the circle of plaits you threaded twelve blood-red ranunculi freshly picked from your sister's garden. How Mahalia became a princess that day, a hot Brisbane one at that. How Gabrielle held her small hand through the singing of hymns. (Did laughter skip and cavort with delight?) And how *you* held your head high.

it splashes, it spills

Flying again

you hold your head high in another place. You and Mahalia in the one city, together at university (Gabrielle doesn't know). The auditorium you're in is hot from many bodies (it feels like a church). Summer. End of semester exams looming, an urgency.

I want to look at the complexities of clotting blood, a lecturer is saying, and you listen carefully. (You're pleased with how this year is progressing, surprised you're able to keep up, surprised too you can remain anonymous amongst the circle of your grown-up daughter's friends.) So you smile and begin to write across the top of your lecture pad in a careful hand — *blood clots saves lives . . . evolutionary adaption to danger* — and think how blood moves between generations. Mysterious ways. How links form, *attractions and repulsions;* how connections float in the wash of these thick streams, *placental memories.* You look towards your daughter there, sitting a few rows in front of you amongst her women friends, but find she isn't listening to the physiology lecturer like you (*are* you?) rather laughing at a joke her neighbour whispers. Laughing, of course! In triplets, in swirls. Her head of hair thrown back wildly just as it should, dark curls flying a trapeze (you've seen this before).

Bursting, bubbling over.

It's contagious, the lecturer looks her way and laughs too
while from behind, you listen transfixed
your head spins under a spell

and you write how blood is a type of connective tissue with a liquid matrix — it splashes, it spills — remembering Mahalia's beginning (your body a gaol of a kind) the haemorrhage while giving her birth, the transfusion . . . *blood clots form when a vessel is damaged, ruptured, when foreign bodies enter the circulating blood* . . . memories a skydive with the lecturer's voice . . . *platelets make a thick jelly with fibres that trap, it prevents excessive blood loss* . . .

deep in those rainforests

It's your father who tells you the story of the leeches (he hides in shadows). (The shadows of women.) He tells you about leopard leeches lurking in the moist leaf-litter of the rainforests of Queensland — Tambourine, Maleny, Mt Glorious — the way they inject a substance preventing coagulation of the blood, the way they suck their fill of the host before dropping off leaving the surface of skin dotted with tiny perforations, streaming with unclotted blood. He says he's known of people who have died . . .

the language of good stories

It's the heat. It bloats
exaggeration.

Crawls with familiarity.
And the moisture
smells of blood.

trickling lines

You let this blood (clotted or not) trickle across the sweet smelling, flower-speckled surface of the paper you make, trace the capillary movement of hearts between generations, the spanning of years, of mothers giving birth in strange places, of latitudes and longitudes, of breasts feeding milk to the hungry, of daughters making choices, the absorption of guilt in their perforated skins.

Tuned to your own voice

— remember and imagine —

you watch the instrument in your hand change in a fanciful way from a calligraphy fountain pen filled with ruby ink (the kind you love), to the quill from an angel's wing, her nib tipped with her blood, trickling lines.

follow your heart

There, Mahalia sits in front of you dressed in black with false hair pinned to her head and strings of rosaries and crucifixes around her neck, doing medicine she says, for the money. (You hold your pen steady.) In the same lecture theatre, there, you're wearing baggy Levi's, your neck adorned with a golden locket, enrolled in medicine you confess, for a personal challenge.

– That's my mum, a voice says, pleased. Mahalia turns and nods. Her friends look back at you with obvious surprise, delight. A laugh. Lips smile.

– We like doing things together don't we Mama? She winks, you blush.

So much for invisibility you think.

only the beginning

The two of you get a take-away for tea. You recall Theo's as you walk around the corner from where Mahalia lives to a classier affair where chic waiters bring out steaming chips on thick china plates rimmed with cobalt filigree leaving you to sprinkle cracked rock salt and wine vinegar to your taste. You can talk for hours on nights like these.

– Let's open a bottle of red wine, you suggest.

– So what's the occasion? Mahalia asks.

– I've got something to give you,

and you pass over stories of your bloodlines folded into a sandalwood box, tied around with plaited banana twine, wrapped up in sheets of newspaper so that what you give her looks like one of those babies full of hot salty chips you adored to hug home from Bribie.

– First instalment, rough draft, you say.

Paper spills, lavenders and the sweet aroma of roses. Spills, the way light fills a room that has been dark.

– So there's more?

– It's only the beginning.

– Around and around in circles we go! She says it with a laugh (you've been waiting) more a smile.

body maps

those hands peeling mangoes

You eat mangoes with her for lunch. Pull, bite, eat, their soft bodies. Wedges of broken bread soak up the sweet juice, soft white sponges bruised orange.

Ripe mangoes, fresh bread.

There's no other food in the house.

The larder is empty. The fridge turned off. For Gabrielle is moving house, large to small, old to new. And you're helping (she didn't have to ask).

from old to new

Gabrielle's hands flick and twist from this to that around the familiar rooms, sorting and collecting. For all her frailty they're freckly, thick-fingered, muscular hands. She doesn't know you're watching but you are, learning secrets of succession from those hard-working, milking hands, the ones you remember seeing years before in a place where she swelled with happiness, in a place on the outskirts of Brisbane, a place alive with the sound of the brush turkeys, their glottal hoo-hoo-hoo echoing across the valleys: there, early morning on a stool, hunched over, holding Berengaria of Navarre's soft pink teats, milking a warm creamy stream.

But things change.

And wet with perspiration, you help her move house.

From old to new.

Large to small.

From a home of familial story to a foreign contour.
A Brisbane weatherboard to a Sunshine Coast
brick-veneer.

of one body

Fingers black with newsprint you wrap the family silver
for her. Pack salt-boats and sugar bowls into small bodies.
Pack into boxes her *life*.

this likeness

You trace a figure of yourself in her body — belly,
armpits, those drooping breasts, those fingers peeling skins,
those hands wrapping silver (does Mahalia do the same,
tracing yours?)
exploring the map of her ageing skin
your skin
pockets of hidden territory
wondering
about the copy of you you see there
hers like yours, yours hers
enough to confuse.

Pam Lewis

Pam Lewis lives in West Hartford, Connecticut, USA. Her short fiction has appeared in *Intro*, *Puerto del Sol* and *The New Yorker*. She is currently at work on a novel.

Potatofah-Minirish

As with most Americans, my cultural heritage is very mixed. We tend to pick out one or two features of our family histories and pass them down. They become the dominant culture although, of course, they are not. For example, my mother was full Dutch, but she spoke very little of her life in Holland. My aunt later told me that in the 1930s the Dutch banded together and were called *Klumpen* after the wooden shoes they left at the door. And this bothered my mother, who had a fierce determination to be only American.

My father, on the other hand, was a little bit of everything, Irish included, and because of the strength of his personality, his stories were the ones that defined our family history. The proudest blood in his line was Mohawk Indian, a tribe from Upstate New York. The chief's daughter, Polly Denny, wed Angel deFerriere, recently escaped from the Napoleonic war. He had been drawn to her because Indians at that time spoke French. When he told me these stories, my father was only one-sixteenth Indian, which made me one thirty-second, but to this day I think of my Indian blood more than any other type.

When I was a young child, my father often said to me, generally when he was in his cups, "You're potato-famine Irish". He always said this in a nostalgic, rather fond way, and the words ran together as one loving and exotic expression whose meaning was never explained. Like all words that are spoken together quickly, they blended into something else. I thought he was saying, "Potatofah-Minirish". It made me special in some mysterious way that would be revealed to me later. Perhaps it had to do with being the youngest or with being the favourite. My sister and brother never had the distinction. It wasn't until I was much older and studying history that I read about the potato famine, and not even then did I connect that tragedy to myself. Then I saw a drawing of bodies lying at the side of the road during the potato famine. I still have a very clear memory of that picture because of the shock. By that time, my father had died and there was no one to ask. But I think it had to do with my father's romantic notion that he was a self-made man, that he had been born into poverty and become an important man.

Somewhere along the line, we were full Irish. There were Fitzgibbons in the family tree, for example. We'd apparently been Catholic too at one time, until the priest made a pass at one of my great aunts, and the whole family left the church at once. After that, they joined Aimee Semple MacPherson's Church of the Foursquare Gospel, an evangelical sect that flourished in Hollywood in the early twentieth century. My father said that at meetings, the flock was invited to pin their donations to a felt-covered board as it circulated, rather than having to fish coins out of their pockets and drop them into a basket, an ingenious way to get more money.

And then my sister married a Tobin, I married a Casey, and we came, if not full circle, at least full loop. My Casey was second generation Irish, the grandson of a woman who had worked as a housekeeper, the son of a father who had owned a hardware store, and himself an executive at a large corporation. That's an Irish story in America, one I believe my father must have wanted for himself. We divorced for reasons that had nothing to do with Irish, Indian, French or Dutch. After a few years, I returned to my maiden name of Lewis. I like the name Casey. It has a sort of raw energy, the antithesis of pretension. My sons are Caseys. And I had developed a very distinctive signature by then, a doctor's envy. But no matter who I met, I was always called Pat. I'd be introduced as Pam Casey, and the next words out of their mouths would be, "So, Pat, tell me . . ."

Lifo

The delivery of firewood finally brought home to me that I was on my own. I ordered way too much of it from my neighbours. Well, neighbours. Chester and Anita Bolduc are a good mile down the road, but theirs is the nearest house. The sign in their front yard says, "hardwood, rabbits, maple syrup". I dropped in on them the day I moved in and asked about the wood.

"Splitting it yourself, are you?" Chester said.

"I guess so," I answered. I wasn't exactly sure what he meant by splitting, but it was important to seem competent. I'd figure it out later.

Chester looked me over, scratched his chin and frowned. "Well all right," he said.

I hadn't a clue what I was getting myself into until a few days later when the Bolducs arrived in their pickup truck with the first load. It wasn't firewood, though, just thick slabs of tree trunk, each about a foot high and maybe two feet in diameter sliced like a sausage. After a few trips up my driveway, which is long, narrow and steep, the truck broke down and the Bolducs finished the job with a backhoe. All day I could hear it grind up and down the hill and then the heavy thud of all that damned wood tumbling into my dooryard. Occasionally, in between deliveries, I went outside and kicked the wood to see what I was in for. Otherwise, I spent my day battling house flies.

It was hot and humid that day, freaky for October. The flies must have thought the sudden heat meant spring, time to wake up. There were scores of them banging against the glass where there'd been none the day before. My original plan for the day had been to caulk all the spaces around the windows with putty and then to bank hay bales around the outside of the house, shovel dirt over the stretch of yard where the water pipe was buried, and finally staple plastic sheeting over the windows that had a northern exposure. I wanted to insulate myself tightly, pack myself into that little house so there wasn't a single crack left open to the outside world.

During one of the lulls between wood deliveries, when no sounds came into the house at all, my ex-husband, Frank Doyle, called me. Had I taken the gravy boat? he wanted to know, his way of letting me know he was having company for dinner. No, I said. And while he had me on the line, how long did I think it was safe to leave chicken at room temperature? I had to fight the instinct to say sure, take it out now and let it sit all afternoon. I could have poisoned them both and gotten away with it, sent them to the hospital instead of to bed.

We'd had an amicable divorce thanks to Frank who had read up on strife-free separation. It was the adult approach to splitting up, he said, without the fights and embarrassing behavior. People simply agreed to end the romance but keep the friendship — all very cool, all very cerebral. We even went out for lunch and laughed about our lawyers after we appeared before the judge.

My petty, murderous response to his call was a kind of failure to live up to the spirit of our agreement, I thought, and it took the starch right out of me. I lost interest in my projects. The next time the Bolducs came with a load of wood, I watched from behind the curtain. Anita hopped from the cab and walked ahead of the backhoe, showing Chester with special hand signals where to turn, where to stop and where to open the bucket and let the wood fall out on top of the pile. They were a real team. When Frank and I drove places together, he'd ask me for directions and then stop the car so he could look at the map himself.

I mixed the caulk with water and poured it into the special cone that came with my caulking kit. But when I tried to squirt it into the crack between the window and the frame it didn't work. It was a mess, too runny. When I added more powder it got too stiff. And it attracted flies. They got stuck, and I had to pull them free with tweezers, carry them outside to the deck and then nudge their little legs free of the gook. That is, until I heard the backhoe arrive with another load of wood and I retreated into the house. I didn't want the Bolducs to see how I was spending my day.

The flies buzzed and crawled over one another on the windowsills where it was warm. They got in my way as I sloshed caulk into the cracks. I vacuumed them up, but there were always more of them. I gave up finally, dropped the caulking gun and slumped to the floor against the wall under the window. I'd never make it. And all that wood in the front seemed to quadruple what was already much too much for me to accomplish all by myself. No one would help me. It scared me that I had been so bold about getting the house. I had only thought about the peace and quiet. Having no one to take care of but me. Now there was someone else in my old house, her feet treading on my plush carpet. Her hands running over the things I'd bought. I felt as though I'd stopped living.

At about five, I heard Chester cut the motor on the backhoe. A few minutes later, he and Anita were standing at my door. They looked like twins. They were both short and squared off, and they had the same wavy pale hair and cheerful, sunburned faces. "All done," Chester said. The wood pile loomed behind them. I wondered how I'd get the car out of the garage.

I asked them to come in and have a beer. It 's what Frank always did with people. But Frank is very outgoing, and when he asked people in for a drink, it was a noisy event with lots of laughing and loud voices and the sound of the freezer chest opening and closing, ice, glasses and bottles clinking. I was suddenly aware that, by comparison, my invitation was more tentative, almost mute. Anita and Chester removed their boots on the porch and padded silently into my house in stocking feet.

I indicated the couch to them. "Please have a seat," I said.

Anita grinned and fell heavily onto the couch with a loud, welcome thud. "Mind?" she asked me pointing to the coffee table.

"Please do," I said, and she hefted her feet up on a stack of magazines on top of the table. Chester landed beside her and squeezed her leg the way he might touch a child whose mischief he thinks is adorable. He liked everything she did.

They were both easy people, I could tell. They were nice to the bone. I felt a swift and dangerous pleasure at having these nice people in my house, at having them as my neighbours, my trophies for making the move. They made the decision to buy the house and change my life a stroke of genius after all. I wanted to say everything at once, tell them who I was and all the things that had happened to me. But I could not utter a word. I could only feel my own smile, and I had enough sense to know it was way too big for the small occasion.

"I'll go get us those beers, then," I said and fled for the kitchen to settle down.

"A loose cannon," Frank used to say of me, and maybe this was what he meant. I felt exactly like a loose cannon — untethered, dangerous, heavy. Tip the deck even a little and I'd crash through everything in my path. When I'd been in the kitchen too long, I went back out to the living room, no better prepared to handle the situation than when I left.

I sat down in a chair, looked into the Bolducs' open, unfamiliar faces. Which was it, I said, the wide rust stripe or the wide black one on a woolly bear that meant a long winter was ahead. I answered the question myself based on a woolly bear I'd seen the previous year and then the length of our winter. It had snowed on April 27. I remembered the date because it was our court date, and we'd had to cancel due to the weather. I told all this to the Bolducs by way of explaining the woolly bear. And then I was on to something else. Was it true that moss only grew on the north side of the tree, just in case I got lost in the woods at some point. How often did the snowplows come through in the winter. Did they get stuck a lot? I talked and talked, and I can't remember a single answer they gave. I have no memory of them saying anything to me, so I must not have given them a chance.

I went on and on about hypothermia. A hiker in Colorado had died of it when his blue jeans got wet. Can you imagine, I said, dying because of wet jeans? Who would have thought it possible? I described my boss as an alcoholic, or so I understood from the gossip around him. How he intimidated his staff through insults and jokes about their work. And then, horrified at myself for having divulged this — what if they knew him, after all — what if they were alcoholics themselves. I switched back to the wood, what kind it was. Maple? Oak?

Anita gave Chester a quick elbow nudge and they both got up to leave. I walked outside with them and when we got to the backhoe, Chester reached into the cab and took out a big metal mallet and two wedges, one big and one small. "You'll be wanting these," he said. He rolled a log out of the pile and tipped it over so it lay flat on the ground. Then he slipped the narrow edge of the larger wedge into a crack, raised the mallet over his head and slammed it down. The wood broke neatly in two. He did the same thing with the two halves until there were four pieces of regular fireplace wood as I knew it. "Trick is," he said, "to raise up the maul and let it fall of its own weight. No need to smash heck out of it. Just tire you out. You'll see. Plenty there to get you through the winter."

Then Chester climbed into the cab with Anita. He turned the backhoe, maneuvering it around the woodpile with such grace and precision it seemed to take on a life of its own. As they headed off down the driveway I could see Anita turn her head to speak to Chester, and I missed Frank. Well, I missed my life in the passenger seat. About twenty yards down the driveway the backhoe stopped. Anita pushed open the door on her side and leaned out. She called something to me, but I couldn't make it out over the roar of the engine.

"What?" I called back, with an exaggerated shrug of my shoulders so she'd see that I couldn't hear.

"Fine!" she screamed at me. "Chester and I know you're going to be just fine." Well of course I am, I thought as I waved back to her and smiled a huge smile so she'd know I'd heard and it was okay for her to leave me there. Of course I'd be fine. I stood at my front door and watched the backhoe disappear down the driveway in the late day sun. The Bolducs told me later, after we'd been friends for several years, that on their way home that evening they gave me until Christmas in that house.

After the backhoe was out of sight I stood still in my driveway and continued to listen. I clung to the sound of it growing dimmer and dimmer in the distance. I knew when Chester down shifted at the main road and turned right. I held my breath to hear the last small evidence of the backhoe vanish and the silence rush in, and then I ran back into the house.

The memory of my wrecked day declared itself when I

went back inside. There were dishes of dried up caulk on the floor, the vacuum cleaner hose and attachments sprawled across the kitchen, the day's dishes in the sink and the empty beer bottles still on the table. I was as weary as the last of the evening sun that fell in dust-filled streaks across the living room. I sank back into the couch in the semi-darkness. Across the valley I could see a faint, comforting halo from the lights and the fog over Montpelier.

Frank had been on my mind all day. Not out in front with the flies, the Bolducs and the wood, but farther back, closer to the nerve. I must have been nursing thoughts of him there because now, alone in my silent house, I was slapped with the vivid image of Frank fanning magazines on the coffee table, placing crystal ashtrays, stacking record albums in the order he would play them. The dog-eared *Bolero* would be close to the bottom of the stack. I saw two chicken breasts thawing on our green Formica.

"The trouble with you," I said. It was how Frank used to preface his remarks to me when he was about to inform me of one of my shortcomings. Frank had a way of making his remarks about me sound as though they were more painful for him to say than for me to hear. He would speak slowly and gently to me as he said, "You're too dependent, or too docile, tough, enigmatic, sure of yourself." In Frank's eyes, I was always too something.

"The trouble with you, Frank," I said again, "is that you're too vicious." The idea startled me. Frank vicious? It was a novel thought, ridiculous, really. I'd always thought of Frank as a nice guy. We both did. Frank and me. He was the nice one and I the difficult, hard-to-satisfy partner. That's how I'd seen us for years, particularly as the divorce drew near. We fell apart because of my regrettable character.

So who was I, the troublesome and unreliable Susan, to call Frank vicious?

"Vicious," I said again just because it felt so good. And it fit rather well, actually. What else was I to make of his phone call? What other motive could he have had than to let me know in a sly, yes vicious, way that I'd been replaced. What better way than to ask my advice? This trait couldn't be new. He must have had it all along.

"Cunning and cruel," I added. As in the dream where you discover rooms in your house you never knew were there, the sudden knowing left me breathless with wonder. How could I not have noticed this about Frank? Like the rooms, this knowledge had been there all along, just beyond a door that was always shut, a door that did not arouse my curiosity in all those years.

I walked right to the phone and dialed the number, my number. The receiver was lifted right away. I heard music, lost my nerve and hung up. But I dialed again immediately and I waited until I heard Frank's voice.

"Amicable, my eye," I said.

"Susan is that you?" he said.

"You know it is," I said.

His end became muffled, the sound of a hand over the receiver, perhaps, as he shrugged and winked at the guest. I'd spent a lot of years on her end of Frank, watching him roll his eyes as he talked on the phone. I was jealous and furious all at once. He came back on the line. "Look, Susan," he said.

"I know what you did. It's all clear to me. You set me up," I said, the words stunning and surprising — instantly recognizable as truth and not just about his dinner that night but about a million other things, including even the divorce itself.

"This is a real bad time, Susan," he said. "I can tell you're upset, but . . . well, not just now." That patronizing voice again, the one in which I'd heard about all my flaws. I pictured him shaking his head, showing the woman the full measure of his compassion. I slammed down the receiver.

He'd stand a moment looking at his receiver as though he'd had bad news, then gently replace it in the cradle, taking a deep breath, perhaps with his eyes closed. I could hear what he'd tell the woman about me. He'd make her think I was unstable to call him on a Saturday night as I had, argumentative and belligerent. Maybe he'd say he tried to let me down gently but there was clearly no way.

They'd talk about me. My call would give Frank what he needed to win her sympathy. He'd shake his head sadly. The woman would ask sincere questions, as though she cared about me, using my first name, no doubt. What does Susan do? Does she have a job? Where does she live? Does she have friends? I couldn't stand it. I'd fallen right into his hands once again. Even at the moment of discovery, I'd continued to play my part, responding with hysteria hours after Frank's cool little phone call.

By then the sun had set and I was sitting in total

darkness. The house had grown cold and I was again aware of silence. It filled the world for as far as I could see. I scratched my heel across the floor. The sound of it scared me. I clapped my hands, a sudden bark that seemed to linger. If noise was to be made, I must be the one to make it.

I said "Ahh", the way I do for the doctor, and then again, practicing the sound sometimes higher in pitch and sometimes lower. Each time, the sound began and it ended, but the louder and sharper the sound, the more likely it was to leave a small echo, a brief tail that came to a tiny point and ended.

I threw on a parka and ran outside to fill up the silence with my own sound. Over and over again, louder and louder, I kept on screaming. I drew in the most breath my lungs could hold, leaned backwards to open my chest for it, and then blasted it out, pushed it out until I doubled over, arms crossed to squeeze out the air. I opened my mouth further than I knew it could go, stretched my cheeks, bared my teeth to the cold.

When I was finished, my fingertips and toes tingled. There was perspiration on my forehead that chilled my face. I sat down, spent, on the edge of the deck and stared up at the black sky, the blacker silhouette of trees rimming it all around. It was very beautiful and cold, and it belonged to me. I owned everything I could see and feel, the night sky, the sharp cold air on my face and in my nostrils and lungs, the faint smell of smoke. As I sat, I began to hear noises as well, small rustlings in the leaves in the distance, an animal cry, the distant sound of a train.

Once my eyes adjusted to the darkness, I could make out the wood Chester and Anita had dumped in the dooryard, so much less daunting at that hour. I went into the garage and flipped on the floodlights. A silver frost had settled on the grass and the bushes. Even the wood glistened. I walked around it a few times, sizing it up, looking for a way in, a piece to separate easily from the rest. I chose a smallish one resting on several others. I rolled it off the pile and over to the cement apron in front of the garage. I felt along the cold, rough surface of the slab for the widest crack, slipped the point of the large wedge into it, lifted the mallet and let it fall, just as Chester had said. It was like hitting a nail with a hammer, only so much bigger. After several tries, the wood split in half in a single, satisfying blow.

It was pleasurable to hit the target time after time and hear that strong iron-to-iron sound echo in the still night. After a while I got a good rhythm. I rolled another log and then another, split them in two with the big wedge, and then into six or eight with the small one. It was excellent wood, so dry the cracks were deep and easy to find, easy to split.

I remember how my world looked and smelled that night. On the forest side of the house, beyond the driveway, was just blackness. On the garage side where everything was well lit and keenly visible, I remember that my summer chairs were stacked on the rafters, their frayed green webbing hanging down in strips. My rake and shovel hung on the wall. It all smelled of fresh damp wood.

From those first slabs I got over thirty pieces of wood,

each one slender enough to hold easily in one hand. I laid them side by side on the ground, the first layer of my wood pile, protected under the deep roof overhang. They looked pale and tender in the moonlight, almost like young skin. Like babies.

Lifo, I thought. It meant last in, first out, and it had to do with taking inventory, a word that had once belonged to Frank. But that night lifo belonged to me. In the next few weeks, if luck and strength held, I'd split the rest of the wood. In just the way I'd seen the Bolducs work, methodical and sure, I'd build my wood pile, layer upon layer until the night's wood was buried and out of sight, until all the wood in the driveway was transformed into hundreds of slender pieces, piled higher than I was tall and extending from the edge of the house to the door.

Pretty soon, even as I continued to add to the wood pile, I'd also be drawing it down. Then, for the next six months, every morning and every night, I'd take a few of the logs until, one day next spring, I would see that baby-colored wood again. I would have survived.

Bronwyn Rodden

Bronwyn Rodden was born in Sydney of Irish and Irish-Scottish parents. After working in various jobs, she moved to Wagga Wagga to study Agriculture. After graduating, she worked as a technical officer before changing to training and development work.

In 1992 she won the Patricia Hackett Prize (*Westerly*), and was selected for the first New Poets Program (Wollongong University) in 1993. She has had poems and short stories published in literary journals in Australia and the UK and was selected for The New South Wales Guild of Bookbinders anthology, *The Poets' Alphabet*. She is currently working on a collection of short stories and a novel.

On being an Irish Woman Writer . . .

It didn't occur to me that I was Irish until I went to Ireland for a holiday in 1990 and found myself surrounded by people who looked just like my parents and brothers and sisters. I realised I belonged to a race of people after all. It grew more intriguing when I stayed with my father's family in Lifford, County Donegal. I was walking down a lane and a man pulled over in his car and asked me who I was and where I was going. When I told him he looked at me closely and then went on his way satisfied. My face was my passport.

I've spent a lot of time in men's worlds: I had five brothers, worked on the waterfront with Customs, studied Agriculture at Wagga Wagga and now work for the New South Wales National Parks and Wildlife Service. I feel I'm able to ask questions some feel are too obvious or odd to ask. I have an interest in the women's view of the world and an interest in detail that is supposed to be female. However, I wonder if it's just an interpretation of what is considered detail.

My mother always said I liked the sound of my own voice. I really like the sound of lots of voices. I've always loved stories and used to invent them for my older sister as we lay in our beds at night. As a child I was crazy about a writing game and bored my family silly getting them to play it over and over. But one of the best times I had was listening to a cousin who had just cycled back from the pub after Mass in Lifford. He was trying to tell us about a woman who'd just bought a new bicycle. The words went round and round in circles and I thought of Flann O'Brien who was born a short walk away in Strabane. We laughed till it hurt and I felt a real sense that I was amongst people who loved words as much as I did.

Nevertheless, I feel Australian as well. I grew up near the bush and spent lots of time there. My work is often inspired by places I've been or return to. This sense of my surroundings seems to me to be a major link between my Australian and Irish backgrounds and at times it's almost tangible.

Tomato Time

I'd always dreamed about life in a cottage, cutting wood for the fire, all alone. Even if I was an old witch in black with a large hooked nose, no one around to disturb me as I cast my spells and wove my magic webs. I could disguise the cottage more and more until it looked like just part of the forest — all twiggy and leafy and an old path hidden behind licheny trees that bear knarled old lemons tough as leather and very bitter. I'd stay there day after day until the hours became meaningless and the days would drift into each other, working around the cottage, the nights for sleeping. Mostly.

When it rained, there'd be no reason to go out — you'd have everything you'd need as it only rains for short periods here and then the sun bursts out like Greek fire engulfing the landscape. It smoulders, the green leaves radiate with yellow light and wild things slip out of hiding places in all the sheltering holes, to shake off their wet coats and dry glimmering in the sunshine.

On warm days it would be work, work, work — lots to do to make it all continue, to keep the roof of the house neatly disguised as wild scrub. And the path, trimming the trees to look like they're all growing naturally and hiding the path leading up to the wooden front door. At night I'd be surrounded by thousands of night dwellers — I'd feel positively lazy, lying in my feather bed while they're out there, working so hard.

But I'm not there yet. It started in that farmhouse in the irrigation country, an hour's drive from the nearest town. I'd look out to see the stars, numerous as the animals on the ground. I'd get up at 4:30 to cook breakfast for the eleven men and women who were the family. They stayed home, mostly, because we weren't mixing people — on religious grounds. And we didn't eat meat. I still don't but it's just habit. You can imagine all the peeling and chopping of the vegetables that went in to make up meals for all those hungry, farm-working people. I sometimes felt a stranger to them and of course in a way I was. I guess what they were was courteous. I wasn't actually married to their father — we never quite got that organised — what with all the fuss over Doris' demise and all the neighbours talk about it being too soon for me to move in. But I did — and they needed me. I guess I became his wife but not altogether. Outwardly, we acted as a married couple to give the children a sense of family — there were so many of them to be orphaned.

It was not a very open-minded community — but small ones rarely are — as if open-mindedness diminishes with the population. They never really accepted us — they never really accepted the family's religion. I didn't think about it — the religion — it wasn't important to me. I did all I was supposed to, but my spiritual efforts went into the cooking pots on those many Saturdays when they'd had their day of rest and my eyes were wet from a dozen onions. I don't think they really thought of me as part of the family. I was convenient — I fitted into a spot they needed. It made the universe tick over somehow and it was as if I was a chink to fit into the wall to keep it from falling apart. It wasn't for a long time that I started to wonder about why we want the walls to fit together — all this fitting together — patching up, like it was something more important than anything for me to do. It led me to wonder about why I did anything at all. And what the walls were and where they came from.

I never saw any of the family naked. I didn't know what they really cared about — except their farm and the motor bikes and their Coca Cola they drank because they couldn't have coffee or tea. They'd sing their dusty hymns to the thin sound of an organ played by the daughter of the house, the only one allowed to work in town. When they chanted bits of scripture I'd look around the room, the good room, with it's heavy floral carpet and dark walls. I'd close my eyes and imagine the countryside. The sky that spread wide over the flat land, the green irrigated paddocks against the summer brown, birds attracted to the unseasonal lushness. I'd think of my walks along the canals, the rice rustling like paper. The air would change when I reached the soybeans, grow moist and alive with grasshoppers.

I was standing by the sink, looking out at boisterous clumps of water melons and pumpkins, when my stomach began to feel like it was floating in the heat. Then, I became conscious of my feet being heavy and stuck to the floor. I am here, I thought, in one farmhouse on one farm in one area of the country Australia, one tiny atom of the universe, playing like a fun park — loud and glary over our heads at night. I thought — I am here. All the hairs on my legs stood up and the skin around the base of my spine prickled — I'm here — ripples played across my shoulders and tingled up my neck until my scalp stung with electricity. I'm here and the watermelons look ridiculous.

I realised I was wearing an apron that had holes worn in it because I'd been working here so long, in this house for these people I really didn't know, and I'd never looked at myself in the mirror at all. I just didn't see the holes.

I couldn't recall them ever asking me what I really liked. Anything. They were too frightened, I guess, that if I thought about it, I might take my chink out of their wall and it would fall around them. I thought they had little to support them, that's why I'd stayed. My clothes, safe and soft and worn and fitting in, meant more to them than I did. They'd remember my apron after I was dead as their heavy tears dried on their sunburnt faces. They'd think of old furniture and wonder where the lace doileys had gone to that they remembered from the early years and not remember that it was their real mother who worried about such things and somehow had energy to starch the linen, wash the nappies and peel twenty carrots for their lunch.

And then I started to wonder about my own wall — where had I come from — where was my wall? It was lost somewhere in the hundreds of kilometres between me and my birth place. And that the distance, the open plains, had swallowed up all of my memories so that I started here without anything. It was instinct, I suppose. When I received the last letter from this man, asking me to join him, I knew, without wanting to, that this would happen. The miles passed along, the red cracked earth soaking up my past until I was as empty as the sky on a November morning.

I relished all the colour of their farm — the vivid green rice waving heavily, the even, feisty rows of soybeans bringing goodness to the world — the magic of produce. Then there was the orchard — perfect fruit falling abundant into our hands. The bright clear days lit up the tomatoes, sweet and spicy as you brush past their leaves and shy yellow flowers, their flesh warm and sweet. I thought about those yellow flowers, standing at this sink, my hands red raw. I felt anger burning into my hands. I couldn't tell for a long time why those flowers made me so angry.

It was then I started to plan. I didn't know what, exactly. I didn't feel there was any use for it — just planning to make the work go faster. And the days flew so fast. It was winter, the windows all misted up with our warm breaths. One morning when I woke up, I just couldn't get out of bed. I made some excuse, which they accepted silently. But nothing was the same after that day. It was only months till I went. They never said anything and neither did I — but they knew I was going. I made my way back to my town — trying to gather up my memories again — battered from their time in the desert, worn and fragile from the beating sun, some I lost forever and maybe I just don't have anywhere to put them now anyway.

I didn't know what I'd find and at first I got so depressed I nearly went back. Then there was a woman who needed a housekeeper in a nearby town — company as well — and that's when I moved into this cottage and realised I liked the cottage more than anything. I loved all its creaks and cracks, the way the light fell in winter onto the leaves outside the kitchen window and the small birds sang to me every morning.

I felt guilty, that I had so little to do. Then, just looking after one other person seemed to fill up all my time. Her name was Wilhelmena and she showed me how she did everything, and I copied her just so I did things differently. We got along fine, I kept to myself and tried not to get in her way. Then one day she said to me, Why do you peel your potatoes just like I do? What? I said. You do it exactly the same way as me. I felt for the hole in my apron, forgetting I'd bought a new one when I moved in here. She came over to me and took the small paring knife out of my hand and put it down on the bench. Now, she said, potatoes all taste like potatoes, you know. It's the same with carrots. They keep coming, looking just the same, and they keep tasting the same. You should try your own way of doing them. Why don't you do the tomatoes? You always leave them to me. They're lovely to prepare, such beautiful flesh, full of life. Try something different with them. They smell so alive, don't you think?

Long Drive to Work
Snowy via Canberra

A rainbow sags in the valley,
sun cuts through the clouds
to trees with just-wet skins,
the car hums,
wipers clack on,
a sweep of light velvets a field,
condensation crisscrosses the hills,
the radio blurts the theme from Love Story.

So many sheep wandering, wandering,
new-shorn pelts exposing
their age:
old ewes' sagging joints.

Four more hours.
I'm getting tired,
turn at a sign saying Michelago,
poplars sky-scrape a fenceline,
find a petrol station in a paddock,
buy a drink and walk outside
away from the looks.
The horizon is black,
I'm leaving the light behind,
cockies flutter like paper rain.

Lamb-marking

they're small and soft like toys
and they make quiet little snuffles
perhaps they haven't found their voices yet

we pick them up in a circle pointing out
their woolly bodies resting on our stomachs
and hold their skinny legs apart

then those on the outside
take up their knives with the hooks
and cut off the base of the scrotum
which hardly evokes a sound
but then
we rip out their testicles with the hook
as they squirm like rabbits and if we
can't get them out we get Janine who
grew up on a big station where she learnt
to do it with her teeth

afterwards she looks like she's
just seen the dentist from hell

a quick hole punch in the ear and
all that's left is the tail and
this only takes one quick slice except
when you miss and get a bony bit
and it grates as you cut and it's
more like sawing if the blade's blunt
and they only lose a few usually

before soon it'll be time for mulesing

Rites

Summer

in striped pyjamas
he taps the brush
on the beach
rubs the green soap slowly
brings the brush up
to his chin

soap smells

he draws the brush around
in an uneven lather
stubble pokes through

he opens the razor
the steel fresh in early light
he looks out the small window
its frosted square ajar

houses bask their
persistent red-tile roofs

on the horizon lies
his thin slice of water-view
its molten glimmer,
he thinks, could easily
be bitumen at midday

he takes a breath of air
swollen with the ripeness of summer
the air unable to stay cold

he inhales the warmth deeply
clears his lungs of winter

the mirror reflects
as the hand draws the blade
across the neck

Winter

all those smooth hills
that peace and
quiet
with cows
overlapping and intertwining
and religious
spirits move
together
at the clouding
of the moon

evening vomits frost
all around
as lovers kill
each other
beneath red stars
folding their hands
around
the scented air
bringing it to their
mouths
they kiss

Bee   Yellow   Native

how many more faces are there in the city
so many
like Sack's woman who remembered everything
as she walked down the street
I should jump into alleys to let it assimilate
but I'm exhausted just seeing us all

lunchtime
the park is luscious with neglected grass
 growing long and wild   accompliced by renegade mallow
heartweed and dandelions
I'm frightened at how distant I've become from it all
in my flat with my potted memories around me
a bee lands near my foot   yellow   native
there's a serenity here despite the dull moan
of traffic behind the trees
an insect could live out its whole life oblivious to it
if only
I roll back the cuff of my jacket
grab my bag

Circling Dublin

On our journey north "Whiskey in the Jar"
feels the same as it did back home,
a twist in the road and the music
becomes a green field ballad with sweet flutes.
Wooden rails are punctuated with gorse,
I smelt it once in Sydney, like coconut oil.
Everything shifts; rubble is pink then grey,
then the sky moves again,
fences become stones and roll away.

The Wicklow Mountains are flat as glass
oriental against the horizon;
sheep are everywhere.
"The grass hasn't started growing yet,"
says Eugene, though it's already knee-high.
We come to the sea, Balbriggan:
light sieves through the boisterous clouds,
leafless trees hang with nests, rags,
mistletoe and buds hiding in parcels,
rusty like the robin's breast.

The Kippure Mountain broods over winter-red
boglands as far as the eye can see.
A relaying tower transmits a greater emptiness.
Tiny cliffs are cut here and there
by the collectors of chocolate-brown peat;
"In summer you'll see cars on the road."

Way below in a valley lies a village,
chunks of humanity in neat rows,
overshadowed by stone steeples.

We arrive at the place of pilgrimage
a century too late.
Seven visits here equal one to Rome;
a large indulgence. They were keen at first,
but the priest emptied the whiskey, broke
their fighting sticks and made enemies embrace.
Heads turn along the path. Stone buildings lie cleft,
dolls' houses we can see into.
We come to the lough Father Kevin
threw the amorous woman into:
she drowned, he's a saint.

Ravens squark in the frozen wood:
a tipsy mountain scene about to tumble.
Its floor is spread with crisp leaves,
lichened stones and tufts of grass.
Skeletons of larch and silver birch sprout
green and brown fingers.
These are farmlands again,
alive with long-fleeced sheep
and spring clumps of shamrocks,
green geometry fenced with gorse,
the smell of coconut everywhere.

Rita Ann Higgins

Rita Ann Higgins was born in Galway in 1955 and still resides in her native city. She began writing in 1982 and has since published four volumes of poetry, *Goddess & Witch* (1990), *Philomena's Revenge* (1992), *Higher Purchase* (1996), and *Sunnyside Plucked: New and Selected* (1996). Her plays include *Face Licker Come Home* (1991), *God of the Hatch Man* (1992) and *Colile Lally doesn't Live in a Bucket* (1993).

She has read her work at Oxford University, Queen's University Belfast, Trinity College Dublin, as well as major arts festivals throughout Ireland.

In recent years she has also held prison workshops in Portlaoise Prison, Limerick, Cork and Loughan House. Her poetry has been anthologised and dramatised.

The Flogger

A man with such a belly
can never ever become a flogger
                The Trial — Kafka

He wanted to be a flogger —
not just any old
swing the taws
Tom-Jack run-o-the-mill flogger
he wanted to be
the best flogger in town.

His father, a fines administrator
his mother, a fine administrator's wife
he knew about the letter of the law.

He longed to flog.
He would flog miserable souls
to within an inch of their miserable lives.

He fancied they would go away galled —
but confident that they were flogged,
not by any Jack-Tom chancer flogger.

They would respond to
how's she cutting greetings,
"flogged" they'd say,
"not by any run-o-the-chancer flogger
by the foulest flogger in town,

and furthermore it was a Double
Special Offer Monday flogging
me and the wife together
me with the left hand
the wife with the right hand
our agonies complete."

When the town flogger
sullied his career
by blind dating a one-time flogged soul,
the fines administrator's son
took the reins.

The slim back
was his favourite
the back to tear a shirt from
the cat-o-nines-delight.

But this flogger,
not just any
swing the mill
run-Jack-over-Tom flogger
was a very fair flogger.

He always gave the choice
"take it off or have it torn off",
that won him acclaim
that, and his Special Offer Mondays.

Like every good flogger
he had his faults,
he had five stomachs
he had to keep them filled
he dipped often into other people's pots.

Eventually he got caught,
his father, a fines administrator
his mother, a fine adminstrator's wife.
The flogger, the fair old flogger
the "take it off or have it torn off" flogger
got fifty lashes
inferior lashes by his standards,
the shame of the flogger
being flogged left its mark,
especially when he met
souls he had flogged
and flogged well,
his shame left him smaller
and red all over.

Prism

After the man
up our street
stuck broken glass
on top of his back wall
to keep out
those youngsters
who never stopped
teasing his
Doberman pinscher,

he put
the safety chain
on the door,
sat at the kitchen window,
let out a nervous laugh,
and watched
the Castle Park sun
divide the light
and scatter it
all over his property.

The Taxi Man Knows

I see them going off there
and hardly a stitch on them
one young thing
I swear to God
you could see her cheeks
another lassie
you could see her tonsils

and they come home then
crying over spilt milk

if she was my daughter
I'd give her something to cry over.

Mothercare

The girls came over
to see the new buggy,
the rainbow buggy,
the sunshine stripes.

OK it was expensive
but it was the best
and welfare pitched in.

It had everything —
she listed its finer points,
underbelly things we hadn't seen.

A little touch here
and it collapses
a little touch there
and it's up like a shot,
you barely touch this —
and you're in another street
another town.

A mind of its own
a body like a rocket
it's yours to control —
just like that.

She swears she'll keep it well
immaculate, she says, immaculate.

When she's nearly eighteen
it will still be new,
Tomma-Lee will be two and a half,

she can sell it then
and fetch a high price,

almost as much as she paid.

Higher Purchase

We saw them take
her furniture out,

the new stuff
her kids boasted about
six months before.

The Chesterfield Suite
the pine table and chairs
the posh lamp
the phone table,
though they had no phone.

When it was going in
we watched with envy
she told her kids out loud
"You're as good as anyone else
on this street."

When it was coming out
no one said anything,
only one young skut
who knew no better, shouted,

"Where will ye put the phone now,
when it comes."

The Flute Girl's Dialogue

Plato, come out now
with your sunburnt legs on ya
don't tell me to play to myself
or to the other women.

"Discourse in Praise of Love" indeed.

Bad mannered lot,
even if I cough when I come into the room
it does not stop your bleating.
That couch over there seats two comfortably
yet every time I enter
there's four of you on it
acting the maggot
then if Socrates walks in,
the way you all suck up to him.

Small wonder Plato
you have a leg to stand on
after all the red herrings
you put in people's mouths.
You hide behind Eryximachus
and suspend me like tired tattle.

"Tell the Flute Girl to go" indeed.

Let me tell you Big Sandals
the Flute Girl's had it.
When I get the sisters in here
we are going to sit on the lot of you,
come out then gushing platonic.

The Flute Girl knows
the fall of toga tune
the flick of tongue
salt-dip and hemlock-sip
eye to the sky tune
hand on the thigh tune
moan and whimper talk
dual distemper talk.

When you played I listened,
when I play, prick up your ears.

Eavan Boland

Eavan Boland was born in Dublin in 1944 and lived in Ireland, London and New York before graduating from Trinity College, Dublin. She has published seven books of poetry. Most recently, her collected poems have been published in the UK and New York. Her prose memoir, *Object Lessons* was published in 1995.

Anna Liffey

Life, the story goes,
Was the daughter of Cannan,
And came to the plain of Kildare.
She loved the flat-lands and the ditches
And the unreachable horizon.
She asked that it be named for her.
The river took its name from the land.
The land took its name from a woman.

• • •

A woman in the doorway of a house.
A river in the city of her birth.

• • •

There, in the hills above my house,
The river Liffey rises, is a source.
It rises in rush and ling heather and
Black peat and bracken and strengthens
To claim the city it narrated.
Swans. Steep falls. Small towns.
The smudged air and bridges of Dublin.

• • •

Dusk is coming.
Rain is moving east from the hills.

If I could see myself
I would see
A woman in a doorway
Wearing the colours that go with red hair.
Although my hair is no longer red.

· · ·

I praise
The gifts of the river.
Its shiftless and glittering
Re-telling of a city,
Its clarity as it flows,
In the company of runt flowers and herons,
Around a bend at Islandbridge
And under thirteen bridges to the sea.
Its patience at twilight —
Swans nesting by it,
Neon wincing into it.

· · ·

Maker of
Places, remembrances,
Narrate such fragments for me:

One body. One spirit.
One place. One name.
The city where I was born.
The river that runs through it.
The nation which eludes me.

Fractions of a life
It has taken me a lifetime
To claim.

• • •

I came here in a cold winter.

I had no children. No country.
I did not know the name for my own life.

My country took hold of me.
My children were born.

I walked out in a summer dusk
To call them in.

One name. Then the other one.
The beautiful vowels sounding out home.

• • •

Make of a nation what you will
Make of the past
What you can —

There is now
A woman in a doorway.

It has taken me
All my strength to do this.

Becoming a figure in a poem.

Usurping a name and a theme.

• • •

A river is not a woman.
    Although the names it finds
        The history it makes
And suffers —
    The Viking blades beside it,
        The muskets of the Redcoats,
            the flames of the Four Courts
Blazing into it
    Are a sign.
        Anymore than
A woman is a river,
    Although the course it takes,
        Through swans courting and distraught willows,
Its patience
    Which is also its powerlessness,
        From Callary to Islandbridge.
            And from source to mouth,
Is another one.
                And in my late forties
Past believing
    Love will heal
        What language fails to know
And needs to say —
    What the body means —
        I take this sign
And I make this mark:
    A woman in the doorway of her house.
        A river in the city of her birth.
The truth of a suffered life.
        The mouth of it.

• • •

The seabirds come in from the coast.
The city wisdom is they bring rain.
I watch them from my doorway.
I see them as arguments of origin —
Leaving a harsh force on the horizon
Only to find it
Slanting and falling elsewhere.

Which water —
The one they leave or the one they pronounce —
Remembers the other?

I am sure
The body of an ageing woman
Is a memory
And to find a language for it
Is as hard
As weeping and requiring
These birds to cry out as if they could
Recognize their element
Remembered and diminished in
A single tear.

• • •

An ageing woman
Finds no shelter in language.
She finds instead
Single words she once loved
Such as "summer" and "yellow"
And "sexual" and "ready"

Have suddenly become dwellings
For someone else —
Rooms and a roof under which someone else
Is welcome, not her. Tell me,
Anna Liffey,
Spirit of water,
Spirit of place,
How is it on this
Rainy Autumn night
As the Irish Sea takes
The names you made, the names
You bestowed, and gives you back
Only wordlessness?

• • •

Autumn rain is
Scattering and dripping
From carports
And clipped hedges.
The gutters are full.

When I came here
I had neither
children nor country.
The trees were arms.
The hills were dreams.

I was free
to imagine a spirit
in the blues and greens,

the hills and fogs
of a small city.

My children were born.
My country took hold of me.
A vision in a brick house.
Is it only love
that makes a place?

I feel it change.
My children are
growing up, getting older.
My country holds on
to its own pain.

I turn off
the harsh yellow
porch light and
stand in the hall.
Where is home now?

Follow the rain
out to the Dublin hills.
Let it become the river.
Let the spirit of place be
a lost soul again.

• • • • • •

In the end
It will not matter
That I was a woman. I am sure of it.
The body is a source. Nothing more.
There is a time for it. There is a certainty
About the way it seeks its own dissolution.
Consider rivers.
They are always en route to
their own nothingness. From the first moment
They are going home. And so
when language cannot do it for us,
cannot make us know love will not diminish us,
there are these phrases
of the ocean
to console us.
Particular and unafraid of their completion
In the end
everything that burdened and distinguished me
will be lost in this:
I was a voice.

Making the Difference

The evening was the same as any other.
I came out and stood on the step
The suburb was closed in the weather

of an early spring and the shallow tips
and washed-out yellows of narcissi
resisted dusk, and crocuses and snowdrops.

I stood there and felt the melancholy
of growing older in such a season,
when all I could be certain of was simply

in this time of fragrance and refrain,
whatever else might flower before the fruit,
and be renewed, I would not. Not again.

A car splashed by in the twilight.
Peat smoke stayed in the windless
air overhead and I might have missed it.

A presence. Suddenly. In the very place
where I would stand in other dusks and look
to pick out my child from the distance

was a shepherdess, her smile cracked,
her arm injured from the mantelpieces
and pastorals where she posed with her crook.

Then I turned and saw in the spaces
of the night sky where constellations appear,
one by one, over roof-tops and houses,

Cassiopeia trapped: stabbed where
her thigh met her groin and her hand
her glittering wrist, with the bright tip of a star.

And by the road where rain made standing
pools of water underneath cherry trees,
and blossoms swam on their images,

was a mermaid with invented tresses,
her breasts printed with the salt of it and all
the desolation of the North Sea in her face.

The light was less now and I could feel
the urgency of their presences making
the difference between the true and the real

but as I watched they were disappearing.
Dusk had turned to night but in the air —
did I imagine it? — a voice was saying:

This is what language did to us. Here
is the wound, the silence, the wretchedness
of tides and hillsides and stars where

we languish in a grammar of sighs,
in the high-minded search for euphony,
in the midnight rhetoric of poesie.

Eavan Boland

We cannot sweat here. Our skin is icy.
We cannot breed here. Our wombs are empty.
Help us to escape youth and beauty.

Write us out of the poem. Make us human
in cadences of change and mortal pain
and words we can grow old and die in.

The Emigrant Irish

Like oil lamps we put them out the back —
of our houses, of our minds. We had lights

better than, newer than and then

a time came, this time and now
we need them. Their dread, makeshift example.

They would have thrived on our necessities.
What they survived we could not even live.
By their lights now it is time to
imagine how they stood there, what they stood with,
that their possessions may become our power:

Cardboard. Iron. Their hardships parcelled in them.
Patience. Fortitude. Long-suffering
in the bruise-coloured dusk of the New World.

And all the old songs. And nothing to lose.

OTHER TITLES FROM SPINIFEX PRESS

Lizz Murphy
Two Lips Went Shopping

Two Lips Went Shopping is a book for anyone who has ever shopped—or worked in shops. But whether you find yourself wincing or laughing could depend on which side of the shop counter you're on at the time.

Find out what it's like to be a young shopgirl, vent your frustrations with today's supermarket society and the advertising and media industries, take a nostalgic trip back to the days of the corner shop.

ISBN 1 875559 96 5

Merlinda Bobis
White Turtle

An anomalous kiss. A white turtle ferrying the dreams of the dead. A working siesta in a five-star hotel. A woman's twelve-metre hair trawling corpses from a river. Or a queue of longings in Darlinghurst. These enigmatic tales of chance and hope are among twenty-three stories set in the Philippines and Australia. Alternately mystic, wistful or quirky, Merlinda Bobis' tales resonate with an original and confident storytelling voice.

Merlinda Bobis writes like an angel. Her characters whisper to you long after they've told their bittersweet tales.

— Arlene J. Chai

ISBN 1 875559 89 2

Merlinda Bobis
Summer was a Fast Train without Terminals

An epic of the old Philippines, lyric reflections on longing, and an erotic dance drama make up this fine collection.

Bobis can produce some genuinely haunting pieces. This is a touching work from an established poet.

— Hamesh Wyatt, *Otago Daily Times*, NZ

ISBN 1 875559 76 0

Sandi Hall

Rumours of Dreams

Beginning in our south Pacific future and stretching back to a Mediterranean past, Sandi Hall's new and startling novel explores a friendship that could affect the history of the world.

Living in 2002, Stella Mante can remember back two thousand years, when she was a 10-year-old girl named Mary whose best friend is a boy she nicknames Santer.

An orphan herself, the young Mary is intrigued by Santer's mother, whose name is also Mary. Her interest deepens when, as teenagers, Santer's mother helps them both secretly flee to Alexandria, the dazzling city of Cleopatra's snowy palace and the greatest university in the known world.

As Santer fights against his destiny, Mary is drawn more and more into mysterious events that threaten both their lives, and trigger her own life quest.

Sandi Hall is also the author of the highly acclaimed *Godmothers* and *Wingwomen of Hera*.

She lives in New Zealand.

ISBN 1 875559 75 2

Suniti Namjoshi
Building Babel

Suniti Namjoshi is an inspired fabulist: she asks the difficult questions – about good and evil, about nature and war – unfailingly bracing her readers with her mordant humor and the lively play of her imagination. — Marina Warner

A unique book which invites the reader to explore ideas on culture and contribution to the Babel Building Site on the Spinifex web site:
http://www.spinifexpress.com.au/~women

ISBN 1 875559 56 6

Suniti Namjoshi
St Suniti and the Dragon

An original imagination full of surprises from Beowulf to Bangladesh.

I can think of plenty of adjectives to describe St Suniti and the Dragon, *but not a noun to go with them. It's hilarious, witty, elegantly written, hugely inventive, fantastic, energetic … With work as original as this, it's easier to fling words at it than to say what it is or what it does.* — U.A. Fanthorpe

ISBN 1 875559 18 3

Suniti Namjoshi
Feminist Fables

An ingenious reworking of fairytales from East and West.
Mythology, mixed with the author's original material and
vivid imagination. An indispensable feminist classic.

*Her imagination soars to breathtaking heights … she has the
enviable skill of writing stories that are as entertaining as they
are thought-provoking.* — Kerry Lyon, Australian Book
Review

ISBN 1 875559 19 1

If you would like to know more about Spinifex Press,
write for a free catalogue or visit our Home Page.

SPINIFEX PRESS

PO Box 212, North Melbourne,

Victoria 3051, Australia

http://www.spinifexpress.com.au